STATIONS

BY THE SAME AUTHOR

The End of the World is a Cul de Sac

Trespasses

STATIONS

LOUISE KENNEDY

BLOOMSBURY CIRCUS
LONDON • OXFORD • NEW YORK • NEW DELHI • SYDNEY

BLOOMSBURY CIRCUS
Bloomsbury Publishing Plc
50 Bedford Square, London, WC1B 3DP, UK
Bloomsbury Publishing Ireland Limited,
29 Earlsfort Terrace, Dublin 2, D02 AY28, Ireland

First published in Great Britain in 2026

A catalogue record for this book is available from the British Library

ISBN: HB: 978-1-5266-6432-7; TPB: 978-1-5266-6433-4;
WATERSTONES: 978-1-03-720552-1; EBOOK: 978-1-5266-6430-3

2 4 6 8 10 9 7 5 3 1

Typeset by Six Red Marbles India
Printed and bound in Great Britain by Clays Ltd, Elcograf S.p.A

MIX
Paper | Supporting responsible forestry
FSC® C018072

For my sisters

And when one of them meets with his other half, the actual half of himself, whether he be a lover of youth or a lover of another sort, the pair are lost in an amazement of love and friendship and intimacy and one will not be out of the other's sight, as I may say, even for a moment ...

Plato, *The Symposium*

Oh I'm missing you under Piccadilly's neon

Jimmy MacCarthy, 'Missing You'

Part One

1

21 October 1982

It was the first time she had spoken to a boy. Red Camelin, a combat jacket over his school jumper, kicking his heels against the wall he was sitting on behind the County Council offices. Watching her, his head cocked as if she had said something funny.

Róisín began digging in the pockets of her gaberdine. Here you go, she said, thrusting the letter at him.

He performed a twirly gesture with his fingers, an expression of exaggerated concentration on his face. Making her wait. Then he plucked the envelope from her hand with a 'Merci' that sounded – deliberately? – like *mercy*, patting the capping on the wall as if it was a sofa. Have a seat, he said.

She hadn't expected conversation, but it would be easier to sit next to him than endure his gaze for another second. She hopped up beside him.

Any smokes? he said, twisting on his arse to look at her again.

She offered him a Consulate from a squashed packet.

They're for pregnant women. Are you with child?

Yeah, I'm expecting triplets.

He lit them both up, sniggering. Minty fresh, he said, shooting smoke out through his nostrils.

She dragged hard, glad to have something to do with her hands.

So, Róisín McCaffrey. Why, out of all the girls in Saint Attracta's College, have you been elected go-between?

She did not know what he was getting at. Or maybe she did, and didn't like it. There were popular girls and invisible girls; Róisín was actively unpopular. She slid into a standing position, pebbledash scrabbing her thighs.

Where are you off to? he said.

You were taking the piss, she said. A lock of hair was hanging in her eye. Her mother's hairdresser was supposed to cut it like the brunette's from Human League, but it was a pudding-bowl style, saved only by her cow's lick. She tried to tuck her hair behind her ear, but it came loose again, diminishing the power of her outrage.

Jesus. I was trying to be sociable. I've no other way of getting in touch with her, it's sound of you to do it.

Red was going out with Tina Doyle; or not going out exactly, as Tina's father had forbidden her from seeing him. Róisín had offered to deliver a letter to Red, not because Tina was her friend – quite the reverse – but because it was prudent to be in credit with her.

Red stood and picked up his school bag, a vinyl one for sports, crackling with newness. He caught Róisín looking at it.

I get the best of everything, he said.

It wasn't a boast, his voice was almost angry. Maybe he hadn't been making fun of her. She wanted to stay now, but wouldn't she seem petulant if she had to be persuaded?

I should go home. Her face felt hot.

Red was flushed too – from the cold, she suspected. I'll walk with you, he said.

They went along the side of the building, past a large office lit by fluorescent strips. A woman in a pink fluffy cardigan came to the window and seized the cord of the blind, frowning at them.

Howaya, love! Red called.

The woman snapped the blind shut.

Róisín let out a snort, surprising herself; she normally found this sort of horseplay moronic.

I made you laugh, he said.

Yeah, you're a comic genius.

He had moved in front of her and was walking backwards. We'll start again. What's your favourite book?

The White Album.

I said *book*.

It *is* a book. By Joan Didion.

He stopped dead. Interesting, he said, cocking his head again. Favourite song?

'Positively 4th Street'.

Mucho mistrust. No surprise there.

She burst out laughing.

He was smiling too, pleased with himself. Favourite film?

On the Waterfront.

No way. That's mine as well. Who's Joan Didion?

She's an American journalist, said Róisín. Or writer, really. It's a book of essays.

Ugh, said Red.

Oh, it's not like the godawful drivel we have to read for English.

Bacon, Lamb and Hazlitt. Torture.

Róisín said it was ridiculous they had to read two-hundred-year-old treatises by men named for meat products, although she liked the Bacon one about borrowing and lending. *The White Album* was not like those essays at all, the first one was about water in California, or maybe the lack of it, which didn't sound that riveting, but the way Didion wrote about it was brilliant. Róisín's favourite was the one about the Manson trial. Joan was sent by a lawyer to buy a respectable dress for Linda Kasabian to wear in court.

She was a little out of breath, and afraid she had sounded insane by calling her Joan.

So there is a connection to *The White Album*, said Red.

Kind of. The title comes from a Beatles album all right, and Manson was obsessed with the song 'Helter Skelter'. But that record you're talking about is officially called *The Beatles*, not *The White Album*.

Róisín McCaffrey has the smarts.

Is that a criticism?

No! Touchy, aren't we?

They were walking again. He told her he'd read a book called *Hitler's Children*, about the Baader-Meinhof gang, another example of sixties peace-and-love gone psycho. Róisín suspected he had the smarts too. She wondered what he talked about to Tina Doyle, who had failed three subjects – including English – in the Inter Cert.

They were on the square that was really just the widest part of the main street, with parking for a few cars. She had never got used to this town on the Dublin to Cork route with its traffic of shitting livestock and rattling buses and articulated lorries. The shops were from another age. A leathersmith's, handmade bags and belts laid neatly beneath bridles and saddles; a drapery, dowdy fashions spreadeagled on pegboard behind crinkly yellow film to prevent fading.

Outside the Sorrento Grill they faltered, inhaling the smell of chips and milky coffee.

I'm famished, he said. Will we pool our resources?

She liked the way he talked. Ironic, slightly formal. Always with the beginnings of a smile. They searched for coins and between them raised 19p, not even enough for a cup of tea. At the only pedestrian crossing she prepared to say goodbye. Red's house, she knew from Tina, was at the top of the town – an expression that confused Róisín, for it was actually south – but he crossed the road with her.

Every few yards Róisín had to bend to deal with her socks, over-the-knee ones she could not pull up fully without hoking under her skirt.

What do ye wear those for? said Red. They're ridiculous.

That's rich! The state of you lot. Moving in drifts of rancid hormones.

He threw his head back and laughed. Jesus, he said. Don't stop now.

You should honestly see yourselves. We can only tell you apart by height, haircut and whatever tragic modification you've made to your school uniform.

'Don't stop now' was sarcasm. And are you saying I don't stand out?

He did. Tall, but not too tall, a blessing as it didn't do to be too anything. Nearly-black hair that stood straight up on his head, a slightly hooked nose. Dark eyes fringed with lashes so thick they could have been false. He was spoken about in giddy whispers at school. The time he drank a bottle of whiskey and had to be pumped out. The time he chucked his school bag out the classroom window and leapt after it, climbing the town's only hill – a man-made one surrounded by a medieval moat – to read a book. Now she had met him his reputation was puzzling. She had expected a delinquent, but he was curious, funny. Nice.

You do stand out, she said. Not in a bad way. Necessarily.

Ah, here. Give us another one of those fags.

She passed him the packet and bent to pull her socks up again. When she straightened he was looking at her. You stand out too, he said.

Because I'm from the north? Or because my da left us.

I fucking wish my da would leave us, he said, louring.

They were at her house. This is me, she said. He followed her in.

The hall had a particular smell, of bleach and soot and the previous night's dinner, that normally comforted her. Today it seemed fusty. Red trailed her as she went through her routine.

Turning on the lights. Stabbing the bank of slack in the grate until it belched smoke. Filling the kettle. She caught him touching the kitchen radiator. The house was heated by a back boiler behind the fireplace and there would be little warmth for an hour or two. He went to the sink and ran the hot tap.

Comfortably numb, he said, rubbing his hands together under the flow. There were white patches on his fingers where the circulation had stopped.

So you like Pink Floyd? she said, firing up the Superser she rarely used because the fumes sickened her.

I do. You?

I'm put off by the people who like them.

That's me told. Where's your ma?

Róisín explained that her mother worked nights and was still in bed. That they took turns to make dinner, and tonight was Róisín's go. Fish finger sandwiches and chips, not very exciting.

That'll do nicely.

She didn't want him to leave, but she didn't want him to sit in their dingy kitchen either. When they moved in, her father had painted the cupboards yellow to cheer it up, but the layers had begun to come away, revealing streaks of the original blue. Condensation coursed down the walls all winter and her mother's frantic cleaning made little difference. Today it seemed all the worse for being cold. She needn't have worried. When she dumped potatoes in the sink he began peeling them, eyes moving from his labour to Róisín, seemingly oblivious to the shabbiness.

Her mother started creaking around upstairs. It was going to be mortifying, the three of them together at the table. And worse, when he heard how she spoke at home he would think there was a want in her.

I have two accents, said Róisín. I talk to my mother in a northern accent.

I don't care, I'm so hungry I'd eat the Lamb of God. But you don't sound like a nordie all right.

Róisín told him they had moved south when she was twelve. On her first day at her new school she introduced herself to each teacher, saying her name, where she had come from. By late morning, some girls – led by one who turned out to be Tina, although she didn't tell Red that – were declaring *Róisín McCaffrey, five miles from Belfast* over and over, in dire mimicry. From then on, every time she opened her mouth there was a chorus of *How now, brown cow* in mangled northern vowels. One Friday she went home and cried all weekend; in school on Monday morning, her northern accent was gone. I suppose you think I'm a fake, she said.

We're all pretending. And that was pure bitchy of them.

Her mother had dressed and brushed her hair, ready to meet the source of the clear voice and sudden laughter, but had the ghostly aspect the night shift gave her, pallid skin and reddish eyes. Red was in Róisín's father's place, sleeves rolled up, buttering bread. He wiped his hands on his school trousers and rose.

Mrs McCaffrey. Enchanté.

Róisín watched, astonished, as her mother's cheeks bloomed with colour. You wee charmer. Call me Una, she said.

After he left, Róisín reconnected the phone line. It trilled immediately.

At long fecking last! hissed Tina. I rang you ten times.

I told you, my mother unplugs the phone so she can sleep.

Stupid bitch, said Tina, with a brittle laugh, although it was unlikely she was joking. Róisín let her away with it. Everyone let Tina away with everything.

Well? Did you give him the letter? Did he open it?

He put it in his pocket.

Jesus! I can't cope. What did he say about me?

Nothing.

He's deep like that, Tina said dreamily. What do you think of him?

Róisín had made a number of deductions about Red Camelin, but knew better than to tell Tina she had been with her boyfriend for long enough to form an opinion.

There was shouting in the background. The father's going mad today, said Tina. When are you picking up the reply?

Red hadn't mentioned the letter after he accepted it, merely saying *Good luck* over his shoulder as he left. Róisín hesitated, dreading telling Tina so, but was saved by Captain Doyle, who was now roaring like a bull, and getting closer. The line went dead. Róisín replaced the receiver.

She went into the sitting room. Her mother was reclined on the settee, feet elevated and resting on the far arm. Well, it's a feast or a famine with you, she said. Bringing a boy home and the phone hopping.

Red's not my boyfriend! Tina's going out with him. Her da thinks he's a bowsie and won't let her out. I delivered a letter for her.

Her mother pushed herself upright, drawing her legs in.

Are you a go-between? For Tina?

Róisín felt herself redden. Yeah.

For God's sake. Where's your pride?

For a moment Róisín was too shocked to answer. My *pride*? she managed eventually, her voice obstructed by a sob that had shot out of her stomach. *My* pride? That's nice. I'll have a rummage in the bin, in case I bucked it out with the scrapings from our plates. I'll have a hunt for your pride while I'm at it. The shite you take from Daddy.

Don't you dare speak to me like that.

Róisín stamped upstairs as hard as she could, leaving the sitting-room door open to piss her mother off. Lying on her bed, she switched on her reading lamp. There was a rule in the house – never let the sun set on your anger – that was broken regularly now. Ironic that it was her father's rule, since he was the cause of most of the strife. Una speaking about him fondly, Róisín calling him a loser, a chancer, a liar. This was different; her mother had looked at her with disgust. Róisín had never admitted how lonely the previous year had been when the girls stopped talking to her, ashamed to let her mother know that she had produced a child so detestable. But Una knew something was wrong, commenting on how quiet the phone had become, coaxing her out of her bedroom. Shouldn't she understand that Róisín had to work to stop it from happening again? Was running errands for her tormentor so bad?

On the wall above her bed there was a clip frame containing a photo taken on a school outing to the Spring Show, the national farming convention. She and the girls had roamed the vast pavilion, between glossy tractors and pageants of blow-dried ewes, hoping to meet boys from around the country. She had felt she belonged that day, but the picture told a different story: it was as though she had been added. She closed her eyes and played the game she had devised the first time her father cracked up. Spelling her whirling thoughts to strip them of harm, pairing their letters to end on an even number. YO UH AV EN OP RI DE moved behind her lids like a news flash as she fell asleep. She dreamt that the framed photograph was of her posing with Stalin-era men in military uniforms. As she looked at it, her image faded until she vanished.

2

6 November 1982

The doorbell rang, three sharp bleats. Róisín stumbled down the stairs, grabbing her mother's buff-coloured raincoat from the banister and slipping it over her nightdress.

Red was on the step, or rather pacing in front of it.

For the last fortnight she had carried a letter to him every day after school, sitting on the wall beside him, smoking and laughing until the damp cold became intolerable. Today was Saturday, but he was in his school uniform, tie trailing from his pocket.

Why is your number ex-directory? he said, pausing and looking hard at her.

Upstairs, a hollow unsticking sound, as Una's warped bedroom door opened. Who's there? she asked.

Róisín stood aside and he stepped into the hall, hands shaking in his pockets as if he was rattling change.

Who's there? her mother said, louder.

Jesus, muttered Róisín. It's Red!

She brought him into the kitchen. Were you out all night?

Producing the envelope she had given him the previous day, he slapped it against his palm. Did you know what was in this? His breath was putrid, cigarettes and drink.

No. What's wrong?

You don't know anything?

No, I told you. Tina gave me the envelope and I gave it to you.

Fuck her. How would you reply to this? he said, waving it at her.

I don't want to read it.

He opened it and shoved it under her nose. The letter was on powder-blue writing paper, the sort Róisín's mother used for school sick notes. Every word began with a capital letter, Tina's idea of a stylistic flourish. It said Tina's father was giving her hell. She had been grounded for weeks and was fed up of it. It would be better to forget all about it all. Red wasn't *Worth The Hassle*.

If I'd known she was breaking it off with you, I wouldn't have handed it over! *Where's your pride*, she thought. Una had been right, of course, not that Róisín would ever admit it.

A pause and he looked at her hard again. You'd have to be some cunt to deliver that knowing what was in it. Are you sure you'd no clue?

Oh, I see, kill the messenger? Do you think I steamed the stupid thing open?

Their faces were just a few inches apart. Minutes seemed to have passed and his gaze was still locked on hers, an expression so open her stomach pitched with fear for him. He must have seen it in her, for he looked away. When he spoke his voice was unsteady. I thought you were sound, he said, rubbing his face, and then I thought you weren't.

She was sure he could hear her heart pounding.

Sorry, yeah? he said, almost pleading, holding her in that look again.

OK. You have shite taste in women, though.

He sat at the table and sighed. I don't even like her that much. She's kind of thick, for one thing.

'Hassle' is spelt wrong. And shouldn't that be 'fed up with'?

It should indeed, said Red. As for 'all about it all' in the third sentence.

Dozens of examples of Tina's stupidity were on the tip of Róisín's tongue. She kept them to herself, but there was one thing she couldn't resist sharing. Tina didn't like the John Hinde postcard with the ginger kids and the donkey, she said.

That was meant to be funny.

Apparently she was a redhead in primary school. She's been using Sun In since first year.

What's Sun In? asked Red.

Spray stuff that makes your hair blonde.

He was looking at her expectantly, as if he was waiting for the punchline. She wished she hadn't brought it up.

Where were you last night? she said, desperate to change the subject.

Out and about.

What did you do with your school bag?

Shite, he groaned. Nathy Phelan will be selling my books for vodka. Red's head was in his hands.

Nathy Phelan's name was regularly to be found on the front page of the *Leinster Champion*, for variously stealing Librium and a Gillette razor from Cleary's Chemist, putting Pascal Conway through the window of his lounge bar for refusing to serve him, and biting an arresting Guard on the ankle.

Perhaps Red sensed her disfavour, for he looked up sharply. Nathy's sound, he said.

It seemed less of a compliment now that he had said that of her.

They went out the back for a cigarette, Róisín leaning from the doorway, barefoot. The box Red pulled from his pocket was tattered, little squares torn from the lid.

Are we all right, Ró? he said, peering at her through the smoke.

Her parents pronounced her name *Rawsheen*, the northern way. In school they called her *Rowsheen* which annoyed her, the way southerners used the fada so literally. No one had shortened her name to Ró before. A light sensation, almost a fluttering in her chest. Yeah, we're all right, she said.

Good. Any chance of breakfast? I'm Lee Marvin here.

Inside, she took down a box of Shredded Wheat and heated milk in a pan. Red pretended to throw up. She told him Danny Blanchflower had eaten it that way in a TV ad for the stringy rusks, saying, 'Pass the hot milk, please,' his Belfast accent cringily refined by his time in England. Red laughed at her impersonation. Róisín was too young to have seen the ad and was mimicking what her father said every morning.

Will your mother not kill you for disappearing? she said.

Something passed across his face but he recovered himself quickly.

My mother won't say a word.

Róisín had seen Mrs Camelin at Mass. She was petite and busty with full coal-black hair and heavy make-up, as if someone had told her in 1968 she looked like Elizabeth Taylor and she had not changed her style since. Still, she was glamorous. Róisín looked down at herself, her legs protruding from her mother's coat like a pair of celery stalks. She went upstairs to get dressed.

The only decent clothes she had were a grape-coloured bat-wing top and jade-green taffeta skirt she'd worn the night they got their Inter Cert results, too much for a Saturday morning. She put on old mauve cords, worn flat at the knees, and a mohair jumper – lavender, turquoise and grey streaked, knitted by her mother – with matching leg warmers because she was frozen. As she went downstairs she made a vow to wear less purple.

Red had put the rashers her mother bought for after Mass on Sunday under the grill. Cool jumper, he said.

I'm like someone who just failed an audition for *Fame*.

That sudden laugh.

They brought mugs of tea and bacon sandwiches to the sitting room. While Róisín lit the fire, Red knelt on the carpet to flip through the records. He took out a Bowie one and held it up.

That's my da's, she said.

Wow. Cool that he has taste like that.

It wasn't cool, it was schizo, she told him. Andy Williams and the Dubliners in there with *Hunky Dory*. Her plasticine father, ready to mould himself into any shape.

You needn't feel sorry for yourself, my ould lad listens to Mantovani and James Last. What happened with your da anyway?

My father, she began, and stopped. She had been sworn to secrecy so long ago she was never even tempted to speak about her father. Why did she think it was a good idea to do so now?

Red was looking at her keenly. You don't have to tell me anything, he said, but if you do, I swear it'll go no further.

She picked at a piece of coal that had burned into the hearthrug.

You asked earlier why our number is ex-directory. It's not because I'm so popular I can't cope with all the calls.

Stop. You're horrible to yourself.

Róisín thought for a second she might cry. Maybe he saw it in her, because he suggested they get out of the house, go for a walk.

He had misplaced his jacket as well as his school bag and put on a sheepskin of her father's that was glossy with age. I look like a fella who buys sick horses, he said, in front of the hall mirror.

Róisín put on her coat, a navy corduroy one with big patch pockets, avoiding her reflection.

It was the first day that felt like winter, a cold clear sky above them. They turned down towards the canal. On their right, the perimeter wall of an Anglo-Irish estate, now a stud farm. On their left, Victorian lodges built for those who worked there long ago: the agent, the gamekeeper, the magistrate. The first time they drove down this road her mother said they would live in one of those houses one day. It depressed Róisín to think of Una's optimism; since coming to the town things had fallen apart.

On my mother's life, she said, if you repeat a word of this I'll put a curse on you.

Her voice felt constricted at first, but loosened as she spoke. On her last day of primary school her parents announced they were moving. Her father, Conor, got a job in a pub. At first he loved it, relieved not to be checking under his car in the mornings or closing the curtains when the street lights came on. His face no longer twitched with tics and the wandering at night stopped. But one of the regulars – a Troubles groupie, her father called him, because he latched on to northerners – asked why he had come south. Her father's explanation that he'd quit a civil service desk job because of sectarianism only made him more curious. What did 'civil servant' mean exactly?

I don't get the problem, said Red.

My father was in the police for a year, she said, a long breath leaving her. An actual sigh of relief.

The RUC? Fuck. So you're a Protestant?

With a name like McCaffrey? Of course not.

My surname is Huguenot. French Protestant from way back.

Very fancy.

Truly.

They were at the waterway. The cold had killed the summer algae and the canal surface was glassy. They crossed the humpbacked bridge to the bank that was in full sun, Róisín squinting, complaining that the rays were too strong.

Such moaning, said Red. Walk in the light and finish your story.

Sometimes she wondered where he'd come out of. *Walk in the light*, loping along in her father's coat like an itinerant preacher.

She told him her mother found night work in the nursing home, sleeping all day while her father applied for jobs at the kitchen table, filling envelopes. One day Róisín came home from school to find him on the edge of the settee, curled like a diver tumbling into a pool, mumbling something over and over, her mother kneeling in front of him. Róisín stood in the doorway until she made out the words. *I'm a broken man. I'm a broken man.* A month later he was gone.

They were at the second lock. Red shunted across the thick, black beam, a drop of fifteen or twenty feet to the water below. Róisín stayed close to the bank, where it was safe.

Why did he join the RUC, though? Red said. I thought it was full of Protestants.

She'd been dreading the question. Her parents had sold the south to her as a sanctuary for beleaguered six-county Catholics but it turned out most southerners were either uninterested or appalled by the north. Even the hunger strike was virtually ignored. Almost nobody signed the condolence book that appeared on the town-hall steps when each of the ten men died, and the four or five boys who'd worn black armbands discarded them before the protest was over.

The RUC is ninety per cent Protestant, she said.

Her father had always had trouble finding work, collecting the dole and picking up shifts in bars owned by better-off friends. For a short time, moderate nationalist politicians encouraged Catholics to join the force to make it less partisan. When the IRA threatened to kill the new recruits most left, but her father stayed on. He was sent to south Armagh, a post that paid danger money because of the likelihood of getting shot or blown up. At first, his fellow officers subjected him to light-hearted sectarian banter, but paranoia soon set in and they fell silent at the sight of him. He came home a twitching, sleepless wreck.

Red lit two cigarettes and passed her one. Jesus, he said softly. That's why ye are ex-directory.

Yeah. And now you have the power to ruin my life.

He swivelled on his backside. Do you think I'm going to tell people? You would not believe how good I am at keeping secrets.

I've been spilling my soul out the last hour and I know fuck all about you. What's your father like?

He's not what people think, he said. Róisín waited for him to say more but there was something in his bearing, staring down in to the canal, lips tense, that stopped her from pressing him.

Commemorate me where there is water, he said eventually.

He was quoting poetry at her?

So you like Kavanagh, she said, unable to conjure a more insightful reply.

I do. I like Yeats too, the ould west Brit. God, I love this spot. We should come here in future.

Róisín had lived by the sea as a child and considered this stagnant ribbon a poor substitute. But it was beautiful, the water mirroring the blue sky and the golds and russets of overhanging trees. Yeah, she said, instead of freezing our holes off on that wall.

I wish a barge would come along. We could drop on to it unseen and start a new life.

Where?

Anywhere. You trust me, Ró, don't you? he said.

Yeah.

She'd only known this haggard boy for a couple of weeks and she'd trust him with her life.

3

4 March 1983

Her mother dropped to first gear as they approached the GAA club. Instead of turning into the car park she stalled about two hundred yards past the entrance. Róisín had given up counting how many times the sun had set since their argument, but reckoned it was close to a lunar month. She thanked her mother's profile – that of a tortured saint – and got out of the car. Her mother didn't reply. These days she only acknowledged Róisín when Red was around.

The club was over a mile from town, where housing estates gave way to countryside. It had been raining for weeks so she walked up the middle of the road to avoid the sopping gullies that lined it. A car lit her from behind and she glanced back. Her mother. Róisín considered flagging her down and begging her forgiveness, but the impulse passed. Stepping out of the way, she kept walking. Her toes were already sore with the effort of keeping on her pumps, shiny black ballet ones with polka-dot bows that grimaced open with each step. They had looked cute, in a forties way, in the shop. Now they reminded her of Minnie Mouse.

Her mother had dithered before leaving, cleaning the hob and hanging knickers on the radiators, and the disco had started almost half an hour ago. Róisín pushed the door open. A pair of sturdy women were by a desk, the wall behind them covered in team photographs, a trophy cabinet to their right. Róisín showed them her ticket but hesitated at the entrance to the hall, self-conscious that she was not just late but alone. One of the women flung a sausagey arm in front of her, shoving her inside with a merry, 'Don't be shy!' A shriek rose from Róisín's left. Tina in her Bananarama phase, hair backcombed to tatty and wearing shredded thermal underwear, outraged at the sight of her.

The Monday after she had delivered the Dear John letter to Red, Róisín walked into the classroom to find Tina with a crowd around her, dabbing at her eyes with a tissue. Róisín went to her place at the front and had just sat down when Tina slammed her hands flat on her desk. The girls had followed, their over-plucked eyebrows raised in fury.

Can you not do anything by yourself? said Róisín. She stared at Tina's hands. Tina moved them to her sides, but she was not fully subdued.

You're a jealous fucked-up bitch, she wailed. I suppose you got off with him.

I didn't, actually.

Well, you've been seen all round the place. Down by the canal, up the town. He's never out of your house!

You broke it off with him, Tina. And got me to deliver the news.

Oh, you were happy enough to carry the letters. Nobody normal would do that. Freak.

Over Tina's shoulder, the poem 'Desiderata' was pinned to the wall.

Go placidly amid the noise and haste, and remember what peace there may be in silence. As far as possible without surrender be on good terms with all persons.

There was no peace in the silent treatment from the girls, or her mother, and sometimes it felt as though they were in league against her.

She had hoped Red would suggest they go to the disco together, but he said he'd see her there. She hated these nights, the charge of anticipation in school on the preceding days, the mortification of the evenings themselves, standing about in the wrong clothes feeling hideous. Tonight the dance floor was heaving. She walked around the perimeter, forcing herself to move slowly lest the girls thought they had succeeded in terrorising her across the room. Where was Red? She was about to do another lap when a fire door ahead of her opened from the outside – since the Stardust inferno, exits were always unlocked – and he came strolling in, a careless sway to his gait. Seeing her, he grinned.

Looking well, McCaffrey, he said, putting on a country accent.

Her hair had been cut in a bob and no longer looked like a mistake. She was in a black T-shirt and jeans, her only concession to the night out little wings of eyeliner copied from a French exchange teacher who was visiting that term. Still, she could not accept the compliment and said her shoes were stupid.

There was a cackle. The girls were a few feet away, Tina doubled over.

Shit, murmured Róisín, instinctively turning towards Red.

Don't mind those fucking eejits, he said. His breath smelled sweet and chemical. He saw her nose wrinkle and opened his jacket, flashing her a glimpse of a Libby's orange juice jar filled with a reddish-brown liquid. Skimmed it off the father's drinks cabinet, he said.

Can I have some?

I'm not giving you your first drink, your ma would kill me.

A pair of New Romantics in white shirts that resembled chef's jackets were swinging their hands low to a Spandau Ballet song. A couple of boys shouted 'Benders!' at them.

I fucking hate being a teenager, she said.

It's brutal. OK, one sup and that's it.

They went through the fire exit to the far end of the building where there was little light. Three boys appeared and assembled around them. Róisín had not been in company with Red before, had forgotten he was the sort of boy others followed. She knew them by sight. Tina's brother Barry; Shay Dempsey, the son of a bank manager; Dessie Nolan, whose father worked for the Office of Public Works. She hated that people were known by what their fathers did, aware that she was known by her dad's abscondment. Red introduced her as Ró. She suppressed a smile, thrilled that he'd called her by the name he used when they were alone.

He passed her the jar. Róisín put it to her lips, tilting slowly because of its wide rim, but it flowed in too fast. She wanted to spit it out but swallowed, hoping the boys could not see her eyes watering at the strength of it. She gave it back to Red.

Barry stepped away, disappearing into a hedge and emerging with three cans of beer he'd hidden during football training. Handing one each to Shay and Dessie, he popped his open. Your health, he said, so gently Róisín found it hard to believe he was related to Tina.

Red did most of the talking. He mentioned her often – *Me and Ró*, *Ró says*, *When I was in Ró's* – the others lapping at their cans and throwing her sly glances the odd time. The beer was soon gone, and Red passed his jar around. The boys relished its potency, Shay exhaling with a *haaa* sound, Barry wiping the back of his hand across his mouth. It took effect quickly and one by one they raised their eyes from the ground. Dessie was first to speak, about a band that had played in the hall the previous summer. Shay joined in, using words like 'riff' and 'bridge' that Róisín had read in the copies of *NME* Red stole from the Emerald newsagent's. The band had played 'Alternative Ulster', 'Needle in the Groove', 'Shadow Play'.

So they're a covers band? said Róisín.

Dessie snorted, a sound that said, What would you know?

Róisín dug Red in the ribs and he threw his arms wide, pretending to spill his drink. All their songs are by other people, right? she said.

Correct, he said, burping.

A covers band, she said again.

They're class in anyways, said Dessie. You probably like Kajagoogoo.

And you weren't there, said Shay.

Would ye all relax? said Red.

She took the jar from him. It went down easier this time, and she liked the mouth it was giving her, arguing with lads she'd never had the courage to speak to.

Back inside, Red pulled Róisín by the hand, half-running, towards two empty chairs. He sat heavily and she perched at an angle so she could see him. Just a couple of mouthfuls had given her a loose, happy feeling. This is great craic, she said.

He was watching her, smiling. God, you're a cheap drunk.

Can I have more?

No, he said.

Sometimes she couldn't stand his gaze but now she held it. No?

As he opened his mouth to reply the lights came down. He looked away.

Róisín loathed the slow set at the best of times, dreading being asked to dance, dreading not being asked, but this was the worst yet. She wasn't sure what just happened but the moment was over, killed by a nausea-inducing interlude of corny music and imbecilic groping.

Beside her, Red had leaned forward, elbows on his thighs, hands clasped between his knees. Nobody will come near you with me beside you, he said, over his shoulder. Do you want me to move?

You'd fucking better not, she said. It was hard to keep her tone steady.

They probably wouldn't anyway, he said, sitting back. You're intimidating.

Tina said that once, it was intended as an insult.

The DJ was playing 'Je t'aime moi non plus'. Drooly Gilhooly, who taught religion and Irish in the Christian Brothers school, was at the edge of the dance floor, eyes sweeping the room like a raptor.

This is like a hallucination, said Róisín. Irish Catholic schoolchildren dancing to a soundtrack of people making orgasm noises in French.

Red sniggered. And Gilhooly ready to bayte them off one another.

Why do they call him Drooly? said Róisín.

Cos he dribbles like a fucking baby, said Barry.

Róisín hadn't noticed that he was close enough to hear their conversation, and regretted mentioning Tina.

Poor cunt probably did it once, said Red.

A Hammond organ, the opening bars of 'No Woman, No Cry', their favourite song. They turned to each other so smoothly it could have been choreographed. Say something, Róisín pleaded silently, do something. A shadow fell across them: Barry Doyle, offering Róisín his hand. She glanced at Red, imploring him now to step in and save her, but he was staring straight ahead. Too much time was passing and the hand was taking on a symbolic quality. She stood up, hoping Barry would lead her far away, but he took just three steps before putting his hands on her waist. She placed hers on his shoulders and they began a slow, revolving shuffle, a few feet from Red.

Róisín was aware of some sort of consternation across the room and looked up to see Tina wringing her hands and being comforted by her lackies.

My sister hates you, said Barry.

That's quite an opening line.

Lookit, I don't really get on with her. Are you drunk?

Ossified.

You're very sarcastic.

For God's sake.

His clothes smelled of Lenor fabric softener, which should have been pleasant but reminded Róisín of his hateful sister. Bob Marley was singing the refrain.

'No woman no cry'. Good motto, said Barry.

Oh my God, do you think it's a break-up song?

What are you on about?

Imagine there's two commas in there. 'No cry' means don't cry. It's a social justice song.

Where'd you hear the like of that?

In a documentary.

He blew air out through his front teeth. So you reckon you know a lot about music?

Throwing 'reckon' in there is bloody insulting.

What?

Wha'? she said, imitating him. You said I *think* I know a lot. Would you say that to a bloke?

The snogging couple beside them, who had been fired up since Serge Gainsbourg, audibly unsucked and looked their way. Why was she in a deathly waltz around a GAA hall with a spotty chauvinist who couldn't pronounce his *th*s? She drew back from him, ready to break free, but Tina, hair like a witch's minge, was eyeing her as if she wanted to kill her. The opportunity to further enrage Barry's sister was too good to pass over and Róisín moved a little closer to Barry, resting her lower arms on the beefy bones of his clavicle. He tilted his head. Was he considering kissing her? She stepped back abruptly until he was at arm's length again.

Confusion was moving across Barry's face, but after they had rotated 360 degrees, he cleared his throat. Does the light in the fridge go off when you close the door, do you think? he said.

She felt as if she'd been on the dance floor for weeks, like Jane Fonda in *They Shoot Horses, Don't They?* If only she could flee without making a show of herself. If only Red would liberate her, but his seat was empty.

On the last beat, most of the slow-dancers moved to dimly lit corners, one or two making for the exit. Barry took her hand and steered her off the floor. He sat in Red's place and – terrified he was going to pull her on to his knee – Róisín took the seat beside him. He mumbled 'Fuck's sake' under his breath. She suspected she had 'led him on', a humiliation her religion teacher, a mad nun, said inevitably resulted in rape. There was nothing to talk to Barry about and seconds passed interminably. When all the girls minced on to the floor for 'Billie Jean', he finally spoke.

You not going to join them?

Oh, fuck off, said Róisín. Delighted to have an excuse to storm out, she rose from the chair and went through the fire exit.

There were more people outside than before, courting couples writhing along the wall. She found Red alone, the jar in his hand, now empty. Did you drink all that? she said.

It's yourself. I thought you were getting romantic with Doyle.

I couldn't say no.

You say anything you like the rest of the time, he said, his enunciation careful.

There were footsteps behind them and she turned to see Barry. Any of that left? he said, studiously not looking at Róisín.

Finito, said Red, look. He lumbered forward and swung his arm back as if for a tennis serve, lobbing the vessel into the darkness. It sounded like a window had shattered and within moments they were surrounded by adults.

Red was swaying, breath coming heavily, Drooly Gilhooly peering into his face. What was he drinking? he asked Róisín.

I don't know.

Red put a finger to her lips to silence her then locked his knuckles together as if he was composing himself. Releasing them, he held his right hand up, touching a digit as he named each drink. Cherry brandy, Kiskadee, Johnnie Walker, Cork Dry Gin, Huzzar vodka.

Are you drunk too? someone asked her.

Not really, she said, and immediately wanted to kick herself.

Cheeky article, said the woman from the desk.

Red had switched hands. Drambuie, Cinzano Bianco, Harveys Bristol Cream, Sandeman's. Pausing, thumb aloft, he slid down the wall.

I'm getting the Guards, said the woman from the desk, he's drunk and disorderly.

He's asleep! said Róisín.

He's pallatic, girl! said Gilhooly.

Barry was gone. What a crap friend, slinking away in case he got into trouble. Someone said she was going inside to phone 999, but Gilhooly lowered his voice, arguing. Right so, said the woman, and left.

Gilhooly pulled Red upright, saying he would bring him home. Róisín took Red's other arm and they propelled him to the car park, his legs giving beneath him every few steps. When they reached his Datsun Cherry, the teacher said, You may get in as well, madam. *Not really*, indeed.

Róisín sat in the back seat and Gilhooly pushed Red in after her. He landed heavily against her shoulder. There was wooden beading on the driver's seat that clacked like an abacus when the teacher got behind the wheel. Red's head lolled on the potholed road, Róisín following his mouth with a Quinnsworth bag Gilhooly had passed her in case he threw up.

Gilhooly didn't ask for directions, Red's was the sort of house everyone knew. A huge dormer bungalow at the end of an arc of semi-ds overlooking an artificial lake. Red had told her the developer built it for himself but went bust and had to sell it for a pittance; his father had thought the purchase a victory when he should have been ashamed. He also said, in the bitter tone he used when talking about his family, the house was fancy, and it was. Wrought-iron street lamps on either side of the front door, flouncy drapes at the windows. A white-painted wall carpeted in a jagged red-berried shrub Róisín's mother called – probably wrongly – cotton easter. Two brand-new cars – a dark metallic Volvo and a white Fiat Panda – on a paved driveway.

Gilhooly parked on the kerb and got out. Come on, son, you're home, he said, opening the passenger door.

Red stirred, opening his eyes wide and squinting in the direction of the lights. When he saw where they were, he said, I'm not going into that house.

I'll go in with you. They'll only be annoyed for a while, it'll blow over, said Gilhooly.

No, said Red, shrinking back until Róisín was squashed against the other door. She and Gilhooly looked at each other. Red was whimpering.

He doesn't want to go in, said Róisín.

Red twisted in her direction, as if he was surprised to see her. Please, Ró, he said. I can't go in there.

He can come home with me, said Róisín.

What will your mother say? said Gilhooly.

Your mother. Did the whole town know her father was gone? She won't mind, he's always in our house, said Róisín.

As Gilhooly drove down the main street, an oncoming lorry flooded the car with light. Red had been slumped against her, but he stiffened, fists clenched. She put her hand over his and whispered, It's OK. She didn't think it was OK at all, but she repeated it until his body slackened.

Gilhooly left the engine running and went up the path. The hall lamp was on and through the glass panel Róisín could make out her mother's taut shape rushing to the door. It opened a crack, then fully. Red was heaped awkwardly across Róisín's lap. She shifted to make him more comfortable, supporting his head as she moved her thighs.

Gilhooly and her mother opened the rear door, hauling Red out. He came to, looking around wildly. Ró, he said, I want Ró.

I'm here, I'm here. She climbed out after him.

She took over from her mother, helping Gilhooly drag Red to the house. His legs couldn't support him and a couple of times the three of them careened off the path on to the wet grass.

Inside, they laid him on the settee. We need to tell his parents where he is, said Gilhooly.

No, said Red, trying to get up.

He almost rolled on to the floor and Róisín knelt beside him.

Shush now, pet, you'll be all right here, said Una, bending to pat Red's shoulder. She left the room with Gilhooly, closing the door behind them.

Red was still, his complexion deathly white against the black of his hair. His lips were pale too and for a moment Róisín wondered was he breathing. She touched the dip in his temple and felt a pulse. The front door clicked shut and moments later Gilhooly started his car and drove away. Her mother came back, standing with her hands clasped, her face crumpled with worry.

I don't know how he got like that, said Róisín.

Do you think I came down in the last shower? Her mother left the room again. She went up and down the stairs and into the kitchen, bringing the duvet from the spare bed, a stack of frayed towels, a basin, two pints of water.

What if he bokes?

Hold the basin under his face!

Róisín raised Red's shoulders and slipped beneath them, cradling his head. Her mother went to the hall to call his parents and was back within a minute. She stood over them, regarding Red as if she had never seen him before. Róisín thought of his house. It was unnaturally perfect. Snippets of what little he had told her about home were assembling in her head and becoming a question, but just as quickly the whole unravelled. An uneasy feeling lingered in its wake.

4

25 June 1983

The queue was along the footpath and Róisín had to inch sideways to reach the counter. Mags, her boss, looked as if she was about to have a brain haemorrhage. She had decided to take in secondhand schoolbooks and sell them on. Today was the last opportunity to offload, and everyone had come at once.

You want to see the shite they're giving me, said Mags through her teeth, smiling psychotically at the line of customers.

Róisín loved working for Mags, who had opened Basin Street Books with so little capital she could scarcely afford to stock it: when she sold a book, she used the profit to buy two. The gaps in the shelves were closing, but the business always seemed to be on the brink of collapse. Still, working there on Saturdays kept Róisín in cigarettes and every week she bought a book with her staff discount, recommended to her by Mags. *The Women's Room*, *A Room of One's Own*, *The Second Sex*. Mags said she herself was not fully 'out' as a feminist, because she was pretending not to cohabit with her boyfriend, a prematurely bald PE teacher called Seamus. They shared a four-bedroom house with another unmarried couple to give the impression they had one room each lest they arouse the suspicion of the parish council – which was partly why she was skint.

Róisín took over at the till so Mags could examine each text and either reject or come up with a price. One batch smelled strongly of salad cream. Some had long lost their binding and were more a stack of pages than a book. Most had been written on. *Fighting for peace is like fucking for virginity. The Who. I love Red Camelin.*

Many of the customers spent the money Mags paid them for the schoolbooks before leaving the shop. The Famous Five and Malory Towers, the Charlie Haughey biography everyone was talking about, the latest Jeffrey Archer. By four o'clock, gaps had reappeared in the shelves and everyone was gone. Mags rushed to the door and locked it, turning the sign to *Closed*. Never again, she said. Let's get the fuck out of here and enjoy the weather.

Róisín paid for the copy of Plato's *Symposium* Mags had ordered for her and went down the town to meet Red. The Derby was on in the Curragh, the street colloped with horse shit that smelled particularly ripe in the sunshine.

Red was on a banquette in the Sorrento Grill, sucking sugar from a spoon.

Happy birthday, she said, handing him the book.

He read the back cover. Thank you. But I never got you anything.

Yeah, you bastard. My ma is at the races with Gilhooly. I'm fighting with her.

Plus ça change, he said. What about this time?

Enda fucking Gilhooly.

It had started after the GAA disco. When Gilhooly wasn't showering the kitchen with flakes of scalp, he was ringing Una, asking if Red was there, if he ever went home at all. Una behaved differently towards Red now, gently interrogating him. Red claimed to be amused by their interest, but he didn't come around much any more. Worse than that, Una and Enda had begun doing things together. Going to the cinema, walking in the Wicklow Mountains, orienteering. That morning he had taken her to the races, coming through the back door when

Róisín was at the kitchen table. She dropped her spoon in her cereal bowl and ran upstairs, standing in the bathroom doorway. Your boyfriend is in the kitchen, she said. Can I not even have my breakfast in peace?

Her mother grabbed a tissue and began blotting at her mouth. I suppose you'll be meeting your boyfriend later, she said.

It was truly impressive how readily Una stooped to her level these days. And she was wrong. Róisín was proud of never having had a boyfriend. Her friendship with Red was on a higher plane than the grubby maulings of their schoolmates, all that boys-and-girls carry-on seemed so petty in comparison. She had ordered the copy of *The Symposium* because they had talked about platonic friendship. You don't understand anything, she said.

Her mother screwed the cap on her foundation and tossed it on to the bathroom windowsill. Just get out of my road, will you?

Sometimes Róisín enjoyed goading Una, watching her struggle to keep her temper. Mostly she felt desolate. Her father hadn't phoned for a fortnight. Una relished in reminding Róisín that when he was in the habit of phoning she usually refused to speak to him. That did not excuse him; after all he'd done he should endure his punishment until Róisín decided it was over.

Red tapped her forehead with his finger. God, I can nearly see what's going on in there. Stop ruminating. Have you any money? I'd love a pint.

Piss off, cows ruminate, she said, opening her wage packet. Mags had paid her an extra three pounds.

Why are you smiling? he said.

Cos I'm fucking loaded.

The town's grimy windows and bad paint jobs looked even worse in the sunshine. She pushed the button at the pedestrian crossing. We could be here forever, she said, and all that awaits on the other side is more of the same.

Profound, said Red.

A bus passed, a tractor, a Hiace van. The green man appeared and they began to walk. A souped-up Ford Escort was idling a few feet away, the three young men it carried watching them cross. If I said you had a beautiful body would you hold it against me? called the driver at Róisín. Red doubled back and went striding towards the car, but the lights changed and the men took off guffawing. Ignorant fuckers, he said.

They went in the side door of the Shillelagh. Four rickety stools in front of the mahogany counter. Behind it shelves of goods she imagined elderly bachelors couldn't live without: firelighters, dried marrowfat peas, mouse traps. Red hit the bell on the counter and Pascal Conway came limping from the lounge next door. Róisín ordered a pint of Harp for Red and a soda water with lime for herself.

She looks about twelve, said Pascal without so much as a glance at Róisín.

Red chuckled and she elbowed him in the ribs. He opened *The Symposium* on a random page and began to read.

Then, said Eryximachus, the weak heads like myself, Aristodemus, Phaedrus, and others who never can drink, are fortunate in finding that the stronger ones are not in a drinking mood. (I do not include Socrates, who is able either to drink or to abstain, and will not mind, whichever we do.)

Socrates me bollocks, said Pascal.

Red closed the book and looked unhappily at his pint. We need to do something wholesome, he said. Will we hitch to the weir?

They bought things for a picnic – Calvita cheese, Ritz crackers, crisps and a flagon of Linden Village – and left Pascal rubbing his knee.

At the top of the town, Red retreated into a bush. Put out your thumb, he said.

An hour ago you were defending my honour and now you're sexually exploiting me.

Who's going to give me a lift? Stop scowling or we'll be here all evening.

Róisín arranged her face into what she hoped was a genial expression, Red laughing from the hedgerow.

A few cars passed before a middle-aged woman pulled up abruptly. I'm only stopping so you don't end up in a gully with your throat cut, she said through her open window.

As Róisín sat in the front passenger seat, Red jumped in the back.

Ah now, the woman said, but she wasn't really angry. She was on her way to visit her father in the County Home, she told them, and they should enjoy themselves while they still had control over their bowels.

She left them in a lay-by, a few miles south. They took a path through a wood, beneath green leaves and flashes of blue sky. As they approached the water, they heard shouts and laughter: the town was forty miles from the coast and this was where people came to swim. Róisín began to complain that she didn't want to be with scores of others but Red was beating a trail through a dense copse of willow. She was about to grumble about that too, but suddenly they were on a bend in the river where they couldn't be seen.

He took off his shoes and socks and stepped in the water, sloshing about. Like his hands, his feet were narrow and long-boned. Elegant. She followed him in, but the little stones on the riverbed pricked her soles and she was out within a minute.

There was just enough room for them to stretch out. The ground had a dank, heady scent and felt almost warm. Red opened the cider and passed it to her. The fizz went up her nose, making her splutter.

I'll never make a drinker out of you, he said.

She squashed pieces from the cheese and put it on the crackers. Red ate fast, washing it down with mouthfuls of cider. Róisín slugged from the bottle again and lay beside him. Red was on his side, his face resting on the crook of his arm. A bird was chirping nearby.

He sang the refrain from 'Blackbird' by the Beatles. He was always quoting lyrics, and they never meant anything. Still...

What the fuck are you looking at? he said softly.

That's what I'm wondering.

What would Plato say?

Plato can fuck off, she thought, but played along, reaching for the book. It seemed to be a series of opinions about Eros, the god of love, given by men lying around gorging on food and drink served by slaves. They talked about beauty and love, the sort of love practised in Sparta, love as a way of ensuring procreation. There did not appear to be anything on what she understood to be platonic love.

Well? said Red.

It's bonkers. A fella meets another fella on the street and says, Were you there the night Socrates was talking about love? And the other fella says, Now, funny you should say that, but I was only talking to a lad the other day and he said he wasn't there, but he knows someone who was.

That's like having a conversation with Nathy Phelan. Give us a look.

She passed it to him and he flashed the cover at her, putting on a serious face. Pretentious, moi? he said.

We're a pair of dicks, said Róisín, going up on her elbow and drinking more cider. She lay back down and closed her eyes. Her head was spinning, not unpleasantly. When she was small she had seen a comedy sketch on television. A man had been buried alive, banging the lid of his coffin and screaming. It gave her nightmares, but perhaps the box was the problem. It felt as though the earth was moulding around her body, holding her, and then Red was shaking her awake.

The light had fallen a little and she was cold. He said she had been asleep for about forty minutes, that he was now practically a classics scholar. That they should go back to town. As they were pulling their socks on, she hesitated. In half an hour they would be loping down the main street and whatever was happening between them here, and there was something, would be over. Red, she said, but didn't know what to say next.

What?

Nothing, she said, wriggling her feet into her shoes. Her mouth began to crinkle. Afraid she was about to cry, she made to stand up.

Wow, he said, pulling her back down.

What? Her voice sounded slightly hysterical.

He kissed her, with his lips at first, then his mouth opened a little, and she opened hers, and it wasn't the revolting intrusion she had seen at school discos, all jabbing tongues and slurping. It felt tender, nice, but he broke away, resting his forehead against hers.

Ró, he said.

She didn't want to hear that it was a bad idea, that they were just friends. She kissed him back. This time he touched her, running his hand from her cheek to her neck.

On the way back through the woods, he went ahead. He didn't speak, except to warn her about briars and nettles. She began to fret that they had destroyed something, but right before they reached the road he kissed her again, more a smack than a snog, she who'd been kissed for the first time half an hour ago discerned. They bickered once more about him making her hitch. She put her thumb out, raising two fingers at him with her other hand, and he watched her from the siding, a half-smile on his face. They were picked up by a man who smelled of fresh Guinness, driving the filthiest car she had ever seen. He was talking about the Derby, but Red's thigh was against hers, and she couldn't concentrate.

They ditched the bag of rubbish in a bin near the town hall and set off for Róisín's house. She couldn't count how many times they had walked this way together, talking and laughing, but a shyness had fallen over them. Twice she felt his eyes on her but when she glanced back he was looking ahead. They turned on to her road and when the house came into view she almost howled: the Datsun Cherry was parked behind her mother's car on the driveway.

By the time Róisín opened the front door she was furious. I thought youse were going for dinner after the races, she said, barging into the kitchen.

'Hello' would have done rightly, said her mother. She was wearing a silky cream dress with diagonal red stripes. Its boat neck gave her narrow shoulders structure and her boobs heft. Róisín couldn't help staring: she was beautiful.

Hello! said Red. You look great, Mrs McCaffrey.

Ach now, said Una, the blush that was washing over her face making her even prettier.

Lickarse, said Róisín.

Enda scratched his head and a skiff of dandruff snowed his sports jacket. What have you been up to the last while, son? he said, turning to Red.

Róisín stared at her mother, willing her to tell Gilhooly to stop, but she was still basking in the compliment.

I've been taking advantage of the clear skies, said Red. Lying under the stars, the heavens like a dome above me. One night a proper tinker invited me into his caravan. It was one of those covered wagons in bright colours with pots and pans hanging all over the gaff. His wife taught me how to read teacups. I'd read yours now, Mr Gilhooly, only Mrs McCaffrey buys teabags. The loose-leaf gear is your only man.

Róisín had stuffed her cuff so far into her mouth to keep from laughing she was nearly choking.

Enda, clearly well used to such lip, pursued his line of questioning. How are things at home?

Marvellous! Sure, it's the happiest house in Ireland.

Jesus Christ! All that's missing is a bare light bulb and him in an SS uniform, said Róisín, tossing her head in Enda's direction.

Una looked like she was going to combust with the effort of keeping her temper. You had better leave the room, she said.

Happily!

Red widened his eyes at Una and walked ahead of Róisín into the hall. Whose side was he on?

Fucking cheek of them, said Róisín as they went upstairs.

Cheek of you. You're like Nancy Spungen.

I was sticking up for you! She sat on her bed.

Yeah. You also wanted to embarrass your ma, he said. He was by the window. He tweaked the blind, surveying the street.

She's a bitch.

There's a pair of you in it, he said.

She felt like all the air had gone out of her. Walking towards the house she had envisaged them alone, him kissing her again, touching her face with that faint tremble in his fingers. Instead she'd revealed what she was really like.

He sat on the bed. I didn't mean it to come out like that, he said. You're not a bitch.

I am.

Only to your ma. And she's all right.

OK, she whined. I'll stop.

Sometimes she was so comfortable in his company she forgot herself, farting, mumbling aloud, then, realising he was there, feeling astonished to see him. Other times, like now, it was as though a crackle of lightning was going between them, like God's finger giving life to Adam in pictures she had seen from the Sistine Chapel. Surely Red felt it too, but he was just sitting there.

When she could finally face him, his eyes were downcast. What we did earlier, he said. Plato would call it vulgar love. You don't really think about me that way, do you?

She didn't reply because she didn't know how to.

After he left she remembered the schoolbook Mags had taken in, *I love Red Camelin* printed inside the cover. IF UC KI NG LO VE RE DC AM EL IN she spelled as she fell asleep.

5

24 December 1983

Róisín moved aside her mother's ornaments – a Royal Doulton balloon woman, a silver rose vase with holes for buds she couldn't afford, a brass tortoise that in its heyday could be wound up and set wandering – to make space for the holly Red had brought.

You found some with berries. I wish we had a real tree too.

Theirs was a fake one, squashed in front of the window, flittery foil branches adazzle with coloured lights and chipped baubles.

Red said he loved it, that Christmas wasn't supposed to be tasteful, a downbeat air about him as he spoke.

They went upstairs. Across his back was the sports bag he had been carrying the day she met him, now cracked, the strap flayed into strips. He dropped it on the floor of the spare room and launched himself on to the bed.

Heaven, he said.

Red had stopped going home before the end of the summer, taking up residence on Nathy Phelan's couch. When he didn't show up in school on the 1st of September Enda visited his parents, who dismissed him as a delinquent, a lost cause. Róisín rarely saw Red now and was surprised he had accepted Una's invitation to come for Christmas. She suspected that even the likes of Phelan had plans and Red had nowhere else to go.

She went downstairs to the kitchen, thinking he would nap, but she heard the shower running. RTE Radio was broadcasting from Dublin city centre, a street trader singing 'Have Yourself a Merry Little Christmas' like she was Judy Garland. Red joined her a little later, his hair wet. Clean, he had lost the rough appearance that had shocked her when he arrived. They spent the afternoon peeling vegetables and making stuffing. Red's mood lifted as he worked, singing along with carols and going in and out of the sitting room to stoke the fire.

In the morning, there were two small piles of presents under the tree. Una had knitted Red a mohair jumper, red and black striped. He hugged her and put it on over his T-shirt. For Róisín there were new jeans that she was too self-conscious to try on, but she kissed her mother anyway. A selection box, diary, socks for each of them. Una handed her an envelope. The card inside had a photograph of a poinsettia and was stippled with silver glitter, *To my dear daughter at Christmas* printed in an old-fashioned script. A hundred pounds sterling from her father in newly minted twenties, more money than she had ever held at once. Róisín gave her mother a Monet calendar and Red a copy of *The Brothers Karamazov*, gifts she'd bought from Mags using her staff discount. Red gave each of them a jam jar containing pieces of paper he said were vouchers for services. Una could avail of *washing the car*, *cleaning the oven*, *cutting the grass*. Her mother exclaimed that it was the most thoughtful and creative present ever, and kissed him on the forehead. Róisín opened hers, trying not to betray her excitement. He'd promised *maths grinds*, *French conversation*, *friendship for life*. She could not read the latter aloud and put it back in.

While her mother gathered the discarded wrapping paper, scrunching it into balls, Róisín scanned Red's face for irony or scorn. I mean it, he whispered. And your reaction was fucking priceless.

There was one gift left. Una picked it up and made for the door.

Whoa, said Róisín, open it here.

Her mother removed the paper carefully, picking off bits of Sellotape, to reveal a yellow anorak.

The relief, said Róisín.

Red told her to stop, but Una was too pleased to care, telling them she'd got drenched the last time she and Enda went rambling.

Her father rang after breakfast. As Róisín took the receiver from her mother, she heard him clear his throat several times, one of his nervous tics. She was flooded with tenderness for him but only managed 'Hiya'. She hadn't called him Dad since he left. How powerless she was, having only that to hurt him with.

Did Santa come? he said.

Yeah. Thanks for the present.

Happy Christmas, love.

Perhaps it wasn't nerves, his voice was nasal and slightly muffled, suggesting a head cold. She tried to muster anger, but the pity was too strong.

Daddy, she said, but he was gone.

The church grounds bore marks left by those who had gone from the pub to Midnight Mass: spilled matches by the gate and a mantle of sick around the crib that was now home to a toddler-sized baby Jesus with limpid blue eyes. Una clacked ahead to her preferred pew by the confession boxes on the right-hand side. Róisín and Red slid in after her. A slap of expensive leather soles made Red stiffen; it was his family. Dolly Camelin was in a green crêpe suit trimmed with gold, Red's father Robert in a trench coat with a brown leather collar. Jonathan, the youngest boy, was in a blazer, not moving a muscle. The middle son, Andrew, was wearing Red's combat jacket and seemed unable to sit still, his backside slipping around the polished mahogany of the bench. He glanced back at Red. His face was bright with fury.

At collection time, Red's father rose to oversee the weekly whip-round for the upkeep of the parish. He waited at the end of each pew for the basket and passed it to the row behind, nodding Christmas greetings to one and all. When he saw Una, his expression changed from jollity to sufferance. Robert Camelin, the God-fearing father of an errant prodigal son he'd gladly welcome home with a twenty-pound turkey stuffed to the point of bursting. When Robert moved on to the row behind, Róisín saw that Red's hands were trembling.

No one lingered when Mass was over, the women in thrall to oven timings, the children impatient to return to their new toys. Una walked quickly, calling over her shoulder that they were lazy hallions for not hurrying. Róisín began to complain to Red, but he had stalled a few feet back. Robert Camelin had an arm around his shoulder, a fatherly, conciliatory gesture, but as he leaned to speak in Red's ear, Róisín felt afraid to her bones; his mouth was twisted in a snarl. Red shrugged free and walked unsteadily towards them.

Can we go? he said, his voice breaking.

Una began rooting in her handbag for her keys, eventually finding them in her pocket, and they piled in. As she started the engine, a car drew up alongside them. It was the Camelins' Volvo. Red's mother was mere inches away. He began to bang the window, but she stayed looking straight ahead. The car moved off and he fell back against the seat and closed his eyes.

You all right, son? said Una when they reached the house.

Yeah, he said, and went to the sitting room, kneeling to light the fire.

Róisín followed her mother to the kitchen. What the fuck was that? she said, pouring cloudy liquid off the potatoes Red had peeled the previous day, covering them with fresh water from the tap.

No idea. Could you hear what the da was saying? said Una.

He was whispering, but I saw his face. Psycho.

That poor woman.

Róisín bashed the lid on the saucepan. Are you serious? she cried. She didn't even turn her head. Glammed up to the nines and pretending everything is normal.

Don't talk about my mother like that, said Red behind them. He looked as though he'd been leached of colour.

I'm sorry, Red, but...

Please, he said.

Una clapped her hands and, full of forced gaiety, put Red at the table with a bag of Brussels sprouts. Róisín switched the radio on but it didn't fill the silence. What a weirdo Red's father was, in his flasher's mac, the toadying, pious head on him as he passed the basket. And his face when he put his mouth to Red's ear. *He's not what people think.* Nor was his mother, clearly, all dressed up for Christmas and blanking her own son.

Una had wanted to roast a chicken, there were only three of them, but Róisín had insisted on turkey, taking responsibility for using all the leftovers. When it was ready, they sat at the table, pulling crackers and putting on the paper hats that fell from them. Una poured them each a small glass of the wine she only bought at Christmas, teeheeing that she was a bad mother for giving drink to teenagers. Red managed a smile but ate without his usual appetite. Once or twice Róisín turned to speak to him. She glimpsed terror in his eyes, the expression he'd worn as he listened to his father.

Una went for a nap after the meal, leaving Red and Róisín in the kitchen. They finished the wine, glugging it in minutes. It affected her quickly and, giggling, she found the brandy her mother had bought for flaming the pudding. As they cleared up they drank mouthfuls of the spirit, humming along to the music on the radio. They were fleet, so attuned to each other it was like a dance. '2000 Miles' came on and Red fell quiet. God, I love that song, he said when it was over.

They brought a tin of Quality Street to the sitting room. Róisín lay on the settee, Red on the floor at her feet. They watched *Flash Gordon*, jeering at Flash's tight, shiny costume and bobbed hair, carping at the soundtrack. He passed her toffee pennies and fudge; he liked the horrid ones, orange creams and nougat. She told him that was the Protestant coming out in him.

They went outside to smoke, standing on the front doorstep. The street was silent, fairy lights twinkling in windows.

Do you miss your family? she asked.

He shook his head as if he was trying to expel the thought of them. Passing her the cigarette, he went back indoors.

She switched channels and settled on *The Return of the Pink Panther*. He was quiet again, blueish light from the television flickering across his face. Why wouldn't he tell her what was wrong? She made tea during the third ad break and brought it to him with a box of USA biscuits under her arm. His back was against the settee, arms resting on his bent knees.

Jesus. More food, he said.

She sat beside him. I don't know what to do, she said.

About what? He was watching Inspector Clouseau crash through a glass roof on to someone's dinner table.

You. You're so sad.

Leave it, Ró. Please.

I'll be your friend for life too.

You won't, he said turning to look at her, and that's OK.

I will.

He reached for her hand. She moved it to his face, placing it on his cheek. For a moment she thought he was going to kiss her, but he laid it gently in her lap. We'll get some kip, he said. You'll be glad in the morning we didn't do anything.

Upstairs, Róisín lay on her bed, feeling the absence of his touch and a dawning shame. *You're so sad* and practically jumping on him when he was upset. You are a terrible person, she told herself. YO UA RE AT ER RI BL EP ER SO N, but the lone N bothered her. YO UA RE AN UT TE RL YT ER RI BL EP ER SO N, she tried, but it was still not right. YO UA RE AN AB SO LU TE FU CK UP had a ring to it. She watched it pass in front of her closed lids, the way normal people counted sheep, and eventually fell asleep.

She woke at six and lay looking at the ceiling, dreading seeing Red. Before nine, she heard him leave his room for the bathroom. Please go back to bed, she silently begged, but he knocked for her, growling, Feed me. Pulling a jumper over her pyjamas she opened the door. He was smiling as though nothing had happened. Downstairs, he chatted and joked. She doubted his mood was much better than yesterday and was terribly moved by how hard he was trying to make things easy for her. They spent the day drifting from kitchen to sitting room and back with turkey sandwiches, bowls of stuffing with HP Sauce, plum pudding fried in butter. Sitting at either end of the settee, stealing the occasional glance at each other.

Enda arrived in the early evening, when they were watching *Eric and Ernie's Christmas Show*. He said they were gone off the boil, that they'd never match the BBC shows of the seventies. Red agreed. Una came downstairs in a black floaty dress with a ruffled hem, smiling shyly when Enda told her she was looking lovely. He was taking her to a party.

You pair, she warned Róisín. Do not go out drinking.

She was barely in the Datsun Cherry when they left for town.

Outside, Red raised his chin and inhaled. God, I love the smell of turf. Aren't we blessed to live on the Bog of Allen?

I do not like living on a fucking bog actually.

He laughed, sounding like himself again.

You're in better form today, she said.

He didn't acknowledge the remark, saying the whole town would be out and that she shouldn't lose it if Tina turned up. Róisín and Red had been friends for over a year, spent hundreds of hours together, and still he fobbed her off with small talk and pleasantries. He knew everything about her, but what did she know about him, aside from his taste in music and books and film? And what had he meant last night when he said she wouldn't be his friend forever?

The pub was a maze of little parlours crammed with china figurines and standard lamps and brocade cushions, a fire lighting each room. It was run by hideously made-up twin sisters in their sixties who were known as Arsenic and Old Lace. The premises were so cute they could afford to be discerning about who they served, but they were too batty to check IDs and the place was full of under-age drinkers.

Barry Doyle was sitting on a stool at the counter. He said hello to Red, ignoring Róisín as he had done since their hapless slow-dance. She listened to them talk for a few minutes, then went off to find a table. They joined her in the farthest parlour, Barry placing a vodka and lime in front of her. She thanked him and he replied with, Your health, sounding even more mild than the night of the disco.

A group of people came in, including Sinéad, who Róisín sat beside in school – one of four in her class, all named for Sinéad Bean de Valera, Irish First Lady throughout the sixties. She fell on Róisín, saying she'd been on the Irish Mist at home and was a bit merry, introducing her farmer brothers. Then she opened her eyes wide at Red's back and whisper-sang the chorus of 'Is She Really Going Out with Him?' into Róisín's ear.

Stop, he's my friend, said Róisín.

Yeah, right, said Sinéad, winking as her brothers tugged her away.

She's cute, said Barry.

The school uniform made most of the girls look awful. Sinéad was going to be one of those you met a few months after graduation and realised she had been a raving beauty all along. She's too nice for you, said Róisín.

Red and Barry drank pints of Guinness with whiskey chasers. Barry rolled cigarettes from a pouch of tobacco, running his tongue across the seal of each paper, handing them around. He did not speak directly to Róisín but no longer had a sulky puss. After they had each bought a round, Red rose, saying they should get back to the house before Una.

Out on the street, three young teenagers were sitting on the bonnet of a parked car. One of them hocked a lump of phlegm on to the path as they approached, the others commending him for his reach.

All the saliva that's projected from the mouths of spotty boys on to the pavements of small towns, she said.

Red didn't answer. He was staring at one of the boys, who came loping towards them, a plastic flagon of cider in his hand. It was Andrew, his brother, childish face contorted absurdly from drink. Red reached for the bottle. Andrew batted his hand away and lost his balance, hitting the footpath as the bottle bounced on to the road. He flapped his arms and legs as if he was making a snow angel, cackling wildly. Red seized his shoulder and hauled him upright. Go home, for fuck's sake, he said.

Andrew poked Red in the chest. Home? he squealed. You left us there.

Red grabbed his brother in a desperate hug, but Andrew pushed him off and spat words Róisín couldn't make out into Red's face. She watched his shoulders drop, as if something had been confirmed to him.

Fuck off, said Andrew, poking him again. Just fuck off and die.

Red, what is going on? said Róisín.

Will you just leave it! he hissed at her.

Barry came out of the pub, holding a bottle of vodka. He took in Red's face and Andrew's hunched figure, now moving away. Clamour from across the road, and a troupe of men in tattered clothes and wigwam-shaped headdresses spilled on to the pavement from the pub opposite. One of them was waving a long stick in the air and whooping. He gave a shout of recognition, and came running towards them.

We're on the wran, he said, leaping on to Red's back and whipping his thigh like a jockey.

The 'straw boys' were the strangest thing Róisín had seen down south. St Stephen, the story went, was betrayed by a little wren that sang its lungs out to reveal his hiding place to the Roman soldiers who were hunting for him. To avenge his martyrdom, men in rural Ireland donned straw camouflage and hunted for a wren on the saint's feast day, parading it on a stick. These days, the hunters collected money; there did not appear to be anything on the end of the thing this straw boy was wielding, but his pockets were jangling.

The man slid off Red's back and removed his headdress. It was Nathy Phelan, his normally bushy hair plastered to his head. Barry showed Nathy the vodka and Red, who ten minutes ago had been about to leave, held his thumb up. The three of them began walking. She had to run a few paces to catch up with Red.

I thought we were going home, she said in a low voice.

I am going home, he said.

Barry and Nathy turned left at the fair green. Red paused for a moment, watching Andrew and his friends until they were out of sight.

Outside Nathy's house, a cooker that someone had kicked dents into was lying on its side. Inside, a stench she thought was bleach but, on seeing the filth of the place, realised was urine. Red sank into a small, saggy couch. My bed, he said.

It was a peculiarly Irish sort of squalor. One room with a cracked window and little Mary statues on the sill. A fireplace, the grate packed with cigarette butts and cardboard beer wrappers. Nothing on the walls but a horse-racing calendar and a copy of the Proclamation. Red had been here for months and it had never occurred to her to ask what it was like. It wasn't that she presumed he was somewhere decent; she had told herself he was fine, that it was an adventure.

Barry was holding up cups and sniggering. One was like a Petri dish, furry growth in its base. He ran the tap and rusty water sputtered out that he swilled around each one. Opening the vodka, he offered her a shot, but she shook her head, afraid she might catch something.

Zero craic, he said sourly.

She wanted Red to protest, but he had drunk his shot and was gesturing for another.

Nathy produced a slab of hash the size of a brick and chipped a piece off with a chisel he said he kept for that sole purpose. Lebanese red, he said.

Barry nodded appreciatively. She would have scoffed aloud but there was something intimidating about the sum of them.

She refused the spliff Nathy offered her. Whatever you like, princess, he said, which Barry found hilarious. Red accepted it and dragged hard, holding the smoke in his lungs. He had ignored her since they arrived. She should go home. Her mother would be back from the party and angry they had gone out.

I'm heading off, she said, Mum will be raging.

Mum, said Barry. Are you fucking English?

Nathy chuckled but then headlights brightened the room and he darted to the window.

Cops, he said, dropping the joint in his drink.

Barry was on his feet, Red slipping the hash under his seat cushion. Nathy opened the door on the third knock. When the first Guard entered the house, bending his long frame to get in, Red raised two fingers to his forehead and said, Ten-Four Roger D.

Watch your manners, said the Guard in a jaunty Cork accent. He was still stooped, the ceiling too low to accommodate his ridiculous height.

Another Guard followed, an older, shorter, wider man. Names, he said, whipping out a notebook.

She was leaving, said Red, you don't need her name.

I'll be the judge of that.

Come on, she doesn't even want to be here.

The lanky Guard had opened the back door and was shining a torch at the yard. What's in that shed, Phelan? he said.

Come back with a warrant and I'll show you, Sticks.

So fast she hardly saw it happen, Nathy was pinned to the wall.

Scarper, the older Guard told Róisín, putting the notebook away.

She walked at first, but broke into a sprint when she was out of sight of the house. It was eleven and the town was already a mess, spilled chips on the pavement, pints abandoned in shop doorways. She paused at the church to catch her breath, then ran all the way home.

The hall light was on. Through the glass she saw her mother's figure on the stairs. Róisín slotted her key in the door and Una rushed to it, flinging it open. She began to chastise her for going out but, taking in the empty path, said, Where's Red?

We went to a house, said Róisín, her breath coming in deep rasps. The Guards arrived.

Whose house?

Nathy Phelan's.

Jesus, said her mother. That dump.

Róisín burst into tears. I didn't want to be there!

Her mother grabbed her keys. I honestly don't understand you, wee girl, she said, slamming the front door behind her.

Róisín went to the kitchen sink and tried to soap away the filth of Nathy Phelan's house but it wasn't on her skin, it was inside her. What was in the shed? Had they found the hash? Had Red been arrested? She made tea and a turkey sandwich and brought them to the sitting room. The fire had died hours ago and there was nothing to watch on television but an episode of *Tales of the Unexpected* she'd already seen. She sat on the settee, unable to focus or eat, and waited.

Her mother poked her awake at half four, still in the flouncy black dress. For a moment Róisín did not remember the night's drama, but Una's anxious face brought it back.

Where's Red, Mum?

Upstairs.

Róisín got up, stumbling towards the door.

Leave him for tonight, love.

The Guards had found stolen jewellery in the shed and a quantity of drugs under a cushion. Nathy had been charged. Her mother was worried they would find a way to pin it on Red too.

The doorbell rang before nine. Her mother got there first and Róisín went downstairs to find her in Enda Gilhooly's clutches, an embrace that became wooden as they realised they were being watched. Una went up to rouse Red, Enda following Róisín to the kitchen.

What were ye at last night? he said, helping himself to tea from the pot.

I've already discussed it with my mother.

He raised his eyebrows, amusement wrinkling his mouth, so impervious to cheek it was maddening.

Una joined them, sitting at the table. Enda put his hand on hers and, inclining her head in a gesture that said *Aw*, she gazed into his eyes. Her own mother making her feel like a gooseberry! They would both take Red to the station, they said, the more responsible adults willing to vouch for him the better.

I'll come too, said Róisín.

They stared at her as though she was insane.

Red was literally hanging his head as he entered the room. Sorry, sorry, sorry, he mumbled. He refused Una's offer of breakfast; he just wanted to get it over with. Sorry, he said again, a tremor in his voice. Róisín was relieved when the three of them left for the Garda station, her mother reassuring Red that it would be OK, he hadn't done anything wrong, the Guards would understand that. He had not even looked at Róisín.

Unable to sit, she took the turkey from the fridge and began stripping it to its carcass, tearing off shreds of meat with her fingers and placing them in a Pyrex dish. Enda and Una thought Red was freaked out because he was in trouble with the police, but they hadn't seen the change that had come over him after he ran into his brother. How had they got here? she thought, emptying a can of condensed mushroom soup over the turkey. Red spooling out of control, a can-do religion teacher thinking he could make it all better and commandeering her mother. Róisín felt a stab of grief for the family they'd been before her father left. She went to the hall and tried his number. It rang out.

An hour later, the others returned. There was no evidence to connect Red to the drugs or stolen goods, he'd just received a caution. Enda patted his back as if he'd won an Olympic medal, saying he was proud of him for speaking so well. Róisín was putting a pastry lid on the dish of leftovers. Una hugged her from behind. It's only early but we should eat it now, she said, giggling as if she'd suggested they do something mad and crazy.

The kitchen felt inundated, the four of them squeezed around the table waiting for the pie. A couple of times Róisín sensed Red watching her, but she resisted meeting his gaze, the pity she'd felt for him turning to enmity. He'd been horrible in Phelan's house and the ensuing drama had kept her mother up most of the night. There was no point in asking why his brother had attacked him, he would just deflect the question. She left the table.

Her mother followed, catching her arm. Are you all right, love? she whispered.

Brilliant!

Una was looking at the hall table, her handwritten directory open on her husband's number in London. Ach, Róisín, do you want to talk about it?

You'd bloody love that, wouldn't you? Any excuse for a conference with Drooly.

She ran to her room and slammed the door, not that the others would hear above the sound of back-slapping. Switching on the transistor radio on her bedside locker, she got under the covers. The eleven o'clock news bulletin finished and '2000 Miles' came on. She wished she was two thousand miles away from this house and everyone in it.

Her mother knocked a while later. Róisín braced herself for a telling-off but Una didn't mention her outburst, instead fretting about going back to work that evening. She needed to rest and was worried that Red was alone downstairs. Enda would come back later to mind them while she was gone.

Jesus! I am sixteen, I do not need a babysitter.

Well then, stop sulking and sit with your friend.

Róisín found Red staring dully at the television. Is this a phase you're going through or are you never going to talk to me again? she said.

I'm so ashamed of my behaviour, he said, wincing.

She was filled with sorrow for him. It's OK.

It's not.

Fuck up. Just stop doing stuff that gets my ma and Gilhooly together. She's falling for him and it's your fault.

He laughed but his eyes looked sad.

They watched television all day, kids' films they showed at Christmas, *Chitty Chitty Bang Bang*, *The Wizard of Oz*. Red said he'd had a recurring nightmare as a child that he and his brothers were spun away into a stormy sky by the witch. It stopped when he was about ten and understood it was the wizard he should be afraid of. She knew he was telling her something important, but her brain was resisting understanding it.

The next morning the three of them were sitting at the table eating Christmas cake, Una still in her uniform. There was a knock at the door and Róisín got up, saying Enda had it bad, calling so early two days in a row. Behind her, Red and her mother were laughing. It was a Guard, the older wider one who had been in Nathy's house. Leaving him in the sitting room, she went to the kitchen.

Who is it? her mother asked.

The chunky peeler from the other night.

He's probably just checking in with you, son, said Una.

The Guard was standing by the fireplace. He said they'd traced the owner of the stolen goods.

Great, said Una. But what does that have to do with Red?

Red didn't seem to be listening, fingers rolling a wisp of fluff that had pilled on his sleeve as the Guard spoke. The jewellery belonged to Dolly Camelin. There had been no sign of a break-in and Red had keys to the family home.

Phelan, Red said faintly, as he sat on the settee.

This is ridiculous, said Una, you have no proof.

What's my father going to do? Red asked.

The Guard said Robert would not press charges as long as Red left the town and made something of himself.

Putting him on the next stagecoach out of town! Are we in the Wild West? said Una. He can live here and go back to school, I'll make sure he doesn't get in trouble.

It's not up to me. And in fairness, his father's willing to help him make a fresh start.

He took an envelope from his pocket and handed it to Red.

After he left, Una sat with Red. Nathy Phelan, the wee bastard, she ranted, he probably took money from Robert Camelin to connect Red to the burglary. Or maybe he'd actually stolen the jewellery himself and seen a way out. They would fight it, Enda would help, they wouldn't let them away with it.

There's no point, said Red, peeling open the envelope.

There was a grand, in crisp new notes.

Part Two

6

24 December 1984

Róisín waited for the other passengers to get off the coach before climbing out of her seat. There weren't many. A woman with three young children she had seen squabbling over biscuits on the ferry. A ghostly man in a tweed jacket who read all through the night. A girl her own age with a permed fringe who asked her if she had a spare tampon at the motorway services in Birmingham. The driver was counting money and didn't reply when Róisín thanked him. Her bag was in the back of the luggage hold and she had to stretch on her belly to reach it. She lit a cigarette and walked towards the street. Her father came around the opposite corner. His clothes were fashionable in a Burton's window way, a confident air about him as he waited to cross. It probably had something to do with him shacking up with a woman twelve years his junior.

When the lights changed, he strode towards her. How was the trip? he said, kissing her on the cheek as if it had been three days and not three years.

Quiet. Normal Irish people *leave* London at Christmas.

It was something the coach driver had said and not intended as a dig, but her father's smile dimmed.

His car – a second-hand BMW, silver, with alloy wheels – was double-parked in front of Victoria Library. A woman came out carrying a stack of books, her hair in a bun, and Róisín caught her sneer at the show he was making of opening the boot. A couple of minutes in and he was already an embarrassment.

He drove down a street of tall white houses, crossed sometimes by squares and private gardens, past a sign for the Tate Gallery, over the Thames. Christmas hits played on the radio as they went through the villages that made up south London, each with a fire station, a Woolworths, a Wimpy Bar. He asked questions about the social science degree Róisín was studying for. She told him about her courses: Evolution of the British Welfare State, Introduction to Political Philosophy, Rural Sociology. He nodded vaguely, tapping the steering wheel in time to the music.

Eventually he parked outside a chemist's, on the crest of a run-down hilly high street. Here we are, he said.

The shop window was bunged with Yardley gift sets, lemon-shaped soaps and Alka-Seltzer. He unlocked a door to the right of the entrance. The staircase was dark and smelled of old wood. The landing suddenly filled with pinkish light and, as he crossed the threshold of the flat, Róisín was aware of a pastel haze beyond him, a blurry frilliness. She stepped forward and a blonde woman was offering her a bundle as if it was a cake. Meet your little sister, she said.

Róisín looked from the infant to her father. Is she joking?

His girlfriend put the baby over her shoulder. Oh, Conor, I told you we should have prepared her, she said quietly.

He's a coward, said Róisín, but you haven't been around long enough to figure that out.

Her father moved his hands from his hips to his face, rubbing briskly. I was afraid you wouldn't come.

You would have been right. Well, happy fucking Christmas to the three of you.

She snatched up her bag and went back down the stairs.

They had passed a train station before turning on to the high street, but she hadn't taken in its name. She asked an elderly man for directions. It had begun to rain. He looked at the sky and said, Penge East, love. Round that corner, at the bottom of the road.

Her father touched her arm.

Get away from me, she said, shaking him off.

Oi, said the man, looking about him as if he was considering shouting for help.

It's all right, I'm her dad.

My bad luck.

She took off, leaving him palms up, apologising. She quickened her pace, but he caught up.

Please, Róisín.

Even that bimbo thinks you should have warned me!

Vexation twitched briefly in his eyes. Her name is Lynne.

Stupid fucking name, she can piss off as well.

He walked beside her, pleading. It would be OK, they could still have a nice Christmas, she would grow to love her sister. She kept her eyes on the British Rail sign at the end of the road, wishing with every cell in her body that he would say something that would make her turn on her heel and walk back up the grotty street to the flat. She charged into the station.

A one-way ticket to London, please, she asked the sleepy-looking woman at the desk.

Jesus, said her father. You don't have anywhere to go.

The woman sighed and looked behind them.

Her father began to empty his pockets. A packet of Rennie's, the Ronson lighter her mother had given him for his twenty-first birthday. A couple of stained tenners and loose change. What will I tell your mummy? he said. His hair was wet, his jacket slaked with rain.

Tell her you have a baby with that tramp up the road.

Someone behind them giggled. He asked for a single to Victoria. He was giving up already? Róisín swiped the ticket and the rest of his cash from the counter and went through the barrier. She stood on the platform, willing him to appear like the father in *The Railway Children*. Even when the train arrived, an old-fashioned one with compartments rather than carriages, she waited until the last possible moment before boarding. Doors slammed and a whistle blew. She lit a cigarette and burst into tears.

Fire escapes and bockety attic conversions, cricket pitches and school playgrounds flitted past. Her sister would grow up here, reared by an Englishwoman and a man Róisín didn't know any more.

Victoria, the final stop. Standing in the centre of the concourse, she didn't know what to do. If she called home her mother would ask why she had stormed off, and it wasn't up to Róisín to deliver the news. Her ticket home was non-transferable, valid only for the 2nd of January. In her pocket there was a twenty-pound note from her mother and not much more in what she had snatched from her father. The only person she knew in London was Red and he had not replied to her last letter. But where else could she go?

She went to the information desk and asked a teenager with a fluffy moustache and a gold sovereign ring on each hand for directions to the last address she had for Red. He told her to buy an *A–Z* and said, Next pulease, in a sing-song voice. The assistant in WH Smith was kinder, showing her how to use the index to find the right page. Red's place was just a walk away.

The clouds were so low it was like a twilight scene, though it was not yet lunchtime. Róisín hadn't eaten breakfast, and dinner the previous evening had been a bag of Taytos and a sandwich on the Holyhead ferry. She passed a taxi rank and dowdy hotels she couldn't afford, an art deco theatre. The pelting rain streamed down her face, leaving a sooty taste in her mouth.

She was on a long street. The entrance to each house was covered by a little portico and it was hard to make out the numbers. As she stepped beneath one to check the door, it swung open. A young man in a shirt and loosened paisley tie came out, a piece of plastic mistletoe in his right hand, pulling a woman Róisín's father would have described as 'well preserved' by his left. They fell on each other, oblivious to her presence. The houses seemed to stretch without end. Some were offices and consulting rooms, marked by discreet brass plates. Others were divided into flats, with rows of doorbells. None looked like a squat. If Red wasn't in number 48, she'd have to go back to her father's place, her tail between her legs. At the thought of him the wrath came up again, giving her purpose.

A little further on, she was distracted by a house across the street. It had a real Christmas tree in the window, ringed with yards of white lights. The one two doors up was dilapidated, stucco crackled, window frames weathered down to the bare wood. She dashed on to the road. A black cab, headlights off, braked inches from her. The driver began pumping the horn. She held a hand up, imploring him to wait, and her bag slid from her shoulder on to the ground. Another hand was there then, seizing the straps.

It was Red, in the black and red mohair jumper. He banged the bonnet of the cab and looked directly at the windscreen. Cunt, he said cheerfully.

The driver bashed the horn once more, half-heartedly this time.

Why are you outside with no coat on you? said Róisín, as they reached the other side.

Why were you running into the fucking traffic?

He had let his hair grow a little and it was standing in black tufts around his scalp. You're like Dennis the Menace, she said.

That's the idea.

They were under the portico. She was so happy to have found him she reached to hug him but he was frowning at a strapless watch. Come in, he said.

Calor gas cylinders were stacked two high along an unlit hallway. Somewhere upstairs a dog was not so much barking as crying, a nervy, keening whelp. Róisín followed Red down five steps to a kitchen. A green Aga in a tiled alcove on which someone had spray-painted the anarchy symbol, a swag of scraggy tinsel taped around the arch. A single window, shrubbery brushing the glass like kelp in an aquarium. Candles burning in tallowy puddles.

It's beautiful, she said.

The last squat in Pimlico. No electric but there's running water, he said, pulling out a chair at a white Formica table with a scribbly black and yellow pattern. She sat and he wheeled a gas heater towards her, lighting it.

His hands were in his back pockets, pushing his shoulders up, but was it possible he had grown in the year since she'd seen him? His face seemed older too, the lower part shaded by stubble like a burglar in a comic, the bones sturdier. And his eyes. Had they always been so dark?

So you finally used my address, he said.

I sent you a seven-page letter in September and you didn't write back!

Bullshit. He had sat opposite her and was crumbling hash on to tobacco.

Why would I make that up?

After he left, they had written to each other a couple of times a week. His envelopes bulged with gig flyers and postcards lifted from museums and galleries. Róisín wrote pages and pages, labouring over every word to make her small life seem big and hoping he would admire her prose. When he didn't write back, she thought he was bored by her.

Why are you here anyway? He glowered at her as he licked and rolled the cigarette paper. Had he always done things so methodically?

They have a baby.

Who has?

My da and that dollybird he's with.

I thought you didn't talk to him.

Róisín's father had taken to phoning her on Wednesdays at seven. She had let herself look forward to the calls, but now it seemed that the regular contact coincided with the pregnancy. The thought that the girlfriend had put him up to it, trying to draw Róisín into their fucked-up new family, made her hate the woman more.

Is it a boy or a girl?

I didn't look at it.

It's not the child's fault.

I'm not angry with her.

Red studied her for a moment. Her, he said. So you did look. What's her name?

I didn't stay long enough to find out. Are you saying it's OK?

You're jumping ahead a few steps, McCaffrey. As is your wont.

She thought of the baby's wizened sleeping face and her father's beaming one. Róisín was nothing to him now. That child would get all the saved-up love that had been denied Róisín since he left, and all his love for evermore, and not even the big-bapped trollop who gave birth to her would get a look-in.

What does your mother think? he said.

I don't know.

Fuck's sake, Ró. You need to phone her.

She took two packs from the carton of duty-free Rothmans she'd bought her father on the ferry, tossing one at Red. It had been satisfying, ignoring the displays of aftershave to buy a gift so impersonal as to be not quite a gift, choosing a brand other than the one he normally smoked. The bottle of Anaïs Anaïs her mother instructed her to buy for the girlfriend was there too. Róisín ripped the box apart and sprayed as if she was dusting crops. The tragic barking started up again as they left.

In the pub, Red gave Róisín two 50p coins and the country code for Ireland. Her mother answered at once, crying, What in the name of Jesus are you playing at? You have me and your daddy distracted!

Róisín was tempted to point out for the umpteenth time that the word she was looking for was 'distraught', but it wasn't a good time to be a smart-arse. Oh, Mum, they have, she said, and stopped. What a spineless loser her father was, leaving Róisín to share his baby news for him. Well, she wouldn't.

It's Christmas Eve, Róisín. I checked the ferry times. You'll not get a boat till the twenty-sixth, if you're lucky, and I'll have to buy you a new ticket. Where are you?

I'm with Red.

Red Camelin?

No, Red Hurley. Of course Red Camelin.

Oh, thank God, said her mother, and Róisín loved her for it. The rest of the parents in the town would have called the Guards if Red Camelin got within ten yards of their daughters.

The phone began to beep. Róisín held her palm out for more money and Red inserted coins, taking the receiver from her.

Mrs McCaffrey, he said.

Róisín didn't need to hear to know her reply: *Call me Una.*

I can't, I'm far too well brought up.

He pawed at the carpet with his right foot, glancing at Róisín a couple of times as he offered reassurances. No problem. Don't worry. We'll be grand. No need. Happy Christmas.

He handed the receiver back to Róisín and went to the bar.

Her mother said she would call her father to tell him she was safe. Róisín said he was a prick. Her mother said she didn't always have to be at war with the world. More beeps and the line went dead.

Róisín took a stool beside Red at the counter. He'd bought two of the worst-looking pints she had ever seen, dark, the head a rusty flotsam. She sipped and her tongue fell from her mouth in disgust.

Sláinte to you too, he said. It's a black and tan, half stout, half ale. You wouldn't give their Guinness to a dog.

He asked her about college. She said she'd made a mistake by not repeating the Leaving Certificate, that she should have tried for law instead of settling for social science. But she had met a couple of girls from Dublin who were nice, and she went to talks and debates sometimes, including one given by a striking Yorkshire miner who'd had his skull fractured by a policeman's truncheon. She didn't say the campus was ugly, sprawling and impersonal and she spent all her time between lectures in the Women's Reading Room, chain-smoking. That Sinéad was in accountancy college and she rarely saw her. That she had panic attacks so bad she had to lock herself in a cubicle until she stopped shaking, two or three a day sometimes, and might fail politics – the only subject she liked – because she couldn't speak in tutorials. That she was lost.

He told her he'd taken over the squat from Dawn, a student at Camberwell School of the Arts who'd gone to Amsterdam. She'd left things in her room and asked him to keep the numbers down so it didn't turn into a dosshouse. Three of them lived there, four if you counted Wilbur the weeping greyhound. He'd been liberated from Hackney Wick Stadium by Greg – a speed-freak college dropout from Arkansas – who saw his owner punch him when he lost a race. Greg erected a tent in his room in which they still slept five months later because at first the animal cowered from light, perhaps because it reminded him of the track.

Greg's ould pair made him go home for 'the holidays', said Red. You should have seen him trying to clean himself up. Three days under canvas with the dog, rattling. And I brought Barry Doyle with me. He's gone home for Christmas too.

He swung off the stool, mumbling he'd be back in a minute. Róisín ordered him a black and tan, and a pint of cider for herself. At home, the pubs would be packed, serving hot port and Irish coffee to shoppers and gallons of Guinness to those who'd returned home for Christmas. This place was grim. An out-of-order fruit machine in a corner, scarcely half a dozen drinkers scattered around the room. A monosyllabic barman framed by tinsel in worse condition than the length in Red's kitchen.

Red came back, smelling faintly of hash. Róisín saw the barman's nose wrinkle and lit a Rothmans to distract him.

How long are you staying? said Red, finishing his pint and raising the new one at her.

My ticket's for the second, but there's a ferry on the twenty-sixth if that's too long.

Don't be fucking stupid.

My da said he'd pay my fare, but of course he didn't. He can't afford us, but he can afford a baby with that one.

I doubt he did cost projections before he rode her.

I could smell it, you know, as I walked in. Talc and milk.

With the next round the barman – his name was Terry – gave them a plate of tired sausages that he called chipolatas. Red ate most of them, explaining as he chewed that her father knew well that if he had told Róisín about the child she wouldn't have agreed to go for Christmas. That yeah, it was a shock, but her father had a new life now, he was with a younger woman who probably wanted babies.

She could feel the drink in her body, the wrong that had been done to her making her righteous. All I know is I walked into an ambush, she said.

Awmmboosh. You sound pure nordie when you say shit like that.

There was footage of the famine in Ethiopia on the *Six O'Clock News*.

She turned her head. Jesus, she said. I can't watch this.

Looking is the least we can do.

Terry switched over anyway. There were trailers for the evening's television on BBC Two. Lena Horne in concert. An English choir singing carols in Bethlehem. *The Quiet Man*, a bit of the Irish, the announcer said in a plummy voice.

Another round. She was finding it hard to keep up. He told her he was studying for the Knowledge, an examination taken by London cabbies. Memorising every street, lane and building within a six-mile radius of Charing Cross. Most people did it by bike or car, but Red was doing it on foot.

Do you want to be a taxi driver?

He began to giggle. Do I fuck.

After another couple of pints they were the only people left. Red went to the jukebox and played Foster and Allen's 'A Bunch of Thyme', an old-style ballad about womanly chastity that had mortified everyone at home when it was a hit in Britain. A bit of the Irish, he roared, and sang along, exaggerating the bog accent on the recording.

Can't you play 'The Frog Chorus' or something? said Terry.

Not a hope, they killed the wrong Beatle.

Out.

Ah, come on.

Terry had folded his arms across his chest and was pointing a finger at the exit like a pistol. Róisín felt sorry for him. She'd been reared by parents who worked unsociable hours; how galling to spend Christmas Eve dealing with drunks. Red drained both their glasses and they left.

On the way back, she paused to admire the beautiful tree she'd seen earlier. A girl in a green dress was at the window. Red pushed up on to his toes and mouthed something. She shook her head almost imperceptibly, and a middle-aged man came to stand beside her. Red shrank back.

You know that girl? asked Róisín.

Just doing the *ho ho ho* thing with the neighbours.

The dog started up before the key was in the lock and became more doleful as Red went upstairs. Coaxing, cajoling, and after a couple of minutes he and the dog skittered uncertainly down to the hall. Wilbur was absurd. A quivering head, all eyes. Slender greyhound legs beneath a chunky body, belly so big he might have been carrying pups.

In the kitchen, Red lit a candle and fired up the heater. He let the dog out the back saying, Have a good shite to yourself, Wil.

Ugh. No wonder the garden is flourishing.

Are you hungry? he said.

Starving.

Taking a tin of Alphabetti Spaghetti from a cupboard, he began stabbing at it with a short knife. He raised it as if he was proposing a toast and poured a slurp of orange noodles into his mouth. The sound was worse than the sight. Want some?

Revolting. Do you have anything else? She tapped the corners of her lips to let him know he had a moustache from the pasta.

Bread. Cereal. Eggs. I wasn't expecting company.

He washed his face over the sink while she ate cornflakes from a bowl with yellow flowers. What do you normally do in the evenings? she said.

Read by candlelight. Wander.

He'd finished Dostoevsky and Kafka and started Sartre, who was really funny. Wilbur came back in and his ripe smell was unbearably strong. Red was teasing her for her tastes, Austen and Eliot and Hardy, and the air seemed to be pressing in on her. Then he was prodding her awake and flinging open the back door; the gas had made her pass out.

This is the first time I've ever fainted, she said, as he helped her up.

You're pretty good at it, swooning to the floor. We should go to bed.

They made weird shadows on the walls as they ascended the stairs. Wilbur's ears, Red's spiky head, her legs from thigh to shin. Greg's room was undecorated except for a huge French film poster – *Orange mécanique, A Clockwork Orange*. The image was horrible, terrified eyes prised open by wire. In the centre of the floor there was a tent, a triangular cloth one befitting a Scout jamboree, that reeked of drugs and dog. Red was having trouble getting Wilbur to go inside and sent Róisín across the landing to his room.

He had removed a suspended ceiling to reveal intricate plasterwork, and stacked the polystyrene tiles in the corner with a sheaf of plastic batons. A marble fireplace, stalactites of molten wax dripping from the mantelpiece. A record player with a cracked lid, LPs that without electricity he couldn't play. The copy of Plato's *Symposium* among a couple of dozen second-hand books.

He's acting up. Don't wait, just get into the bed, he called.

What would she wear? At home, she had taken to sleeping in just her knickers, a habit her mother found wanton and potentially scandalous – what if the house caught fire! Would Red think her tragic if she put on the nightdress she had packed for her dad's? She removed everything but her T-shirt and underwear and got into his bed. The linen was very cold but dry, sheets that practically snapped.

Fuck's sake, he said as he came into the room. She tried to look nonchalant while he undressed.

They lay side by side, Red lighting the stub of a joint. She glanced at him, surprised to find they were almost touching. Almost.

Thank fuck I found you, Red, she blurted.

It was open to interpretation, and as she waited for him to reply she wished she'd phrased it differently. She'd meant it in all the possible ways, of course. Thank fuck she'd brought him Tina's letter. Thank fuck he was outside the squat when Róisín arrived. Thank fuck they were together again.

He stretched away from her to drop the butt in an ashtray. No worries, he said.

She rolled on to her side and made herself as small as possible, trying to harness her own body heat. Scenes from earlier kept her awake. The girlfriend's open smile as she offered the swaddled newborn. The contents of her father's pockets. All he had to say was that Róisín was his firstborn and would always be his favourite. But how could she compete with a baby? And Red looking up at that window. Who is the girl in the green dress? she wondered. WH OI ST HE GI RL IN TH EG RE EN DR ES S? WH OT HE FU CK IS TH EG IR LI NT HE GR EE ND RE SS?

Red woke with a start, looking at her in surprise. Christ, I forgot you were here.

She'd been so addled by him she'd not slept. Happy Christmas, she said.

Nollaig shona duit.

They dressed quickly in the mist from their breath and brought the dog downstairs.

Red made tea and toasted bread against the grille of the gas heater. It was so comforting she was able to overlook its petrochemical flavour.

Santa didn't come, he said.

Bastard.

He laughed for a while, mirth that felt disproportionate to the joke. Maybe the spliff he'd almost finished was making him giddy. Could it do that? She'd had a single pull of a joint in the college bar.

She put the ham from her mother on to boil. He told her about all the things she needed to see while she was in London. St Paul's, the Post Office Tower, the Tate. He was still so easy to be with, although when he checked his pocket watch from time to time she wondered did he want to get away from her.

There was a rap at the door. Red jogged up the steps and cold air flooded the kitchen. A brisk clack of heels and the girl they'd seen at the window swept down ahead of him.

Every idiot who goes about with 'Merry Christmas' on his lips should be boiled with his own pudding and buried with a stake of holly through his heart, she said, dumping a hamper on the table.

A Christmas Carol, said Red. Ró, this is Octavia. She lives in the house you were gazing at like the Little Match Girl.

Hiya, said Róisín.

Octavia ignored her. She was their age. Thick, wavy hair, most of which was tossed over her right shoulder, blending into the chestnut-coloured fluffy collar on her tweed coat.

What's all this? said Red, pointing at the hamper.

Canapés and a mutilated Stilton into which a vandal sloshed port. And the dregs of some vino collapso. She sniffed the air. Christ, are you boiling a head? It smells like Dennis Nilsen has moved in.

Red chuckled.

I brought a slipper of ham from home, said Róisín.

Octavia had taken the joint from Red. Slipper! she said, her eyebrow raised.

Red was at her heels as she went back up the steps, a nervous energy on him that reminded Róisín of Wilbur. Whispers, then Octavia exclaimed, Marvellous! Beats sitting in a bar in somewhere ghastly like Deptford. The front door banged shut.

He returned patting his back pockets, a satisfied smile on his face, as if he'd put something right.

Who the fuck is that one? said Róisín.

Her father's a Tory MP. Aubrey Hammond?

He was in the north for a while. Security mad, he was. Can I have a drag? She reached for the joint.

No. Stick to the fags.

He was treating her like an annoying little sister. She would tell him so, but was afraid he'd laugh at her again. She opened the basket. There was a cylinder of blue cheese, its centre gouged out and jammy. Marzipan fruits and chocolate truffles in tinfoil clumps. A disposable platter of tiny quiches, things on cocktail sticks, miniature sausage rolls. And four bottles of wine with only a little gone out of them.

We need to go round there, said Red.

Round to Octavia's? I forgot my ball gown.

To your da's.

He can shag off. So can Octavia. Slippah! Fucking cheek of her.

7

31 December 1984

The hamper fed them for a couple of days. When it ran out, Róisín hacked pieces from the ham, frying it with eggs, flittering the offcuts into spaghetti with crumbled Stilton, putting it between slices of white bread slathered in mustard. Red said she had a way with food. She said it was all the butter and he said she still couldn't take a compliment.

They walked miles, always beginning by the high, murky river. At first they brought Wilbur. Róisín marvelled that he did not need to be put on a lead and Red said he was an unlikely candidate for bolting as he had to be inveigled out of the tent. As the traffic returned in the days after Christmas the animal became timid and they left him behind, crying. Red told her things. About architects and artists and writers. Floods and plagues and executions.

Sometimes he left her in the squat, saying he had to run an errand, often returning empty-handed. Without him, the house felt decrepit, and so cold. A cold that made your nose drip constantly, that made peeing feel like passing boiling water. A cold that at first made you alert but, as it set in, became all you could think about. Well, almost all. Alone, she wondered where Red had gone, afraid he was escaping her, and why he never put a hand on her. One day when he had been absent for three hours she left the squat, unable to stand her own company. She called her mother from the pub, wanting – for once – to hear the jumpy pep in her voice, and felt dejected when she didn't answer. Afterwards, she rang Sinéad, telling her about her father's new family, the pink baby and the floozy girlfriend she had taken one look at and walked away from.

But where are you? said Sinéad.

I'm with Red.

With him? In the biblical sense, like? Oh my God.

Róisín coughed delicately, saying, Ah stop. To her own ears it sounded false, but Sinéad was shrieking; she'd fallen for it.

So have you done the dirty deed?

Róisín dropped her voice to a whisper. I can't talk now.

Shit, he's beside you! You better ring me back, I'm demented for the details.

After she'd hung up, Róisín felt even worse.

On New Year's Eve they left in the early afternoon. Red took a detour at the Tate Gallery, bringing her to a railing by a block of flats. Beyond it the ground sloped sharply to a trench covered in old flagstones, nylon clotheslines criss-crossed above it.

A sluggish ditch deposited its mud at the prison walls. Coarse grass and rank weeds straggled over all the marshy land in the vicinity, he incanted.

What's that from?

David Copperfield.

She thought of Octavia prancing down the steps spouting Dickens. Red knowing the reference. Oh, she said.

This is what's left of Millbank Prison. It was so bad the inmates got every disease going. Cholera from the Thames. There was even a plague of typhus, scurvy and dysentery all at once. The Tate and all these houses are built over it. Can you not feel it? All those wretched lives layered up underneath us.

He was staring into the trench with a scattered expression that made her want to run. How do you know all this? she said, hating herself for her perky voice.

From walking and looking.

There's a word for that.

Unemployment.

No. I'll have to look it up.

What are you gawping at? someone shouted. A man with the close, doltish face of a woodland mammal was leaning from a window on the second floor. Red held up his middle finger as they walked away.

Distances she would have baulked at a week ago were nothing to her now, and it felt good to be in the fresh air. On Oxford Street, red and white banners screamed *SALE*, then they were on streets that seemed to narrow with each step, buildings falling in on one another. Windows full of curios and prints, neon signs for adult cabaret and peep shows. A couple of teenage boys were outside a sex shop, leafing through a porn mag like they were looking for the free gift in *Roy of the Rovers*. The woman on the cover was licking her lips at the sight of her own hard, rosy nipples.

Ró! Red said, as if he was repeating her name. Jesus, you're blushing.

She stepped around the boys. It's really sleazy round here, she said.

It's like taking a nun out for the day.

He was still laughing when they entered a wonky pub on the next corner. It was ancient, lit with globe-shaped glass lamps and fitted with over-polished mahogany and under-polished brass. Red went to the bar. There was no room to lurk behind him, so she backed herself against the wall. The patrons were a varied lot: men in tweed, an old lady with a little dog, girls with fuchsia lipstick, a couple of scruffy boys like Red. A few tables away, two men were speaking intently. She had seen the older one on a late-night arts programme talking about photography. He was regarding his young companion with such tenderness

Róisín could have cried. She must have been staring, because they drew away from each other, sitting up stiffly. It made her feel terrible and she looked at Red instead. She liked being able to watch him. In the house, she sometimes found herself mooning and had to focus on something else. He was making the barmaid laugh, dimples appearing in her middle-aged cheeks. The hang of his jeans and the rise of his shoulders as he pulled twenty quid from his pocket. Holding up two glasses and bowing slightly before leaving the bar.

Any craic? he said.

A fella over there has fallen in love with someone he shouldn't have.

Takes all sorts, he said, handing her a drink. The barmaid didn't know how to make a hot port so I got us port and brandy.

Napper Tandies, my da calls those.

A couple left and they took their seats. He told her 'Soho!' was the hunting cry of the duke who had owned the land here when it was just fields. It was her second-last day, she wanted to say, and she dreaded leaving him. She lit a cigarette, not bothering to offer him one; he wasn't really a smoker, unless you counted the joints he toked from morning to night.

Your woman Octavia never came back, she said. Even speaking the girl's name made her furious and it was hard to keep a neutral tone.

She's in Venice for a Hogmanay party.

That's the most obnoxious thing I've ever heard.

It's fairly odious, all right.

It was as near as he'd come to criticising Octavia, an opportunity to remind him Róisín was here and that upper-class wagon wasn't. In forty-eight hours I'll be on the coach, she said.

You will.

If she hadn't turned up he'd have spent Christmas with a suicidal greyhound. Would it kill him to say he'd miss her? Not ardently – *I am praying for a blizzard* – just an acknowledgement that it was better having her around than being alone. If that even was the case.

Will you miss me? she said. God, she really couldn't help herself.

You can come back in the summer. Get a job.

I could go on the scratcher.

He tutted. What are you like. It's shit being on the dole.

You're doing OK.

On their third drink, a young blonde woman in a cream bouclé wool coat that swept the floor came through the door. She paused, looking uncertainly around her. Her eyes lingered on Red for a moment, but she walked past their table, towards the back of the pub. Róisín glanced at him, wondering if he had noticed, but he was rising, muttering about going to the jacks.

She looked around the room again, but everyone appeared so easy in themselves it made her self-conscious. Even the arts-show man she'd been staring at had resumed cooing into his young friend's face. She lit another cigarette.

Red came back and the front door banged shut. Through the window, Róisín saw the blonde girl walking away.

That girl. You followed her to the loo.

He sipped his drink and leaned back against the leather banquette. Don't worry about it, he said quietly.

She turned to face him. What does that mean?

It means don't worry about it, Ró. His cheeks were pink, whether from the Napper Tandies or her question she couldn't tell. The hash-and-fry-up scent of the jumper her mother had made him. Look, I'm selling the odd ten spot, he said. It doesn't make me Larry Dunne.

She thought the people who said cannabis use led inevitably to heroin addiction were hysterical, and she didn't care that he was breaking the law. It was the sneaking around that bothered her, nipping out on various pretexts, not trusting her with the truth. Why didn't you tell me? she said.

Fancy you turning up, Róisín, by the way I'm a drug dealer, like? I didn't tell you because it would have sounded bigger than it is.

For the last week there had been something shifty about him, glancing at the face of his watch before disappearing. But at least he hadn't been leaving the house to get away from her.

That's why that Octavia one came round. God, I'm thick.

It wasn't the only reason, she's a mate.

It was worse hearing this than that he was dealing. The whispering in the hallway on Christmas Day, keeping his voice low so the naïve little cailín from the old country wouldn't hear. Octavia hadn't been discreet, declaring Red had spared her from going 'somewhere ghastly', as if she had wanted Róisín to know. Floating in all dressed up to collect something she wouldn't lower herself to buy on her own.

Just forget about it, Ró, please? Come on, I'll take you somewhere cool.

Lights and red lanterns strung between buildings, a Chinese pavilion in a run-down square. Shop windows displaying unfamiliar ingredients and cooking implements, restaurants offering menus in Cantonese. He chose one because the exterior was in the red and black of his jumper. Most of the premises were painted in those colours, but it was good to hear him being silly again.

Red held the door and she entered first. At home, there were two restaurants: a steakhouse that fed the horsey people and a takeaway called the Wok Inn, neither of which her mother could afford. Róisín could only recall them eating out once, when her parents had taken her for chicken in a basket after her confirmation. Now, as the waiter approached, she didn't know what to do. Red did, stepping forward to shake the man's hand. Table for two, he said, you can have it back by eight, we're here for one course. She often forgot he'd had a middle-class upbringing. For most of the time she'd known him he'd been homeless.

The waiter's face relaxed into a smile. He was probably amused to hear such patter from a teenager with holes in his clothes.

The room was full of Chinese people picking white things from bamboo baskets. Red asked for what everyone else was eating and two glasses of wine, refusing the offer of cutlery. Róisín studied how the nearest diners were holding their chopsticks, but when their food arrived, copying them was beyond her. She tried to lift a dumpling but managed only to impale it. I need a knife and fork, Red.

You'll never see any of these people again, just eat.

She put it in her mouth, raising her head when she had finished chewing. The angles of his face, the black curling lashes. She hoped the lighting made her pretty because he was so beautiful to her then she could hardly stand the sight of him.

Afterwards they walked to Leicester Square, riding the escalators down to the Piccadilly line. There were tiny mice darting among the tracks. Róisín was frightened of them but could not avert her eyes.

They're happy enough running about, I suppose, she said.

That's blind panic, said Red. A charge of dead air rushed in and the mice scattered.

They crushed themselves into a train just before the doors closed. There was little space and their bodies were touching. A soughing in her chest, nerves or apprehension. They changed at Green Park to a quieter train, the armrest putting distance between them.

When they got to Pimlico, Red said she should call her mother, but the payphone in the station was out of order and so was the one further up the street.

We'll go to the pub, said Red.

The one we got chucked out of?

It'll be grand.

The crappy garland had already been taken down, and an exhausted-looking Terry stood sullenly behind the counter. Róisín went straight to the phone. She dialled her home number, slotting in change in small denominations, all she had left apart from a five-pound note.

Róisín! said her mother.

You sound all giggly. What's going on?

I have news, but I need to tell you in person.

If you're pregnant I'm going to commit suicide, I can't handle any more surprises. Tell me now.

A moment's silence, then her mother's voice dropped to a girlish whisper. Enda proposed, she said, sounding slightly loopy on the last syllable.

Was this why her mother had been so keen for her to go away? Enda was in the house often but he had never stayed over. Still, Una had replaced her candlewick bedspread with a duvet and floral covers and her over-washed granny knickers with a seven-pack of pastel-coloured 'briefs'. But marriage? To Drooly Gilhooly?

Róisín? Are you still there?

Yeah, I am. Forgive me for being momentarily fucking speechless but you're married already and there's no divorce in the Irish Republic.

Look, we won't talk about all this now, we'll have a chat when you get home.

When I get home, Enda will be hanging about and we won't be able to talk!

I'm looking into getting an annulment.

You must be bloody joking.

It's the only way. Enda's faith is so important to him.

Well, as long as Enda's happy that's all right then.

Jesus, Róisín, he's not more important than you! But your father was able to move on, and I should be too. Your daddy left *me*.

He left me as well and I'm not marrying a dribbling religion teacher with chronic dandruff. Feel free to move on. Without me. I'm sick of the lot of you.

She slammed the receiver on the hook. Red was at her side. Calm down, will you, he'll bar us for good.

I can't go home, Red.

Wilbur cantered into the kitchen and nosed Róisín briefly in the crotch. It felt like an electric shock, and she reddened, horrified that the touch of a dog was reviving her horniness. Red let him out into the back garden and began to roll a joint. What's the story? he said.

My lovely ma, as you call her, is planning to marry Enda Gilhooly. Because he is a Catholic freak, he expects her to annul her marriage to my waster of a da. Pay thousands to the Vatican to prove the union was flawed, based on lies, or never truly existed.

You can't begrudge her that, it's shit there's no divorce at home.

An annulment would render any issue from said union illegitimate, i.e. me. They got married. They had me. For a while they were happy.

She burst into tears.

His arms were around her then, a hand on her lower back, the other below her shoulder. Shit, he murmured, rocking her gently as she sobbed, Wilbur jittering beside them.

Upstairs, she undressed and got under the covers, waiting for him to settle the dog.

It's like having a baby, he said when he came in, removing his boots and jeans and getting in next to her.

He hadn't brought a candle and she was a little below him, unable to fully see his face. A few minutes ago he had held her and if she didn't do something the chance would pass. She rolled a little until she was on her side, lying against him. He didn't shove her away, but he wasn't responding either.

Red, she said. Her voice sounded like it was coming from the corner of the room. As he turned his face she put her mouth on his. He did nothing at first. She was fretting that as usual she had misread him, but his lips opened and he began to kiss her back. His body was touching hers and she could feel his erection. She slid her fingers under her mother's knitting and traced the line of his spine up towards his shoulders, but the sinews of his back tensed.

What do you want me to do? she said. That weird voice again.

Too drunk to fuck. Must be the Napper Tandies.

The words were surprisingly coarse. And they sounded rehearsed, as if he'd stored them up for when he needed them. He reached away from her. The click of a lighter, the pungent aroma of hash smoke. Lying on his back, he found her hand and squeezed it. So you're staying, he said.

Yeah.

Good.

He wants me here but he doesn't want *me*, she thought, her want for him so abject it hurt. HE WA NT SM EH ER EB UT HE DO ES NT WA NT *ME*. An even number of letters. Confirming it was the truth.

8

1 January 1985

They had come apart in the night, Róisín now curled forlornly beside Red. Something had gone wrong when she touched him, he had been in actual physical discomfort. She'd never had full sex, just a dry hump from a boy after the Freshers' Ball the week she started college. Maybe she was terrible at it, creeping up Red's back like a spider. Afterwards, when he touched her hand, she felt better, but then he just lay there. He looked so gorgeous now, the tip of his nose bright from the cold, those lashes brushing his cheeks. She edged across the mattress, careful not to startle him, and assumed the position she'd been in last night. There was a change in his breathing: he was awake. It felt like perpetrating a sexual assault.

Top o' the morning, he said.

Happy New Year.

That too. We didn't make it to midnight.

I did, she wanted to say. I lay against you for hours willing you to want me.

Wilbur let out a yelp. Red rolled away from her and swung his legs out of the bed. The clump of his boots across the landing, his hushed entreaties as he unzipped the tent. *Time for a dump, Wil. Come out, pal, those cunts won't hurt you again.* Wilbur's paws scrabbling on the stairs, the high scrape of the back door as Red hauled it open.

She dressed and followed them down. Red was shuddering, his arms and legs like a plucked turkey, clicking at the gas heater. Christ. We're out and the shop's closed till tomorrow.

We can go somewhere warm. A gallery or something.

It's New Year's Day, nothing's open.

She went to the sink and filled the enamel water pot.

Don't bother making any for me, he said, sitting at the table with his pouch and papers.

You always have tea.

He was glaring at the knot of tobacco between his fingers. You can't stay here, Róisín.

He wants me here but he doesn't want me*?* He didn't want her at all. Worse, he'd wiped out all their history with a single word: Róisín. She turned off the Primus and made for the steps. He caught the tail of her T-shirt. Will you just listen instead of storming off?

That was plain enough, even for stupid bitch me. Unhelpfully, she had begun to cry, great snattery blubs.

Ah stop, I meant you can't stay in London. You're wrecking your life. Go home and suck it up, finish your education.

Red, I really can't live with her, she said, her voice risen to a yawl.

Fuck's sake. She'll think it's my fault.

She won't, she loves you.

You can stay. On one condition.

Anything.

Make up with your da. It's too hard to survive here on your own.

You're doing it!

She meant it as praise, but he let out an ugly laugh. Do you think I'd be here if I had a choice? I can't even set foot in the town, never mind my own home. His voice was unsteady now too.

She didn't know what to say. She never knew what to say.

* * *

Outside Victoria station, two men were in an exhausted tussle over a bottle, so drunk it appeared to be happening in slow motion. The younger one got control of it and took off running at impressive speed. The other man fell backwards, skull audibly colliding with the wall. At first he seemed unconscious, but then his mouth opened like a wound and he began to sing.

I wish I was in Carrickfergus
Only for nights in Ballygrand...

I wish you was in Carrickfergus too, you old soak, called a man in a British Rail uniform by the station entrance.

Don't mind that bollocks, Micksy, we're listening, said Red.

Encouraged, Micksy rolled his shoulders back and took in a breath. His voice was a raw but rich baritone and a small crowd was gathering. The final verse always moved Róisín and Micksy did it justice with his beseeching:

I'm drunk today and I'm seldom sober
A handsome rover from town to town
Ah but I'm sick now, my days are numbered
Come all ye young men and I'll lay me down

At the end of the song, the people began to move off, but Red stepped towards them.

Pay up, you miserable bastards, he said.

One couple practically ran away, but the rest went through pockets and purses and in their shame tossed Micksy fifty-pence pieces and pound coins that tinkled on to the ground. He reached for them and toppled sideways, looking up at Red. Have you a shmoke, son?

Róisín here has loads of them.

She found a pack in her bag and went down on her hunkers. Micksy's hands were jerking so violently he had to seize his left one with his right to steady it. Just as his faecal reek and the dirt of his fingers were overwhelming her, he gave her the saddest smile she had ever seen. The blessings of God on you, Róisín Dubh, he said.

Their train was leaving in four minutes. They bought tickets and ran across the concourse and along the platform, leaping into a compartment right before the whistle. Dirty upholstery and wooden walls, peeling flooring. Murder on the 15:05 to Bromley South, said Red.

That man. Jesus Christ.

Poor auld Micksy.

Those people were afraid of you.

Proper order. Tight fuckers.

I'm not afraid of you.

Are you just saying the first thing that comes into your head?

Forget it.

As the train passed Battersea Power Station he told her Pink Floyd floated an inflatable pig above it for an album cover only the pig broke loose and wreaked havoc with British aerospace. She wanted to tell him she wasn't afraid of him because she knew he was kind and good. Instead she reminded him she didn't like the sort of people who liked Pink Floyd.

In the chemist's window, discounted Christmas gift sets sat among laxatives, Lemsip and cylinders of Cambridge Diet shakes.

She pressed the buzzer. I feel sick, she said.

They waited for a couple of minutes.

Come on, so, said Red. At least you tried.

The door opened suddenly. Lynne's top was spattered with white stains, her face free of make-up, revealing a speckled complexion which suggested she was naturally a redhead. Posing as a blonde, like Tina Doyle. I'm so sorry, I just got her down, she whispered. Come upstairs.

Lynne fluffed a couple of cushions and switched on a lamp on a side table. The room smelled of spilled milk and washing powder. Your dad's at work, Róisín, she said, pronouncing it *Rawsheen*, the way her father did. He'll be back at fiveish.

We won't be here that long.

Red thrust his hand at Lynne, saying, Red Camelin, I'm Ró's friend.

Lynne Page, she said, beaming.

It was like a stage name for someone in musical theatre, thought Róisín.

Lynne asked Red where he lived, exclaiming that Pimlico was lovely, but awfully expensive. He said it wasn't expensive to break into a vacant property. Róisín was ready to launch into a polemical defence of squatters' rights, but Lynne said the country was in a right state with all the unemployment and that it was great to have a bit of get up and go.

The baby – the child with whom Róisín shared a father – began mewling. Lynne seemed to deflate before crossing to a Moses basket in the corner of the room.

You've got windypops again, little Mary, she murmured, lifting the child and holding her against her chest.

They'd called her Mary! After Róisín's grandmother. She had died the year after they moved south, of renal failure, her kidneys salted up with Dromona butter and bacon. That Mary would never meet her didn't make Róisín feel better. Something had been taken from her; bearing their granny's name would give her sister a connection that Róisín didn't have. Still, she couldn't help staring at the child, the trippy whorl of hair at her crown. Black hair, like Róisín and her father. Their father.

So have you got all the services in the squat? said Lynne.

Just mains water, said Red.

I forgot to turn the immersion heater off and there's a full tank, boiling it is. You're both very welcome to have a shower.

Róisín had never heard anything so ridiculous. She widened her eyes at Red, expecting to share a sneer, but he was taking off his jacket and asking for a towel.

Have a seat, lovey, said Lynne when he was gone. She lowered herself on to an armchair and, drawing the baby's blanket around her upper body, put the child to her breast. She winced. I'm trying to wean her, she said, but she loves a little nursey.

Róisín sat on the couch. Terrified of catching a glimpse of her father's girlfriend's mammary glands, she took in the room. A rack of baby clothes drying by the window. A bunch of magazines that came free with Sunday tabloids on the coffee table, wan-looking presents under a Christmas tree. Through a low arch there was a galley kitchen, a single run of worktop with a microwave oven, toaster, kettle and a Milton sterilising unit, dirty dishes taking up the rest of the available space. Róisín felt a pang of sympathy for Lynne. In case it got out of hand and she began to like her, she reminded herself this was the slapper who'd stolen her father. When she looked back, Lynne was asleep.

Red returned and offered Róisín his towel.

No.

Cop on, he hissed. You haven't washed properly for over a week.

Snatching the towel from him, she went to the bathroom.

She rubbed the mirror with her sleeve. Her eyebrows were in danger of meeting in the middle and there was a week's deposit of liner beneath her eyes that soap had not removed. A bamboo shelving unit was crammed with bottles and jars, most of which were marked *Tester*. She used Lynne's cleanser and toner, plucking Neanderthal hairs with her tweezers. Afterwards, she dried herself and smeared her body in as many products as its surface area would accommodate, her heart racing.

In the sitting room, Red was placing a mug beside Lynne, a tea towel printed with penguins and snowflakes over his shoulder. Soap suds were bubbling over the rim of the sink and the dirty dishes were now clean and upside down on the draining board. Róisín was ashamed she'd binged on Lynne's things. There was something trusting about the woman – she found Conor McCaffrey plausible, God help her – and Róisín should have respected that.

Lynne reached for the steaming drink and the baby jerked, making herself cry.

I'll take her, said Róisín, the words out of her mouth of their own accord. She scooped the child up and laid her against her shoulder, rubbing her back in a circular motion.

What was Róisín like, being jealous of an infant? Mary would never eat iced fancies in their granny's neat, smoky house, or hear her quivery voice sing Doris Day songs. Maybe Róisín could tell her about their Nana Mary. If their father didn't keep doing stupid things that made her want to banish him from her life.

The child issued a rich belch that could have come out of a grown man.

Spectacular, said Red, peering at her. You burp like Micksy, little lady.

Who's Micksy? said Lynne.

He's a wino.

Lynne hooted with laughter.

Red sang to Mary.

They sweated blood and they washed down mud
With pints and quarts of beer.

And now we're on the road again
With McAlpine's Fusiliers.

The shunt of a lock. Why did her father have to arrive when they were all getting along? He kissed first Róisín then the baby on the head, withdrawing quickly as if they might lash out. The whiff of beer wasn't surprising – he was a barman – but it was on his breath.

Red introduced himself.

Conor, her father replied. Thanks for putting Róisín up, or putting up with her.

He'd long since lost the right to tease her and Róisín was annoyed when Red laughed.

Cans of beer fizzling open, talk about the day's football results. It was the 1st of January, the day of derbies, big away wins for her father's favourite clubs. Celtic beat Rangers at Ibrox with goals from Johnston and McClair. Spurs stuffed Arsenal at Highbury, a magnificent Hoddle doing the groundwork in midfield for goals by Falco and Crooks. Red had little to contribute and she prayed her father wouldn't subject him to the starter-for-ten thing and quiz him on sports trivia.

Rawsheen, Lynne said, taking the baby from her, you haven't opened your presents.

The gifts under the tree were for her? Red pointed his beer at the gaudy parcels, urging her to open them. She sat on the floor, a surly, oversized Christmas fairy. Her father knelt beside her and retrieved four small packages, placing them together. She knew what they were. After he left the RUC he worked – until he was intimidated out of the place – in an east Belfast office with a tiny fierce woman who said modern children were spoiled rotten, that in her day they were happy if Santa left an apple, an orange, a pencil and a rubber. He delivered the punchline – the woman was called Miss Jingles, named for Christmas but too dour to enjoy it – and got the usual laughs, but Róisín hated that he kept flicking his eyes in her direction, looking for approval. She began to rip open her other gifts. A box of mint-flavoured Matchmakers, a notebook, a giant jar of Marmite, paisley tights and a book about Georgia O'Keeffe.

Thanks, Daddy. And Lynne.

Your mum was in on it too, she popped a couple of things in the post when I went into hospital.

My mother knew you were having a baby?

Lynne looked at Conor in panic.

We wanted to tell you ourselves, love, he said.

Róisín got to her feet. Since the three of youse are all palsy-walsy, I suppose you know she's getting an annulment.

Is that an operation? said Lynne.

In other circumstances she and Red would have fallen about laughing, but he was glaring at Róisín. Desperate for solidarity, she took Mary from her mother's arms. The tiny eyes opened.

We are the spawn of fucking idiots, Mary McCaffrey, Róisín told her silently, and it's already rubbed off on me. You are our only hope.

The baby rootled at her conspiratorially and went back to sleep.

9

7 January 1985

Seated at the kitchen table was an extraordinarily tall young man. It wasn't just the top hat on his head that gave him stature. His legs, though crossed and drawn towards the chair, were endless, his fingers the longest Róisín had ever seen. His face was long too, freakishly so. Her granny would have said it was like a Lurgan spade.

Gregory Cartwright the Third. How do you do? he said in a drawl that sounded like parody.

Grand. Róisín McCaffrey.

Red had lit a joint. Róisín's staying, he said, passing it to Greg.

Cool. How were the holidays?

She felt a pang of anxiety; Red's answer would reveal how it had felt to have her around. Before he could reply there was a rap at the door.

I suppose I'm getting that? said Red.

I have jet lag. Anyway, it's for you, I'd know that knock anywhere.

You're lazy, man.

Octavia was ahead of Red like last time. Plucking the spliff from between Greg's fingers she drew hard on it. She opened her mouth, watching the smoke waft in front of her face. It went on for a long time. Christ, it's my breath, she said. This house is bloody freezing.

The way she spoke, teeth almost closed, pronouncing 'house' the way Róisín's mother did: *hice*. Lady Di had made the same sound when she said she'd met Prince Charles in a *plighed* field.

There's snow coming, it's going to get worse, said Red.

Róisín felt like screaming. She had endured the cold for a fortnight, but one complaint from Octavia and he was treating it as an emergency.

Shall we go on an adventure? said Octavia.

Don't forget to bring Julian, Dick, Anne and George with you. And Timmy the dog, said Róisín huffily.

Greg sniggered – sarcasm was clearly the way forward – but to Róisín's horror, Red was getting to his feet. Do let's go on an adventure, he said. Or let's do, or whatever the fuck one says.

I'm going to sleep all day, said Greg, stretching. You kids have fun.

Róisín trotted after them. Red and Octavia talked about the vile occupations of London's past poor, mudlarks and toshers and nob-thatchers, Red particularly taken with the latter. Sometimes he hung back to include Róisín, but mostly they ignored her. On High Holborn, Octavia led them into a laneway so narrow Róisín was able to touch both walls at once, the grey sky like a roof above them. A sharp turn and the street opened on to a square. They went left, where the uniformity of a terrace was broken by a cluster of houses that looked gloriously wrong. As they entered through the middle one, a discreet sign said they were at Sir John Soane's Museum.

The narrow hall had columns and busts in recessed alcoves, the next room books and art and more busts and an astronomical clock. A guide seemed to step out of a wall, so slim Róisín wondered had he been employed because there wasn't enough weight on him to throw around and break things. He pointed out a vase from the fourth century BC and said the room was painted in a red shade that matched a piece of plaster Soane took from the ruins of Pompeii. Red, who – stoned a few days earlier – had staged a one-man protest about the Elgin Marbles outside the British Museum, was nodding enthusiastically.

Octavia seized Red's fingers and tugged him further into the house. They were holding hands! An only child, Róisín was uncompetitive, but this could not be tolerated. She charged after them, the guide practically spinning in her wake, but when she caught up they were apart. Octavia's had been an instinctive gesture, performed without thought. Róisín's approaches were always planned, so cloying in comparison.

Worse, Octavia was giving a better tour than the guide, pointing out portraits of Napoleon and a dog called Fanny and the domed ceiling overhead made of tiny mirrors that intensified the effect of looking. Another dome, in a chamber that cut through three floors, engorged with so many objects it was impossible to take in. Octavia said Soane was a teacher, an architect, a collector. During the Napoleonic Wars, when it was not possible to do the Grand Tour, he brought his students here. It wasn't a bad substitute; there were Corinthian columns holding up a mezzanine, an Egyptian sarcophagus in the basement. Róisín left them and went outside, lighting a cigarette that made her head swim. It felt as though she had been beaten in a race, unable to withstand the conditions.

Red came bounding down the steps. Come in or you'll miss it.

Miss what?

I don't know but Octavia's creaming herself in there.

He was making fun of Róisín's rival. She had won him back.

Inside again, everyone was crammed into the Picture Room, the guide now in white gloves. He began to flip up latches and fold back panels, saying Soane designed the gallery to accommodate three times as many artworks as the space could hold.

Pictures were disappearing and they were looking at *A Rake's Progress*, eight paintings by Hogarth. They told the story of a young man who inherited money and let it ruin him. Straight out of the blocks he was a shit, reneging on a promise to marry a girl he'd got in trouble, staggering from brothel to gambling den to prison to asylum. Red had moved away and was beside Octavia, as close as they could get to the canvases. Peering at each one with a look that bordered on desperation.

Fuck, said Red when they were on the street. Tom Rakewell. Even the name.

He destroyed himself and everyone around him! said Róisín. The poor one-eyed woman he married and cleaned out and him eyeing up her maid. Sarah at his deathbed like a lapdog. And the brothel scene is ridiculous, everyone is fully clothed.

His face was like Una's when she found cigarettes in Róisín's room: disappointed.

Octavia appeared, presenting Red with a paper bag. Inside were eight postcards, *A Rake's Progress* in gift-shop miniature. Red was thrilled, thanking her again and again. As they walked back it was as though he had forgotten Róisín. Sometimes familiar names reached her. Byron, Shelley, Wollstonecraft. Mostly she had no idea what they were talking about. To compound her misery, when they got to Pimlico, Octavia walked straight past her own house and into number 48.

Wilbur didn't start up, clearly cured of depression by Greg's return. Octavia sat regally at the kitchen table and reached for Red's pouch. He fired up the heater and dragged a chair beside hers, the way he normally did with Róisín. It was devastating, but it would have been too melodramatic, even by her standards, to march upstairs.

She set about making tea. Behind her, Octavia was telling Red that *A Rake's Progress* was Hogarth playing with Bunyan's *The Pilgrim's Progress*, telling it in reverse: a journey from redemption to sin. Red was saying *hmm, hmm* urgently, as if it was the most interesting thing he'd ever heard. In fairness, it was riveting to listen to her. The minute and ghastly details of Hogarth's *Gin Lane*. The sign that read *Drunk for a penny, dead drunk for two pence*. The swinging corpse of a tailor who'd just hanged himself, a man fighting a dog for a bone. She was telling them about the Mohocks, a band of young gentlemen who ran amok in London in the 1700s cutting people's noses off for fun, when Barry Doyle walked into the house.

Where'd you hear the like of that? he said, ripping the tinsel off the tiles. He was in a woolly plaid jacket lined with fake fleece, face and hands veiled in dust.

My father has a satirical print from 1745, said Octavia.

Was she actually blushing?

Well for him, said Barry.

Ha! said Róisín.

Barry flicked her a look and she waited for him to comment on her presence. Are they sitting here talking shite since I left? was all he said. Why wasn't he surprised to see her?

Long enough to smoke four of these, said Red, holding up a spliff. He sounded as if he'd had his mouth frozen by a dentist.

Idle cunts. I travelled all night and did a day's work. Taking the joint from Red, Barry sucked greedily. Fuck, he coughed, I thought you kept this for the customers.

Needs must. How was Christmas?

Champion. Everyone was home.

Red raised an index finger. Except me, Doyle.

You're missed, man.

It was said gently, as if it was a simple fact. Red bowed his head in gratitude.

Barry passed Róisín the joint. Red, who never let her smoke hash, didn't seem to notice. She pretended to inhale, afraid of making a show of herself by choking.

Octavia rose, saying, My father's having people for dinner. She had been quiet since Barry arrived.

The hostess with the mostest, he said.

Red saw her out, bashing into the wall and giggling at the top of the steps.

There's days you wouldn't be in the humour, said Barry, throwing an exaggerated eye roll over his shoulder in the direction of the hall. Róisín could have kissed him.

Red, back at the table, began to make another joint.

You're fairly going for it, said Barry.

Each to their own, Doyle.

Barry went upstairs, saying he needed to clean up and change. Róisín opened the book she'd been reading, Red's copy of *The Reprieve* by Sartre, the second novel in a trilogy that she wasn't enjoying as much as the first. Maybe it wasn't as good. Maybe it was. As long as Red was bewitched by Octavia, Róisín would never enjoy anything again.

Then they were all there. Barry in stiff new Wranglers and an argyle-patterned jumper, probably Christmas presents. Greg in his top hat – how was she going to live with these idiots? – and a notably zen Wilbur. Barry gave Greg a tenner for beer and kebabs, as if he was sending his son down to the shops for sweets. Even Red, who was alone in the world and now apparently a petty criminal, seemed like a kid beside him.

Are you going looking for a job or will you be hanging around the place with these layabouts? Barry asked her.

I want to work. I got a National Insurance number this morning at the DHSS office. A demented pensioner called Stanley fucking Robbins was terrorising the whole room, wasn't he, Red?

Red was looking at the table, mouth contorted in an imbecilic gurn. Fuck him, she thought. It was a good story. Barry chuckled as she described the tiny angry man roaring that he'd lived through two world wars and fought in one, threatening to wipe the smirk off her lazy Irish face. Like how did he know where I'm from? she said.

You couldn't be anything but Irish. Barry was eyeing her sidelong. She instinctively raised her hands to her cheeks.

He told her not to get her hopes up about work. It was better than home but lots of the jobs were shit, literally: he'd spent a month laying sewage pipes in the City. There were jobs going in the Docklands, demolition work for unskilled labourers like him. She felt her prospects diminish as she listened. Barry wasn't stupid, he'd done better than Róisín in the Leaving Certificate. If all he could get was a job on a building site, what was the equivalent for Róisín? Cleaning arses or urinals?

So it didn't work out with your father, he said.

What do you mean?

Meeting the kid, like.

Who had told him that? He'd only just arrived and Red was stoned beyond speech. Registering her confusion, Barry was blushing now. My neighbour works with your ould one, he said, she told my ma.

So that was why he hadn't been surprised to see her. Una's workmates had known about Mary before Róisín did? She'd probably told everyone she planned to get married again as well. And if Barry knew, his hateful sister did too.

My mother should keep her trap shut.

He nodded slowly, as if he was trying to understand, and she felt mean for snapping at him.

You didn't miss much anyway, being away for Christmas, he said eventually. Just a couple of mad nights.

Yeah?

When Greg came back, Róisín was laughing at Barry's description of Shay Dempsey at the end of a party, 'like a dying swan, with a bun burger stuck to the back of his head'. Róisín got plates and forks. Barry ripped the bags open and passed everyone a can.

These are gyros, said Greg, moving around the food as if he was inspecting a buffet in a country club. I always go to the Greek-Cypriots across the river.

Red was licking the corners of his mouth, still with that moronic look in his eyes. Róisín felt so abashed as she ate that her head began to bob, a bouncy little tremor that used to come on her in the college canteen. But she was hungry and it tasted good, even though the sight of Wilbur slurping a sliver of processed meat from Greg's palm confirmed its resemblance to Pedigree Chum.

Barry asked Greg and Red when they were going to get the electricity sorted. It was miserable in the winter and when the summer came their food would spoil and they'd smell like derelicts. Greg said English bureaucracy was Kafkaesque and it would fuck with his mind. Red, in a rare moment when his eyes were actually open, shuddered as if harrowed by the very thought.

I'll do it, said Róisín, eager for an ally. Tell me where to go.

Sound, said Barry. We won't know ourselves.

When the six-pack of beer was finished – Barry drank four and Red, fit only to poke chips in his face, none – there was a brief debate about whether he should open the whiskey he'd bought on the boat. But then he was yawning, and so was Greg.

Barry shook Red's shoulder. Bed for you, he said. Red's elbow slid off the table and he began to laugh. Róisín couldn't bear to see more.

She went upstairs to the bathroom. If it hadn't been the only one in the house she would have bolted herself in for the night. When she came out, Red was slumped against the headboard. On the bedspread the Hogarth postcards were laid out, except for *The Asylum*, which was in his hand.

* * *

She woke with her body against his. She shifted to the other side of the bed but it was so cold she snatched her legs back, kicking him.

Go easy, will you? he said.

She was tempted to kick him again. Reaching for a second jumper, she saw that her belongings were all around the room. His room. Perhaps the mess was irritating him. She got up and began to fill her bag with dirty clothes. Red propped himself on his elbow to watch, as if her packing was a performance to get his attention.

What are you doing? he said.

Tidying up, what does it look like? She pushed the last of her things in the bag and zipped it closed.

Stop, will you? Sit down.

What? she said, staying on her feet.

You need your own room, Ró. Dawn says you can have hers if you promise to take care of her art.

When had he spoken to Dawn? Not today, surely, it was just after nine o'clock in the morning; and not yesterday, Róisín would have known. He'd been planning to get rid of her for days while she lay beside him, her heart in her throat at the nearness of him. I'll move out altogether, she said, in tears now. You'd probably prefer that.

I want you here, he said, his voice squeaking on the second word. Please, I can't handle this stuff.

Snow days at home were clean and new. Here, the inch that had fallen overnight had been soiled by a Westminster Council gritter that was moving slowly towards the river, the crust on the pavement already trodden to ice. She didn't have anywhere to go. Lynne said she would always be welcome, but her father would soon get sick of the cutting remarks that left Róisín's lips unbidden, especially now that he had a gorgeous new daughter.

Feet slithering around the footpath, she made her way to Victoria. Micksy wasn't there, and she hoped he was somewhere warm. She bought a paper cup of tea and asked for the change in coins. At the payphone, she dialled her home number but clicked off before it had a chance to connect. Her mother had made her choice; she didn't want Róisín either. She dialled Sinéad's number, bracing herself to explain to Mr or Mrs Flanagan why she was calling so early, and almost wept with loneliness at the sound of her friend's voice.

Why are you up? said Róisín.

It was my turn to do the milking. Why are you up?

Red doesn't want me.

I'm delighted he doesn't, you might see sense and come home.

But I can't come home.

Ah, Róisín. Piss or get off the pot. If you're insisting on staying, make the best of it. Go down and see your sister. Barry's there, isn't he? He's nice, you can hang around with him. And get a bloody job.

Have you ever heard of sympathy?

You know I'm right. I'm going to send you a long letter telling you why. What's your address?

10

6 July 1985

Octavia was at the kitchen table, or rather on it, the hair twirled into a glossy rope that hung over her shoulder. She had on a sailor-style dress with a white yoke, toes pointing to the ceiling to keep on a pair of battered silk slippers. On anyone else it would look tragic, but she appeared sepia-tinted, like one of the last Tsar's daughters. Here's the Little Match Girl, she said.

Red licked the gum on the joint he was rolling and chuckled. He was amused that the nickname he'd given Róisín was being used to make her look stupid?

Are youse here for the day? said Róisín.

Why, are you entertaining? said Octavia.

Clearly not as entertaining as you. Róisín left the room.

Ah, Ró, called Red after her.

She stomped up the two flights to the second floor and sat on her bed. The high notes of Octavia's laughter reached her and she slotted a cassette into the cheap personal stereo Lynne had given her for her birthday. The foam earpieces had begun to disintegrate and a couple of tracks in she heard a wary knock.

Piss off.

Barry's head came round the door. I hope you were expecting someone else, he said.

I wasn't expecting anyone.

She rarely saw Barry. Some mornings she heard him leave, clopping about in his work boots, waking Wilbur. In the evenings he often came home late, leaving aromas of beer and batter or ghee lingering on the landing. When they met in the kitchen or hallway they had little to say to each other.

Amazing paintings, he said, looking at the pair of almost life-size artworks on either side of the fireplace. A willowy nude woman in a forest clearing, bleary as if seen through heavy rain. In one she was walking into a dense wood; in the other she was running away from it.

Those are photographs, printed on board, actually.

What was Róisín like? Six months in an art student's bedroom and she thought she was Sister Wendy.

What are you listening to? said Barry.

Lloyd Cole and the Commotions.

Student shite. Do you want to go to a lido?

Yeah. What's a lido?

He smiled and for a moment looked carefree; Róisín's mother would have said he'd given his face a holiday. It's an outdoor pool, you'll need togs. Ten minutes, yeah?

When she went downstairs, Red and Octavia were by the door to the drawing room, Barry behind them. It had been locked since they moved in, apparently because on the first day they had found monstrous droppings in its corners.

Kick the door down, said Octavia.

Do not, said Barry, I'll have a go. He rattled the key, simultaneously rotating the knob back and forwards. A click and it opened. Róisín hung behind him, expecting to be set upon by giant rodents, but the droppings were just the husks of dead woodlice, a false ceiling the only offending feature. At Christmas, Red had refused to open it for Róisín, but Octavia could persuade him to do anything.

The four of them stood in the room. It was enormous, reaching from the front of the house to the back.

We can put the telly in here, said Barry.

Telly! said Octavia.

Snotty cow, what does she call it? Róisín asked Barry as they left.

Micksy'd had a shave and a haircut but his eyeballs and complexion were yellow. Róisín crouched to give him a cigarette.

Róisín Dubh, he said.

As she rose, she got a full-length eyeful of Barry. Jeans baggy below the knees, tight at the thighs and crotch – please God he hadn't seen her looking – biceps bulging beneath the sleeves of a Rory Gallagher T-shirt.

The smell off him would make your eyes water, said Barry. Fair play to you.

I take a deep breath.

He insisted on buying their train tickets, something old-fashioned about him as he flashed them at the barrier. An announcer from inner-city Dublin was calling out the stops, mangling the place names so thoroughly it sounded almost subversive. 'For Folkestone, or anywhere out that direction, go to Platform Five,' she finished.

My father lives *out this direction*, said Róisín as they boarded.

Is that where he ran off to?

He didn't run off. He came here for work.

Must be weird. Him having a new family.

It was at first. Just as well the baby is cute or I'd still be raging.

The lido had the biggest pool she had ever seen and she almost ran to the changing room. Stripping quickly, she put on a candy-striped bikini she'd salvaged from a bag of Lynne's cast-offs (mostly ra-ra skirts and Lady Di blouses). Her breasts, it turned out, were larger than bosomy Lynne's. She stretched and pulled but there was so little fabric to work with it was pointless.

Outside, she dived straight in, coming up too close to Barry. She took off, a prim breaststroke, resting against the tiles at the other end to wait for him. He was a sloppy swimmer with his flailing crawl and thrashing legs, lips pursed like a hen's hole to keep out the water.

You're showing off, he said as he reached her.

I'll do a doggy paddle from now on to spare your feelings, she said, making paws of her hands.

I'm just jealous. Where did you learn? His forearms were on the edge of the pool. They were deeply tanned, like his face, the rest of him white as milk.

My father took me swimming every week and when I was eleven my class had lessons in the posh Protestant school next door. It had a wee pool.

Wee. You don't usually have a northern accent.

It was slagged out of me by Free Staters.

Róisín waited for him to get annoyed that she had used the pre-Republic 'Free State' to refer to the south of Ireland, proud of herself for not naming his sister as her main tormentor.

Hmm, was all he said. He was staring at a spot just in front of her. She looked down. Her breasts were above the surface of the water, the bikini practically transparent, her aureoles and nipples raised and dark. For a mad second she imagined him untying the strings and ravishing her. She swam away from him. This time she did show off.

I could teach you how to do a mean front crawl, she said on her return. You can swim out of your depth, you'd learn in no time.

Go 'way, will you.

Do you not take advice from women or something?

He laughed. A shy laugh. Maybe I don't want to make an eejit of myself in front of you.

Look, she said, flipping on to her belly. She cut three strokes through the water and turned her face to the left for air, cutting three more and turning to the right. Barry was reclining against the edge, watching her. It was intense, being looked at like that. She kicked away from the tiles. He was swimming alongside, taking panicky gulps of air, but a calmness came on him and he reached the far end pouting with the effort of not smiling to himself.

They stopped for a drink a few streets away. Like most London pubs it was disappointing, the Victorian exterior offering something cute and historic, the interior presided over by a female version of Terry. A mostly male clientele supping beer from dimpled tankards and laughing like maniacs at their own jokes. On hearing Barry's accent, a couple of them fell quiet.

Róisín found the beer too strong and could only manage sips. Barry demolished his in a series of long swallows, his Adam's apple going up and down like a ballcock. He set his glass on the counter, too loudly, and pointed at it. The landlady put it under a tap.

Why do you want to stay here with them all gawping at us? whispered Róisín.

Because fuck them.

His swagger seemed stupid to her, especially since one of the men, a rifle bisecting a Union Jack tattooed on his arm, was stepping forward. Róisín held her breath, but he just eyeballed them for a moment and went to the gents.

Your face, said Barry.

What about it?

Scared and disgusted at the same time, he said, and lowered the second pint in three tilts. He asked the barmaid for another. Róisín left her unfinished beer on the counter and walked out on to the street.

He came rushing after her, a freshly lit cigarette in his mouth. Jesus, you're some woman for running off, he said.

They didn't want us there.

That's generally the case for the like of us living here. Come back in, I'm busting for the jacks.

Any bloody wonder, you're averaging a pint every three minutes. Do what you like, I want to go home.

OK, we'll go so.

He paid for both their tickets again, mumbling something about getting a train 'out that direction', imitating the announcer they'd heard earlier. His impersonation was rubbish and she didn't like being beholden to him, but at least he was trying. As the train pulled in, she saw their reflections, expecting them to look like they could not possibly know each other, but they fitted together. They looked Irish – her pale and green-eyed with dark hair; Barry freckled, with thick brown hair that glinted reddish in the sun.

In Micksy's place there was a puddle that smelled of Jeyes Fluid, as if he had been sluiced away. The British Rail employee she had seen goading him before was watching. You looking for your dad? he called.

Barry started towards him, but Róisín pulled him back. Stop, I have to work in there.

What's it like?

Working in Sock Shop? Fabulous. Women from Sidcup treating a ladder in their tights as a national disaster. I sold a pair of fishnets to a middle-aged man, though.

They were probably for his wife.

Unlikely, the way he was whispering.

All your education. You could get something else.

I dropped out of college after three months. I'm no more educated than you.

You know what I mean. All the books you read.

The only true wisdom is in knowing that you know nothing.

You've lost me.

Socrates, maybe.

You're an intellect.

Intellectual. And I'm not. All the reading is making me mental. God, isn't it fucked up being poor in an area like this?

Where would you like to be poor?

Nowhere. It's not that I want to be rich, but wouldn't it be great to be given a place to live and vouchers for basics like food and books and smokes?

And drink. Speaking of which... They were opposite the Bull and Crown. He waggled a thumb at it as though he was hitching a lift.

Terry raised his eyebrows at Barry in greeting, but at the sight of Róisín shook his head. Barry spoke to him quietly and eventually Terry plucked a couple of glasses from the shelf.

Find a table and don't open your mouth, said Barry out of the side of his face.

Róisín was so stunned she did as she was told. What was that about? she said as he placed their drinks on the table.

He's barred Red for dealing and he thought you were his girlfriend.

No way is he dealing in here.

Barry lifted his pint and took a long gulp, eyeing her over the froth. For someone so smart you can be awful fucking dim. Red's dealing everywhere, Ró.

She shifted in her seat with irritation. No one but Red ever called her Ró.

You pair, he said. Always in cahoots.

Bullshit. He's in cahoots with that disdainful cunt from two doors up. He's hardly spoken to me since she turned up again.

Youse don't even need to talk. There's a charge in the air the rest of us can nearly see.

Very poetic.

His colour deepened and he lit a cigarette.

I'm sorry, Barry. Talking about them is putting me in bad form. I shouldn't have brought it up. Although it was worth it for 'disdainful cunt'.

Barry was knocking down factories and warehouses on the Isle of Dogs. Filthy work that raised nuclear-looking clouds of dust, but there was double pay on Saturdays so it was worth putting in the odd extra morning. His father, an officer in the Irish Army, wanted him to apply to the Cadets. Weird, he said, considering he hasn't been right since he came back from Lebanon. Shelling and landmines for months and then one of his men cracked up and shot himself.

She knew Barry and Tina's father had been on UN peacekeeping duties but had never considered what that meant. Now it seemed they understood what it was like to have your father turn from a normal person into a wreck. Not that she'd ever share that with him.

Barry wouldn't let Róisín buy the next round, saying she should stay put and not remind Terry she was there, but she suspected he was being chivalrous, in that ould fella way he had. Drinking visibly relaxed him, enabling him to smile easily, meet her gaze. She talked for too long about the book she was reading, Ibsen's collected plays, borrowed from the library, and he called her a poser. His admiration for Charlie Haughey, the former Taoiseach, made her indignant, but as long as they avoided mentioning Red they got along. She went to the ladies expecting to appear attractively spent from swimming and alcohol, and saw that her face was burnt.

Back at the table, she held her cold glass against her cheek. I'm fucking roasted.

You're grand, he said, giving her that slow side-eye.

The door to the drawing room was ajar. Aside from the shutters, one of which had been prised open, it looked untouched.

Hello? called Barry. When no one replied, they went to the kitchen. He took a bottle of wine from his bag. I bought it from Terry while you were in the jacks. Stowells of Chelsea, made just up the road.

Surely it's imported, she was about to say, but he was smirking.

She told him she had food to use up and he was welcome to have some. He divided the wine between two pint glasses, staying close while she trimmed the outer layers from an onion and chopped it with a floppy carrot and sprouting garlic. She fried it all up with greying mince, adding Worcestershire sauce, tomato ketchup and a stock cube. He peeled potatoes, like Red had that first evening in her house. It felt like so long ago.

How come you know how to cook? he said at the table.

My mother works nights. She hated it anyway, and it showed, so it suited me not to be eating her slop.

You don't go home, he said.

I will sometime. I'm not very forgiving.

He swallowed before replying. She imagined his soldier father shouting at him to not speak with his mouth full. Gilhooly's all right, you know, he said. There's worse cunts your mother could be with.

It's not just him. My father has Lynne and the baby. Maybe I'm pissed off because they're all OK and I'm not, she said. Hearing herself admit it made her mournful.

He must have seen it in her because he murmured, Ah no.

Jesus. I've spent months trying to figure this out. I never thought I'd have a moment of clarity drinking with Barry Doyle.

Barry Doyle. That makes me sound like a caricature or something.

I didn't mean it like that, she said, and she hadn't. She used Barry's full name when talking to Red; even when he wasn't there she addressed everything to him.

She brought their plates to the sink. Barry joined her, lifting a tea towel. If they're not clean I'll drop them back in the bowl.

I used to do that to my mother. God, I was a pain in the hole.

He was drying the last dish when the front door opened.

Where did you pair disappear to? said Red from the top step. He was agitated, pulling at a thread on his cutaway sleeve, and his jeans were hanging off him. Greg had started using speed again a month earlier. At first Red scoffed at him, saying it was muck, but within a couple of days he was at it too.

We went to a lido, said Róisín.

Why didn't you ask me?

Cos you were with the English one, said Barry.

Fuck's sake, said Red. We are in England.

Not by choice.

Red looked hard at Róisín and went into the drawing room.

Róisín wiped the draining board and draped the cloth over the tap. Red was more difficult to get on with than her mother. I'm going to bed, she said, afraid that a contraction she felt in her throat betrayed her. She climbed the stairs to her room, careful not to run. It was exhausting appearing not to mind.

Picking up the copy of *Time Out* she'd bought at Victoria, she read the listings for free things to do in London. She could take tango lessons, swim in the pond at Hampstead. Or see Mary more often, Lynne made it easy for her.

Feet on the landing, the timid knock. Would this help? Barry said, coming in. He was holding a bottle of vodka.

You're a walking off-licence.

He sat beside her on the bed. Red's being a cunt, he said, slugging from the bottle and passing it to her.

I'm so sick of this. If Enda Gilhooly wasn't hanging out of my mother twenty-four-seven I'd go home.

The chlorine had irritated her eyes and the spirit briefly scorched her corneas as she threw it back. He had insisted on buying her train tickets, been unfazed by the squaddies in the pub. And his working-man's tan in the pool.

He placed the bottle on the floor. Don't go home, he said, and pulled her on to his knee.

11

13 July 1985

The brush of a rat or mouse. A feral scent from the bedclothes she hoped wasn't coming from her, a grazed feeling between her legs. The rat, which she now realised was Barry Doyle's hand, twanged her nipple like a guitar string. Her head was throbbing, unable to assemble an account of how they had ended up in bed again.

After the lido, they had spent twenty-four hours doing just about everything – not that she was an expert – but fucking. Late on Sunday he left for his own room, saying boxers weren't allowed near women before a fight and he'd be unfit for work if they didn't stop – but not before he slathered her in baby oil and masturbated her until she came with a bovine maw he would probably impersonate in the pub. Never again, she vowed to herself and managed to avoid him all week. But now his mouth was on her neck, his fingers stroking her hips in circular movements. His cock – so very hard! and a little wet, and soft like satin – was poking into her kidney. She pressed against him and when it slipped into the cleft at the base of her spine, she gasped. For a moment, neither of them moved. Then he rolled her on to her back and threw the covers off.

His mouth tasted like a bucket of slops into which someone had emptied an ashtray, but his kisses were deep and rhythmic. Even his congested breath was turning her on. Are you sorted? he said, drawing away from her. Protected, like.

Yes.

She thought Red would be the first, that he would say something profound and unforgettable afterwards. But she had lost her virginity to Barry Doyle. Still, it was momentous, and the next words spoken would carry great weight. Barry cleared his throat. Róisín kept her eyes on the ceiling and prayed to Jesus, Mary and Joseph and all the holy saints it would not be something ridiculous that would make her laugh.

You OK? he said.

Yeah, she said. Maybe she was.

She fell back asleep and woke to the sound of Annie Lennox singing 'There Must Be an Angel'. Barry was putting dirty clothes in a cotton sack. Behind him a tin sign, a pelican eyeing a pint of Guinness, was on the mantelpiece and empties were crowding the hearth. He kissed her and left for the launderette, padding out of the room in too-white boot runners. She went to the bathroom, showering and dabbing foundation on her peeling nose. Apparently Dusty Springfield was so overwhelmed by fame and attention she never took her make-up off, layering it up day after day until she felt safe, masked, shielded. Róisín put on a second coat but still felt as if she was walking downstairs stark naked.

Red was up a ladder in the drawing room, ramming at the fake ceiling with the shaft of a brush. Every few strikes a tile came away, raining dust and dead insects down on him. He descended and relit his joint.

You OK? he said.

It was the second time in an hour she had been asked that question.

Why wouldn't I be?

He fuzzed his hair to free it of a spider's web. You were really drunk last night, Ró.

So? You're chewing the face off yourself the last month.

He scratched his hand. It was already raw. At least I'm not falling about the place.

Oh, just fuck off.

She found paracetamol in the kitchen and swallowed two dry. Greg was watching from the table.

How's our dirty Little Match Girl today? he said.

Had Barry told him? Or worse, had everyone heard them?

Red came down the steps and washed his hands at the sink. He filled the electric kettle, another gift from Lynne. Róisín waited for him to finish, hanging back as if he had something contagious. When he moved away she drank two pints of water. Without the pot and Primus his tea-making ritual lacked grace. Everything seemed slapdash and ordinary now.

Barry returned, putting bags of shopping on the table. He must have dropped his clothes off for a service wash; Róisín could only afford to sit in the launderette for hours watching her smalls getting tossed around a coin-operated machine. She was resigned to being ignored by him, he'd hardly looked at her from Monday to Friday, but what he did was much worse: placing his hand on her shoulder he began stroking her neck with the side of his thumb. She could only sit there and tolerate it, and it didn't help that it felt good.

Greg took a queen cake from the bag, an eyebrow raised as he sank his teeth into it.

You must be hungry, said Barry, producing a sausage roll that he pointed too close to her face. She snatched it from his hand and took a bite, cursing God that Red was there to see.

Barry switched on the television and fiddled with the aerial – a wire coat hanger – until there was reasonable picture and sound. Charles and Diana were taking their seats above the toilets in Wembley Stadium; Live Aid was about to begin.

Geldof on his feet for 'God Save the Queen', the big Blueshirt, said Barry, patting Róisín's head as if she was a racehorse in a parade ring.

Ha, Blueshirt, said Greg.

Red tutted. The Blueshirts were Irish fascists, Cartwright the Third. Come on, Barry, he can't exactly sit on his arse when everyone else is standing up.

I thought your one Octavia would be in the Royal Box, said Barry. She must be down among the plain folk.

Red left, spewing words Róisín couldn't make out.

When Barry's beer was gone he gave Greg money for more, telling him to pick up his service wash. At first she'd been baffled by Greg's subservience, until she realised he wasn't entitled to dole. Red spent most of the day in the drawing room, coming in sometimes to make more tea. Watching the television as he waited for the water to boil, he tossed out comments so apt she wanted to shout, Yes! When Bono disappeared for ten minutes he said the rest of the band looked like they didn't know if he was alive or dead. *This is an abomination*, he said about Jagger and Bowie's murder of 'Dancing in the Street'. *Oh shit, Bob*, he murmured when Dylan said he hoped a million or two of the money raised would go to US farmers. And he was in the kitchen when Barry gave a languorous yawn and said, Bed?

Red's eyes were practically boring a hole in the screen. Fuck you, she thought. Slipping her hand in Barry's, she slunk out behind him.

On the first-floor landing, he walked past his door, but she pulled him in. His bed was rumpled from their earlier exertions and he began to straighten the blankets, plumping the pillows with his fists.

She went to the window. Beyond their tangled garden there were yellow boxes of light, figures moving around distant houses. All done, he said, and crossed the room to her. He began to undo the buttons of her blouse, a fitted one in oat-coloured linen she'd bought in a charity shop. Her skirt was off next, then her bra. It felt like visiting the doctor and having things done you knew were necessary and did not enjoy, but as he pulled her knickers down she saw their reflection, her naked body and his fully clothed one. She unzipped his jeans.

You're champion, he said, walking her backwards and pinning her to the wall.

Afterwards, in his bed, he turned her face to his. So you and Red. What's the story?

She felt so physically comfortable it was appalling, her hand splayed on Barry's stomach, feet tethering his ankles. Shut up about Red.

There's something. The head on him earlier like.

Róisín didn't trust herself to reply.

He won't talk about you either, said Barry.

Why would you want him to talk about me?

He looked at her mouth. Maybe I like you.

When the intensity was becoming too much, he lifted the covers and peered. I've a horn again. What do you reckon?

At first, they went slow, with more touching and kissing, too slow for her liking, he was rolling her breast with the heel of his hand as if he was making a hot cross bun. She guided his fingers to her crotch.

Fuck, he said, going up on one arm to shove his cock inside her with his free hand. It almost slipped out and she grabbed his arse cheeks, pulling him close. Róisín likes it hard, he said – if only he wouldn't say things like that – and began thrusting. He came quickly, a stupefied, faraway glaze in his eyes, and buckled over. Róisín felt squashed and frustrated but he did something with the joint of his thumb that made her climax almost immediately.

For a while she felt a woozy euphoria, but as it wore off, all she was aware of was the thudding and battering from downstairs. Last weekend, after the lido, Barry had gone up the next flight to her room; this evening they had practically canoodled in the kitchen and shagged with abandon in the bedroom next to Red's, which was also directly above where he was working. She pictured his skinny arms bashing upwards, over and over, heart thumping. Even after dawn lit the gloom, the noise continued. Róisín lay parched and guilty, wishing he would stop.

Barry made a clucking sound in the back of his throat, his mouth gaping like someone in a stroke awareness poster. His alarm clock said it was almost ten. Róisín drew the covers back. The pale sheets had creamy traces. Semen. Not very much, because most of it was inside her, trying to fertilise her eggs with a thick Kildare accent. What had possessed her to let Barry Doyle strip her in front of the window? To encourage him to do it! She tiptoed across the room and gathered up her clothes from the floor. Dressing quickly, she went downstairs.

Red was up the ladder with the brush, wearing the T-shirt he'd had on since Friday.

Why aren't you talking to me? she said.

Away with your shite.

Yesterday you talked to the walls and the lads and Bob Geldof. Not to me.

He jumped down and loomed into her face. Barry Doyle, he said. Really, Ró? Is he your boyfriend now?

No!

Well, you might want to tell him that, he said, rubbing his eyes and opening them wide. His pupils were so dilated there was only a thin rim of brown around the black.

What's it to you anyway, and you spending all your time with that horrible bitch, she said, her voice shaky.

Octavia is like me.

Maybe Barry Doyle is like me.

Yeah, right. Did he tell you you're champion? *That was champion, Róisín.* Róisín McCaffrey and the Leinster Champion, together at last. He was speaking very fast, twisting the shaft of the brush as if he was screwing it into the floor.

You're demented.

Barry's boot runners on the floorboards, the slam of the front door.

Fuck! said Red, tossing the brush aside.

She ran upstairs to get her bag. Greg had come out of his room. He was passing a burst tennis ball back and forth between his hands.

Spy in the house of love, he said, grinding his teeth.

She shoved him out of the way.

Why had she told Barry she was 'protected'? It was Sunday. If she didn't get herself to a doctor by tomorrow morning she would be in trouble, but she didn't have a GP in London. She wanted to call Sinéad, bawl down the phone at her, but she had gone Interrailing. There was only one person she could ask for help. She left the house.

Micksy was in a nest of newspaper, Charles, Di and Freddie Mercury peeping from under his arse. Róisín Dubh, he said.

I've no smokes, Micksy.

Arra, loveen, he said, pulling out a flattened pack of Sweet Afton. He thought she was asking for a cigarette! She took one, filthy to her core and not in a position to judge the dirt of the hand that offered it.

Róisín had practised what she would say, but at the sight of Lynne blabbed, I need a doctor, please don't tell my daddy.

Upstairs, Mary was in a Winnie-the-Pooh high chair. She began to slap the plastic tray.

Pick her up, Rosh, she's happy to see you, said Lynne. Conor, will you buy bread and bacon for lunch?

She'd used 'Rosh' last time too. Róisín had thought it was a liberty, but today she could only hear affection.

Hello, love, her father said, a hum of stale lager on him she could smell from five paces. He wandered to the bedroom and back as if trying to remember what he'd been asked to do. There's cash in my bag, said Lynne, a curt nip in her voice.

He removed a tenner from her purse with the sleight of a pickpocket. Was he taking money from her all the time?

Whatever is the matter? Lynne cried when he was gone, rushing to Róisín.

I need the morning-after pill.

Well, thank fuck that's all!

Mary bounced and clapped her hands. Her first word is going to be fun, said Lynne, carrying the phone into the bedroom.

Mary's hair was held off her face with a pink ribbon, her widow's peak as pronounced as Róisín's. We're dead ringers for Eddie Munster, sis, she said, tickling under her chin.

What time? called Lynne.

I don't have a watch, it must be nearly one?

Oh my days, I meant what time did you do the naughty thing?

Ten on Friday, said Róisín, tracing a circle in Mary's palm that made her giggle.

Rosh!

What?

Sorry, petal, but she needs to know if it was more than once.

Just once, said Róisín. She felt sick. It was five times that she could remember.

Lynne came back. She said the pharmacist lived around the corner and would be here in a few minutes to make up a prescription.

Thanks, said Róisín.

Was it Red?

No. Róisín began to cry.

Did anyone hurt you?

Just me, thought Róisín, I hurt myself. No, Lynne, she said.

Oh, matey. Must be hard without your mum too.

My mother is the last person I'd talk to about this kind of thing.

Can't you make it up with her? It's been going on ever so long.

No, I can't. Anyway, even if we were on speaking terms she'd die of disgust. And it's hard to get contraception in Ireland. Until four months ago, you could only get condoms on prescription.

Gracious!

Róisín suspected Lynne didn't believe her.

The doorbell rang. Lynne went downstairs and came back a few minutes later with a palmful of pills. Take two of these now and two in twelve hours, she said. The stray one is for nausea, I've got more if you need them. Oh, and Sheila, the pharmacist, wants to check your blood pressure in the morning.

Róisín swallowed the tablets. Thank you, she said. I had nowhere else to go.

It's all right. You don't want to get up the duff at your age.

Her father returned with lager twinkling in his eyes. He clattered about the kitchenette for half an hour and served them 'sarnies', the English abbreviation sounding pitiful in his mouth. They watched television all afternoon, Conor sipping from a can, misty smiles forming when his eyes wandered from the screen to the couch. My three girls, he said a couple of times.

Lynne insisted Róisín stay overnight. It was a relief not to face the lads in the house. Red swinging between derangement and silence, Greg making her feel like a whore. And Barry Doyle. She never wanted to set eyes on him again.

In the morning, she fed and dressed Mary while Lynne got ready for work. She helped them downstairs and watched Lynne hurry towards the train station with a bag of bottles and nappies hanging from the handle of the pushchair. Conor was still in bed.

Sheila, the pharmacist, was a Belfast woman. She sat Róisín in the dispensary and put a cuff around her upper arm, pumping until it felt like it would burst.

Your blood pressure's at the high end of normal, nothing to worry about. The morning-after pill isn't a form of contraception, it's for emergencies. There's a new disease that's spreading like wildfire. They're saying it's only affecting gay people, but they don't know enough about it yet. Get him to use these, she said, giving her a box of condoms.

Sheila's accent unexpectedly devastated Róisín. She no longer knew who she was; she didn't even speak the way she had as a child, the way she still spoke in her head. A couple of tears spurted, and Sheila, perhaps thinking she had been harsh, gave Róisín a hug.

Ach, love, she said. Wise up and go on the pill.

Róisín ran panting into the shop. Alison, her boss, emerged from behind the pop socks with a man in a blue suit. He had a clipboard in one hand and a felt-tip pen in the other.

Ricky, area manager. Rosin? he said. The mispronunciation was a new one on her.

I'm so sorry. I couldn't phone, I was on a train.

He nodded, scribbling her out of every shift.

You're sacking me? Alison, this is the first time I've ever been late!

Alison was now behind the counter with a bundle of CVs.

Tell your mate not to come back either or I'll call the police, said Ricky.

Did he mean Micksy? He'd called in a couple of times, Alison had been disgusted. For a moment Róisín considered upending the place, but a feeling of relief washed over her. Never again would she hear Alison complain about Ken Livingstone or declaim *I am a Fatcherite*. Or have to evade the bizarrely personal questions

Alison tossed out as if she was asking if Róisín took sugar. *Do you bleed after anal intercourse? Are you a spitter or a swallower?*

The pair of youse can shove your socks up your holes. And by the way, rosin is salve you rub on the bow of a violin.

You'll have plenty of time for playing Irish jigs now, love, said Ricky.

Róisín walked out. The station seemed so disorienting in that moment, with its franchises and information boards and announcements. A place of transit in which you weren't supposed to linger. How had she stuck working here?

Where the fuck were you? said Red in the hallway, seizing her arm. A stye was glowing on his left lower lid, his lashes crusty.

Sydenham, she said, trying to push him off, but he tightened his grip.

I looked everywhere for you. Those cunts you work with put me out. He was speaking even faster than yesterday, almost shouting. The deposit of tartar on his lower gums looked like a crop of baby teeth.

Red, you're a fucking mess.

He let go of her and clutched his chest, visibly wilting. I feel like I'm going to explode.

She led him upstairs. He was so close to her they were almost abreast, knocking against the walls and banisters. His room was foul, floor strewn with rolled-up paper, joints left to burn out where they'd fallen. Records and books were tossed around as if he'd been looking for something. On his bed there were other books, academic tomes on the Georgians, a huge glossy Hogarth catalogue.

Red was pacing, hands on his hips. Will you hold me? he said, bending over.

All the times she'd reached for him, willing him to say that. Now she couldn't bring herself to touch him.

Please, Ró.

She lay down with him, the reedy scrape of his voice still in her ears, and wrapped him in her body. He put her hand on his heart. She began to move it in gentle circles, as if she was winding Mary. How long before it wears off? she said.

A couple of hours maybe. I'm scared for when it stops.

I'll stay.

You're going to leave me.

It's not like I have anything else to do. I don't even have a job any more.

It was meant to be a joke, but he flipped on to his other side, taking her face in his hands. Please, he said, his eyes wild and black. I don't care if you fuck all the Barry Doyles in the world. But please don't leave me.

Later, when he'd fallen asleep, she opened the copy of *Childe Harold's Pilgrimage*. Red had marked some lines with a green colouring pencil.

Nor sought he friend to counsel or condole, / Whate'er this grief mote be, which he could not control made her cry for him.

...though he loved but one, / And that loved one, alas, could ne'er be his made her cry for herself.

12

3 August 1985

Róisín's instinct was to find fault with Lynne, and today there was a lot to work with. The baby-pink top, elasticated neckline pulled down to expose her shoulders. Strappy gold sandals, Farrah Fawcett flicks. Her greetings were over the top too, flinging her arms around Red and telling Mary to kiss her stunner of a big sister. But as Róisín watched, she understood something that had begun to dawn on her when she'd come here for help: Lynne was the best person in her life.

Mary had graduated from a ribbon to a sparkly hair clip. She was gnawing a teething ring, a sadness in the downward slope of her eyes. Red put his finger under her chin and tickled. A giggle, then she changed her mind and griped. My God, said Red, glancing at Róisín. The resemblance is terrifying.

Pink carnations on the table, a card tucked among the blooms. Róisín could not help reading, to see what milestone or joy had been celebrated. *Sorry*, it said, in her father's hand. Lynne saw her replacing it and seemed about to speak. Instead, she began removing dishes of food from the fridge. They helped her carry them down the fire escape.

A patio made of crazy paving dusty with new cement. A lawn sprouting in patches like chives, a couple of geraniums in plastic pots. The rest of the garden was more tangled than the one in the squat. It had Róisín's father stamped all over it. The sense that nature had been beaten back briefly but had ultimately won.

She thought of the *Sorry* card, worried that her father had done worse than give up on the garden.

Brussels pâté in a blue ceramic ramekin, bought from a supermarket. Cereal bowls of potato, rice and pasta salads, cold chicken drumsticks. Bread rolls and a glass dish of butter that looked as if it had melted in the sun and been put back in the fridge.

They sat on mismatched seats, Red sprawled in a stripy nylon deckchair. There was still a harried look about him, and he'd said a couple of times he was depressed. It scared Róisín, because he used to say he didn't believe in boredom or depression. She told him it was the powders and dragged him out for walks he had no interest in any more and to matinee screenings of summer blockbusters. She made stews and pots of soup and helped him strip varnish from the mahogany overmantel in the drawing room. It felt as though she was managing him; God knew what would happen when Octavia came back from her travels in the Far East.

Mary was leaning from Lynne's knee, jolting back when she tilted too far.

Can I have her? said Red.

Lynne passed the child across the table. Red held her at arm's length then raised her over his head. Mary laughed, but as he lowered her, she hit herself in the face.

Jesus, said Róisín, give her to me.

Ah, come on, I'm getting into it. He jiggled her on his knee until she had forgotten the earlier assault. She began to tilt forward again, slowly this time, looking at Red with great sincerity, and clamped her gums round his mouth.

Mary, you little flirt! laughed Lynne.

She's no flirt, she loves me. First baby I've ever held too.

What's the verdict? said Lynne.

She feels light but important.

Lynne blinked quickly, as if there was something in her eye. Out of the blue, Red could say something that killed you.

They had been drinking raspberry-coloured wine that was slightly fizzy.

Heaven, Lynne said, placing her empty glass on the table. Beneath the flush of booze she looked drawn. Can't remember the last time I sat down to eat. Conor works so much.

He also spent a lot of time in bed, thought Róisín.

When the garden was in shade, they went back up the fire escape to the flat. Red and Róisín washed up. God, it's good to get out of the squat, she said.

Yeah. Nice day for it.

That wasn't what she meant. It was hell being around Barry. Until they had sex Róisín had seldom seen him, but now he seemed to be at home every evening. For a couple of weeks, he'd been seeing a nurse from Kilmacrennan he'd met in the Crown in Cricklewood. She looked like a postulant but roared 'Slap me, hai' as she came, a demand that carried all over the house.

They had more fizzy wine and ate strawberry tarts from a china plate with Prince William's baby face on it. Lynne fell asleep first, then Róisín. Her father's voice woke her.

You're like Jim Jones with them passed out all round you, he was telling Red.

He had been fully Lynneified. Hair cut short over his ears, a little longer at the back. A blue shirt with a red check so fine it looked pink, off-white trousers held up by a canvas belt in the same shade. Most atrocious of all, there was a silver identity bracelet on his wrist. Róisín was filled with sadness for him, his weakness and malleability. He must have sensed a softening, because he bent down to kiss her. How's my Róisín? he said.

Great, Dad.

Beer bottles gasping open, Red at the stereo, slagging her father and Lynne over their terrible cassette collection. Not one but TWO copies of *Brothers in Arms*... Phil Collins, somebody shoot me.

Lynne insisted they stay, getting blankets for Red, telling Róisín her bed was always ready. Her father followed her into the room and looked from the cot, where Mary was sleeping, to Róisín. God bless my daughters, he said.

A little later, the smell of tobacco smoke wafted through the open window. Red and Conor were on the fire escape.

Did she have to be dragged down here? her father said, toking urgently on his cigarette.

Mary's quite a draw. But it's hard for her.

Aye. How long have you been in London?

Two years in January.

You were young leaving home.

Sixteen.

I knew your da. When I worked in the pub.

I suppose you're going to tell me he's a great man altogether. First to the bar and cigars all round. Hail fellow well met.

No. I thought he was... Her father inhaled, slowly this time.

What?

Never mind, son.

The clang of metal and the door closed.

Róisín lay awake. It wasn't her usual insomnia, thoughts cantering about her head generating cinematic scenarios that got more noir by the hour, but a general dread. Deep in the night, Mary made a weird gurgle. She slept on her back and, afraid she was choking, Róisín lifted her gently and brought her to the kitchenette, heating a bottle in the kettle.

Suits you, said Red.

You frightened the life out of me! Maybe I'll get pregnant. They'd give me a council flat and I could get away from you lot.

Red raised the blankets, drawing them over when she was comfortable. She eased the teat into Mary's mouth. Put your arm around us, she said.

He did as she asked and a mangled cry convulsed his whole body.

Ah, Red, I was only joking about getting away from you.

He didn't reply.

Mary drank, milk hissing and bubbling in her bottle. When she was finished, their breaths fell into sync, two baby breaths to one of Róisín's. The bones of Red's ribcage were so thin they felt like an X-ray, but his head, resting on hers, was heavy. He wept noiselessly into her hair until dawn. The salt from his tears made her want to rip her own scalp off.

Mary woke, shifting about on a full nappy. Róisín lifted Red's arm away, trying not to disturb him, but he sat upright with a start.

Go into the wee bed, said Róisín, you hardly slept.

Neither did you, he said, running his finger across Mary's cheek. She grabbed it and tried to put it in her mouth.

Hold her for a sec, I'm thirsty.

She stumbled a little as she went to the sink, stiff from being in the same position all night, and filled two glasses with water. Red was rocking Mary in his arms and raised his head as Róisín approached. He resembled a photograph she'd seen in one of her granny's true crime magazines of a murder victim whose eyes had been gouged out.

Then Lynne and her father were there, giggling about staying up so late and thanking Róisín for the lie-in.

You're a bit the worse for wear, son, her father said.

Red was trying to assemble his face into a smile, but he couldn't manage it. Róisín passed him a glass. Drink this, she said, taking Mary from him. We'll get out of here soon, go for a walk or hang out, anything you want.

He sat looking at the floor.

Lynne made tea and toasted a stack of bread. Róisín went on to the fire escape to get her father. He swung away from her, placing something behind the zinc bucket he used as an ashtray. Coming now, love, he said over his shoulder.

He joined them at the table, rubbing his hands. It was a gesture that suggested vigour, but as he reached for a slice of toast, he was quaking. There was something slippery about him. His marbled complexion, the way he was dodging her gaze... he'd been drinking a can of beer outside. The last time Róisín was here, Lynne said it was easier to get herself and Mary ready each morning than ask Conor for help. Róisín had got seven good years out of her father; her baby sister wasn't going to get one.

13

14 September 1985

Sinéad was telling her Interrailing stories. Waltzing by the Seine with an elderly man, sleeping in Milan train station to catch the early service to Florence, riding a moped through Naples. A year ago, Róisín had imagined such a trip for herself, never thinking she would drop out and her quiet friend would be the one to travel around Europe.

Barry raised Sinéad's chin with his finger and kissed her. She had asked Róisín for a dispensation a few hours after she arrived, saying she really liked Barry but wouldn't go near him unless it was OK with her. Róisín insisted she didn't mind at all – what else could she say? It wasn't that Róisín was jealous, although Barry did seem more attractive now that Sinéad liked him. Nor did Róisín worry that he'd detail the particulars of the sex they'd had, or her enthusiasm for it. What bothered her was a feeling that she had breached her own privacy by sleeping with someone so close to home; now that her best friend was with him she felt even more exposed.

Octavia, of course, had been Interrailing, at sixteen. She listened politely to Sinéad – or at least she listened, more than she'd ever done for Róisín – then said she'd had her arse licked clean by a pig in a 'rather basic lavatory' in Phuket. Róisín tried to catch Sinéad's eye, intending to yawn theatrically, but she was laughing. Everyone was.

Greg passed Róisín a joint. How had she ended up between him and Chilly, Barry's soft-bellied builder mate? Across the table from Barry and Sinéad and, worse, Red and Octavia. After Sydenham, Róisín had been afraid to leave Red alone. He accepted her ministrations with a gratitude that verged on abject, slipping into her bed in the night and asking her to hold him, fretting when she was out of his sight. Octavia reappeared, golden-limbed and intriguing, just as he was coming out of himself. It had been less than a fortnight and he'd gone back to wandering. When he wasn't at that he was lounging with Octavia in the drawing room, now strewn with beautiful patterned cloth she'd collected on her travels. Róisín looked at the spliff between her fingers and had an urge to grind it in Octavia's face, or Red's or Barry's, even Sinéad's. She put it in her mouth and dragged.

Chilly's claim to fame was that he was from the next town over from Ballinspittle, where the moving-statues mania began.

Ballinspittle! cried Octavia.

That's an anglicisation, said Róisín, it doesn't sound ridiculous in the Irish language.

Interesting. What is it in Irish?

Róisín could only glare in reply.

If you gawp at anything long enough it'll start moving, said Chilly. And there was plenty of bobs made from selling tea and sandwiches.

I don't know. The weather at home has been so wet it's like the apocalypse. The farmers have taken in no hay. Like it's so bad our neighbours are clubbing together for a silo. People are suggestible when they're afraid. Realising everyone was listening, Sinéad's hand flew to her mouth. Farmer's daughter here, she said, sorry.

There's no farmers' daughters like her round my way, said Chilly to Greg, leaning across Róisín.

Right? said Greg.

Sinéad must have heard, but didn't react. God, when did she become so cool?

Maybe the statues *are* moving, said Greg. He was rolling another joint on his knee beneath the table.

Come on, man, said Red.

Come on yourself, man. Maybe the people have faith.

That's like saying if we believe this table is moving, then it is, said Róisín. Some things are objective truths. It is objectively true that statues are made of stone or plaster and can't fucking move.

Ha! said Octavia. Introduction to Philosophy, Michaelmas term.

You can fuck up, said Róisín.

Octavia beamed sweetly and moved her hair on to the other shoulder.

Greg reached the joint across the table, offering it to Sinéad. I'm afraid of getting busted, she said, they'd bar me from the accountancy body.

He nodded without calling her square, which was what he threw at Róisín when she wouldn't get milled.

Sinéad whispered something to Barry, her lips touching his ear. He was pushing a beer mat around in circles with his index finger, regarding the table as if he wanted to fuck it. Octavia and Red were almost mirroring them, but Red's expression destroyed Róisín; he was serene.

Another pint was put in front of her, then another. She accepted a toke every time Greg offered and didn't realise how wrecked she was until she tried to get out of the bench to go to the toilet. She was aware that she was comically slow, not trusting her body to do her bidding, but succeeded in standing without falling over.

In the corridor that led to the ladies, she attempted to pass a couple of girls, but one put her arm out, blocking her. This is the queue, she said.

As the line moved, Róisín slithered along the sweaty wall, increasingly aware of her bloated bladder. To distract herself, she looked in the crackled mirror, a bad idea because she was like one of the undead. Finally it was her turn. She charged into the cubicle and did well to get her drawers down in time, her head light. Bent over the bowl, fingers down her throat, she couldn't raise so much as a retch. She needed water.

The bar was two-deep. When a gap appeared she tried to push forward, but someone always got in ahead of her. She gave up, blundering back through the crowd. At the door that led to the beer garden she smoothed herself down, straightening the lining of her dress and tucking her hair behind her ears. Red was in the corner with a man she'd never seen before. She toddled towards them, as though her feet were running away from her.

I'll be done in a minute, said Red. His voice was sharp.

The man was rat-eyed, thirtyish. When she didn't leave at once, he looked at Red expectantly.

Go, said Red, and turned away.

In the beer garden, it was as though the volume had been hiked up, pints everywhere and delirious laughter. Greg's face had become enormous, his expression ecstatic.

Do you like this dope? he said, passing her his joint.

She inhaled and held it in her lungs.

It's opium-based, Red's diversifying.

How she hated his drawl.

Sinéad and Barry, the neck she'd concealed beneath the bubbled collar of a school blouse slender and white, his lips parted like a vampire. Chilly dancing 'Shoe the Donkey' with Octavia, step-a-one-twoing its mazurka tune. The beer garden flooded with light and everyone was rising. Then they were gone. Róisín tripped into the bar. It was empty, a lone man lifting stools on to tables. A bouncer appeared. He kicked open a side door and deposited Róisín on the street.

A seethe of people outside. She lumbered across the road and into Camden Town station, clinging to a green-tiled pillar. The porcelain felt greasy but the cold of it was soothing. Then Red was shouting at Greg, who was shouting back. Sinéad was shoving them aside, crying, Jesus, Róisín, what the fuck? Octavia and Barry watching everything. Seeing a gap, Róisín made for the escalators but she couldn't get her feet to step on. She grabbed the handrail, holding fast against the surge that was building behind her until someone pulled her away. More shouting, Red insisting, Will ye all shut the fuck up! A man saying, She's a danger to herself and others and I should call the police. Sinéad grabbing Róisín's face, imploring, Look at me, look at me. The press of bodies, a tiled tunnel of peeling posters. The bars of a railing, vomit on her shoes. The sky a massive dome, tilting on its axis.

She coughed, releasing a foul taste. She curled into the recovery position, hoping it would help, but even tiny movements felt monumental. Her back and front were itchy and hot, her arms too. Someone had left water beside her, in a glass with a beer logo that made her stomach heave. Glugging it down, she was hit with a wave of nausea. She ran down a flight to the bathroom, retching brown paste until all that was left was bile. She poured bleach into the toilet and brushed her teeth, avoiding her reflection. The door of Barry's room wasn't fully closed, a rhythmic panting rising that she wished she didn't recognise.

She brought her water glass downstairs. In the kitchen there were signs of a small party, empty bottles and an overflowing ashtray, the crusts of sandwiches Sinéad had probably made. There was music playing low in the drawing room. She pushed open the door. The room was lit by a single candle and, as her eyes adjusted to the dim, she made out Red's shape on the couch. Octavia in his arms.

* * *

It's unreal up here, said Sinéad, handing Róisín a mug of tea and sitting on the edge of her bed.

Everything is Dawn's.

Those are yours, Sinéad said, pointing at the mantelpiece. Róisín had placed a chunky glass vase swirled with green and blue beside a seed pod picked from a garden up the road, a stack of old Pelican paperbacks on their right.

I just put them there.

For a moment Sinéad said nothing, then she turned to Róisín, her eyes bright and worried at once. Let's get out of this fucking house, I'll buy you a rasher sandwich.

I'm dying, said Róisín, and she was. Not from a hangover, she'd thrown up the pints by midnight; she was dying of anguish.

Get. Up.

Róisín was sure she'd seen the Regency Café on television, its walls in rosy pink and mint green, the chequered floor.

How do you know this place? she asked Sinéad.

Barry brought me here a couple of times.

It wasn't Claridge's, but he'd taken Sinéad out. Róisín had settled for carryout in the squat.

Sinéad ordered them fry-ups with everything and a pot of tea. So what are you going to do?

Nothing.

Sinéad's jaw was jutting. She was trying to keep her temper.

Their food arrived. Beans and eggs together are fucked up, said Róisín, and mushrooms are rank, they grow in the dark.

Don't eat it so. Jesus Christ, Róisín, last night you didn't care what you were putting into your body.

Neither did you.

She watched Sinéad's eyes flicker with confusion and, as she understood what Róisín meant, gape open. You can be really fucking horrible.

Sorry, but that was sanctimonious, even for you.

Sinéad slammed her cup into the saucer. I am trying really hard to be your friend. Red and Octavia are getting into serious stuff.

Serious stuff, mimicked Róisín. Spoken like the Leinster Champion.

You know well Red's selling opium, and fuck knows what else. The cut of you last night.

That's a bit dramatic. And Greg laced the spliff, not Red, said Róisín, too loudly, because the men at the next table were looking at her.

Sinéad leaned forward. They've made your drawing room into an opium den, for fuck's sake, she hissed.

The scene Róisín had worked all night to banish, two-spelling inane affirmations until Sinéad came into her room, bloomed so fully in her head it could have been unfolding again. A Bach record revolving slowly on the stereo, Glenn Gould audibly humming as he played the *Goldberg Variations*, a dense, intimate smell in the air. Red's naked torso in the amber glow of the candle. His face lit by rapture.

You're not a squat person, said Sinéad, taking advantage of Róisín's silence. Fussing about the electricity bill and cleaning the kitchen cupboards.

It was almost a relief to hear it. She'd tried to fit in, drinking cider and going on the dole, but she hated the uncertainty. Her happiest days were pottering about the flat in Sydenham.

And what about your mother? said Sinéad.

Oh, get it all off your chest, why don't you.

You're skint. You fucked your education. Go home, Róisín. Sort things out with your mam.

There's nothing at home!

You can come back to London with a plan. Get a job, study at night. Something visual, I can't believe your room.

I put things on a fucking mantelpiece, said Róisín. Anyway, where would I live?

My cousin is looking for someone to share a flat in Islington. Just get away from Red. Please.

14

22 September 1985

She knew before the man opened his mouth that he would order a black and tan because he couldn't stomach what they did to the Guinness here. She knew before he patted his breast pocket that he would produce a packet of Gold Bond, the nearest you could get to Carrolls Number 1. She knew he'd light his cigarette with a safety match because a box of Swan Vestas lasted no time in a mouldering bedsit.

Will you have one yourself? he said, pointing at her glass.

I've one here. Thanks but.

Are you long over?

Since Christmas. What about you?

Nineteen fifty-four. Thirty-one years. It went quick at the start. Slower now, he said. He took a drink.

Shtart. Shlower.

You're from the west.

I'm a Roscommon man. Scramogue. You probably never heard of it. Where are you from?

The north, originally. Kildare now.

Horse country.

It is. We used to get a week off school for Punchestown races.

I won money on the big race this year. A horse called Galmoy. Are you doing well?

She wanted to tell him she had walked away from an education. That her father was in the process of destroying his second family and that her best friend was destroying himself. I'm doing all right, she said.

Good girl yourself. I worked on the roads.

Do you get home often?

'Seventy-eight was the last time, for the mother's funeral. The brother's funeral this time.

Sorry.

I'm the last. There's a small farm.

Are you going home for good?

He didn't answer.

People were standing to leave. She opened her handbag and found her ticket. See you over the road, she said.

The man took a slow sup of his pint. I'll follow you shortly, he said. It came out as *folly*.

She crossed to Victoria coach station, in the footsteps her father had taken on Christmas Eve, nine months ago, when he came to pick her up. There was a long line of people heading for Dublin, mostly students returning to Ireland after a summer of work. She sat three-quarters of the way down, on the side that had a view of the road outside.

The driver walked the length of the aisle, counting passengers.

There's a man coming shortly, she said. She looked out the window and waited for him to appear on the street. After a couple of minutes, the driver came back and spread his hands at her.

But he has a ticket.

Sorry, love. I can't wait for him.

The door closed and the engine thrummed to life. The man came out of the pub. He'd seemed taller inside. From up there she could see how sparse his hair was, the scarring on his scalp from working outdoors. Surely he knew it was the coach he was meant to be on, but he didn't look up. He paused and hoisted his canvas sausage bag over his shoulder. It was blue like hers. There was a piece of paper in his hand. He looked at it for a moment and began to rip it up. As the coach swung on to the street, he sprinkled the confetti he'd made of his ticket home into the bin.

Róisín said goodbye to the girls she'd met on the ferry, three physiotherapy students who'd spent the summer cleaning the Royal Brompton Hospital. She stepped on to the gangplank and searched the pier for her mother. She found her at once. It wasn't just the brightness of her yellow anorak, the Christmas present from Gilhooly, it was the set of her. Head forward, narrow shoulders rounded against the breeze. Seeing Róisín, she raised her hand.

Róisín managed not to cry when they embraced, even as her mother wept, but when she dropped her bag in the boot of the car she was overcome by a feeling of release so strong a choked sob left her.

Ach, Jesus, her mother said. You're home now.

The route took them past the entrance to UCD, the college she'd dropped out of. She felt neither regret nor failure as she watched a number 10 bus swing across the flyover and into the campus. Still, for a short time she had been on this road twice a day, as close to knowing Dublin as she ever had.

At the start of the dual carriageway, where tractor showrooms and builders' providers gave way to fields, her mother spoke. Are you in trouble?

Pregnant? No!

Some other trouble then?

Nothing like that.

Is it Red? Did something happen?

No.

Róisín had been so determined to avoid Red she'd become the third wheel in Sinéad's romance. Barry was kind and it felt crap that he knew Róisín was sad and felt sorry for her. When Sinéad left, three days before her, Róisín had gone to Sydenham. Lynne paid for her fare and gave her extra for a meal. An hour before the coach was due to leave, Róisín had returned to the squat to pack, hoping to find Red frantic for her, but he was in the drawing room with Octavia. If he knew Róisín was there he didn't give any sign.

The house had its late-summer look, the one Róisín liked best, the lone hydrangea and sheafs of montbretia along the lawn giving it the last colour of the season. Inside, there were still aromas of coal smoke and mould, but the old-dinner smell was gone. Her mother was thin, had she stopped cooking altogether?

Róisín went upstairs to unpack. There were Hoover tracks on her bedroom carpet and the bed was made neatly. College books that had briefly excited her – Basil Chubb's *The Government and Politics of Ireland*, Paul Harrison's *Inside the Third World* – were still on her desk and above it, pinned to a cork board, were the cards and flyers Red had sent her from London. They'd given the impression of a better life than the one he had, or maybe Róisín arrived as things started to slide. The vouchers he'd given her that Christmas were there too. *Friendship for life.* The image of him with Octavia was forming again. She unzipped her bag and began filling the laundry basket.

Her mother tutted as she placed Róisín's things in the washing machine. It was the second-hand clothes, she saw them as a sign of material want, not an aesthetic choice. Róisín opened the fridge. There was milk, butter, and a tub of dried Parmesan bought a year earlier that smelled like baby sick. Do you not eat any more? she asked.

I take my dinner in work. We can do a shop tomorrow, buy anything you want. I thought we'd get a Chinese takeaway tonight.

What's your roster this week?

I'm on holiday. Nothing to do till next Monday.

No mention of Enda Gilhooly. She didn't need to say it was over. It was in the empty fridge, in the pounds she'd lost.

A fast-food joint called Yankee Chicken had opened beside the Sorrento Grill, a rooster wrapped in stars and stripes painted in its window. There's someone put through that glass every weekend, said her mother. Pops and Posters, where Róisín had spent her pocket money on Blondie singles, was gone, replaced by a shop selling car parts.

They parked and went into the Chinese. There were a dozen empty tables set with red cloths, a smell of garlic and frying. Róisín studied the menu and asked the woman behind the counter for dim sum. Don't have them, she said flatly. Róisín felt silly. She didn't even like them, she'd been trying to impress her.

They ate in front of the television, the fire blazing. Her mother opened a litre of Italian red wine. Like Róisín, her face went pink as she drank. At nine, she switched to BBC One, an adaptation of *Tender Is the Night*.

I was mad about Scott Fitzgerald in school. *The Great Gatsby*.

I'm mad about Peter Strauss since *Rich Man, Poor Man*.

A teenage actress was mooning over Strauss's character. 'I could love that man', the girl told her mother, who replied, 'Wound yourself for him'.

Dear God, said Róisín.

I can see her point.

Jesus!

It was a joke.

It's awful. I don't think it's even in the book.

Róisín threw a couple of peat briquettes on the fire. The episode was finished and so was the wine. It had been lovely to laze about the house with her mother, but there was something unreal about it. Neither of them had acknowledged the fact that

Róisín had been out of touch for months, let alone why, Una carrying on as though she'd come back from a day in Dublin.

The next morning, they went to the supermarket. Her mother deferred to Róisín's choices as if she was a sophisticate, an arbiter of good taste, not an unemployed teenage squat-dweller. She was enjoying bringing her around, introducing her to the butcher as *my daughter home from London*. She'd been as lonely as Róisín. A whole sea between them, when they could have had each other.

I missed you, Mum, she said at the bakery counter.

Your daddy is the fun one, replied Una, squeezing a Vienna roll.

She thought so little of herself it was exasperating.

They were eating dinner when her mother finally said it, looking up from her plate of lamb chops and carrots: I'm not seeing Enda any more.

I'm sorry. He was nice.

Her mother gave a short laugh. Don't be getting carried away, you despised him. But he was nice. *Is* nice – Jesus, we're talking about him as if he's dead. It wasn't anything to do with you, in case you're inclined to blame or flatter yourself. I don't love him. The annulment seemed like an awful lot of trouble to be with someone I don't love.

Do you love Daddy?

Of course.

Is that why you never gave out about him?

You were entitled to your good opinion of your father.

The next day, when Róisín was mowing the lawn, her mother brought her a glass of lemon barley water. I sent you ten letters, she said, poking at a clump of grass with her foot. Did you read one of them?

I thought you didn't want me any more.

I thought you didn't want *me*, you find me so stupid and annoying. Enda did seem to want me, maybe I lost my head a wee bit. She bent to pick up the clod of grass and jerked upright.

Is it your back?

Aye. And old age.

You're thirty-nine, stop writing yourself off. You could...

A pause, and her mother said, It would be very hard for me to listen to you telling me what I could be doing.

The television was on from early evening, Una in the armchair with the weekly listings from the Sunday paper, working her way through the programmes she'd marked at the start of the week. Lionel Blair was presenting *Name That Tune*.

He's so tanned he looks like he's been dunked in gravy, said Róisín.

He tried to kill himself, said Una, without taking her eyes off the screen.

Lionel? I feel bad for slagging him off.

Your daddy. When he came back from Crossmaglen. You were at school. The ruts that appeared between her mother's eyes when something worried her were deep.

I didn't know that.

Do you not remember seeing him in Purdysburn?

Róisín recalled visiting him when he'd been admitted with a sore leg, a vague ailment she accepted without question. Purdysburn was a psychiatric hospital; at seven, she was too young to tell the difference.

Why are you telling me this now?

Because you think I'm a martyr. I'm not. I didn't ask for any of it.

And so they went on, throwing out truths without eye contact, the words so powerful neither of them could bear to behold their effect.

* * *

On Thursday morning, Sinéad came in her mother's rusty Fiat 127.

I suppose you passed the test, said Róisín as she brought her in.

With flying colours.

Una had come out of the kitchen. Ach, did you drive here? she said, nodding at Sinéad's keys. Róisín, I'll get you insured in my wee banger, you'll be on the road in no time.

They said goodbye and got into the little green car. Sinéad tied up her hair and checked the mirrors. I can't see with this mop otherwise, she said. In national school myself and my sisters were called the Hair Bear Bunch.

Róisín burst out laughing.

Fucking bitch, said Sinéad, giggling as she turned the key in the ignition.

At the traffic lights, Sinéad looked at her. Your mother thinks you're staying.

I never told her that.

Are you?

I don't know.

They went out the back road to Blessington and parked at the viewing point for the lakes. The sun was strong but low in the sky, picking up the copper and bronze and red of the trees on the lakeshore. In London, she'd not noticed it was autumn.

Sinéad had brought a flask of tea and buttered brown bread wrapped in foil.

I suppose you made this yourself, said Róisín.

At seven this morning. It's a fucking farm, I keep telling you. How are you getting on with your mother?

She tortures me for about an hour every day with a terrible revelation, but at least we're not fighting.

She's a dote, your mam.

Yeah.

You and Barry, said Róisín, eyes on the water. You like him.

He's lovely. Pity he's an alcoholic.

He's eighteen, he can't have a drink problem!

Matt Talbot was an alcoholic at thirteen.

Barry's the most together person in the house.

That says it all. I'm not able for the chaos. Not like you, lapping it up.

Maybe I'm not able for it either.

What are you going to do?

I can't stay here, I'll die.

The Late Late Show had switched from Saturday night to Friday. The country was still in uproar over the lesbian nuns a couple of weeks ago – ridiculous, said Una, sure what else would they be at in a convent? The show's big guest was Bob Geldof, looking like he hadn't changed his clothes since Live Aid. What a weekend that had been.

On Saturday night Róisín refused to go out with Sinéad, sick at the thought of explaining herself to people she hadn't seen since school. Of the hundred-odd girls in their year, scarcely ten had got into university and she'd lasted a single semester. She lived in a squat with Red and, no, she wasn't *with* him. Barry lived there too, and it was none of their business if she'd been *with* him or not. She'd only managed to get a job in Sock Shop and hadn't been able to hold it down. Weirdly, the only thing she wasn't ashamed of was Mary.

You should have gone to confession yesterday, said her mother as they walked into Sunday Mass. I doubt you've set foot in a church since last December.

Róisín put on a long-suffering face and blessed herself. Her mother smiled and, picking up a copy of the parish bulletin, slapped Róisín's hand with it. But she had been in church. Several times she'd fled the squat for Westminster Cathedral, looking up at the blue-sky ceiling, pleading with God to make Red want her or come back from wherever he'd drifted to or stop hanging out with Octavia.

She used to resent being dragged out of bed on Sunday mornings. Now she was almost enjoying walking up the side aisle in her oxblood leather coat and paisley minidress. Their particular scent, of mothballs and faded cologne, pleased her, a smell that had not been diminished by days flapping on the clothesline. They sat in her mother's usual pew. Róisín said there should be a plaque on the end with her name on it.

Like the Prods, said Una.

The brusque clip of well-heeled shoes. She knew without looking it was the Camelins, but there was only one boy with them, the youngest. He was at least fourteen, old enough to be in rebellion, but was a diminutive version of his father, dressed for a committee meeting at a golf club. Róisín could not stop staring, as if there might be a physical mark on them that explained their shrinking family. At the sign of peace, Robert shook Una's hand, her body tangibly flinching. Dolly took Róisín's, looking at her almost brazenly, and squeezed, briefly but with force. Robert's hand appeared in Róisín's field of vision. A visceral aversion came on her at the prospect of touching him and she swung to the people behind, slowly gripping every hand along the pew. When she turned back, everyone was facing the altar again.

Andrew Camelin wasn't there today, said Róisín when they were home. She was preparing a roast, a fat piece of pork loin her mother bought presuming she would know what to do with it.

No sign of him the last few weeks. Did Red say anything?

No. Anyway, Andrew blamed Red for leaving them.

They worked on without speaking, Mícheál Ó Muircheartaigh on the radio, still raving about Kerry's defeat of Dublin in the All-Ireland final the previous weekend.

You haven't mentioned Red once, Róisín.

I did just now.

Don't be smart. What happened?

Nothing.

Are youse not together?

No.

But you'd like to be.

Róisín began to grab handfuls of parings from the sink, dropping them in the bin. Jesus, Mum. Yes, I would like to be with him, but he doesn't like me that way. I don't know if he likes me at all.

Ach, love. But he's all right, is he?

Róisín had bitten down on the inside of her cheek so hard it was like gristly mince. He's fine.

She made an apple pie. Rolling the base, laying it over the pin for lifting on to an enamel plate. Apple slices and sugar, a couple of cloves. The lid, slit in the centre, ringed by pastry leaves made from scraps. It was how her Nana Mary had made it. Thinking of her made her think of her sister. You knew Daddy had a new baby and didn't warn me, she said.

It wasn't my story to tell. Your father said he'd do it, and I had to accept that.

Why have you been so accepting of Lynne and Mary?

Because I wouldn't wish it on anyone to see what I saw the day he tried to kill himself.

They were looking at each other now.

15

10 November 1988

Aside from the trading floors, which were open-plan bedlam, each of the bank's twelve storeys was a series of offices encased in smoked glass. The one Róisín worked in was so cold it was like being in the vegetable drawer of a fridge. She got up and rotated the dial on the air conditioning from fourteen to twenty-two degrees. Eve, her self-appointed supervisor, turned it back down and, taking four packages of microfiche from a drawer in the filing cabinet, tossed them one by one on to Róisín's desk. Françoise, their manager, lifted her shoulders and mouthed, Oops! Róisín wished she would have a word with Eve and get her to stop being a bitch, instead of offering pointless shrugs of solidarity.

Róisín opened a pack and spread out its contents. She had a system: alphabetical by company name, then date order. Lynne, who worked in recruitment, had been begging her for ages to get her typing up to forty words a minute so she could place her in a better job, but Róisín had resisted. Though the work was soul-destroying, it left her mind free to wander. Sometimes she envisioned terrible scenarios for Eve: her house collapsing into the Channel Tunnel she'd been pestering Ted Heath, her MP, about, taking her with it to France; or a hot flush so fiery she dissolved into a talking puddle. Sometimes Róisín imagined she was in number 48 putting food on the table, Red with an appetite and flesh on his bones sitting down to eat. Today she had an essay to write. Drawing a spider plan in her head, she wrote 'Cultural Capital' in its centre.

At 12:59, people in other glass boxes were leaving their desks. She picked up her bag and, as she stood, Eve's perfume filled her nose, an incongruously heady corporate-sexy scent that reminded Róisín of marzipan.

Where's you off to, matey? said Eve, wearing the rage-smile that came on her when Róisín behaved like an independent human being.

Lunch?

Best to wait till one, said Eve, then looked momentarily stunned. At first Róisín thought it was because she had answered back but Eve's panstick make-up had begun to curdle. Róisín left her to see out her hot flush alone.

She took the lift to the staff lounge on the top floor. Almost nobody else used it, and she had come to think of it as her space. She laid her packed lunch, notepad and textbook on the coffee table and, leaving her bag on one of the blue institutional-looking couches, went to get a hot chocolate. The machine sputtered purplish liquid with the ashy smell of burnt coffee.

Putting her personal stereo on, an actual Walkman she'd saved for, she began to eat her sandwich. A man came in and sat disturbingly close. Tall, judging by the jut of his legs. Slender. Light brown or maybe auburn hair. He was speaking to her. She removed her headphones.

'Marmaduke', he said.

What?

Charlie Parker. *Savoy Sessions*, if I'm not mistaken. Great number.

Numbah, she repeated.

He laughed. There's a film about Parker coming out in a couple of weeks. *Bird*.

Angular features including a slightly broken nose, probably from rugby with an accent like that – Londonish, posher than Lynne's but not as posh as Octavia's. Shirtsleeves rolled up, his forearms creamy-toned as if he tanned easily, colouring you rarely saw on an Irish person.

May I? he said, pointing at her book.

Sure.

He picked it up. *Distinction: A Social Critique of the Judgement of Taste*, he read aloud. Scandalous Marxist blueprints. Worse, it's by a Frenchman. Are you a sleeper? A saboteur?

I'm taking night classes. Unfortunately there isn't much scope in my job to wreak havoc with global banking. What about you?

Mergers and Acquisitions.

So you buy up little family-owned factories and promptly close them, decimating small towns in the north of England.

Jesus, he said. I vote Labour, if that means anything.

It's OK. I aid and abet you by putting microfiche of company accounts in alphabetical order.

I'm sure it's more interesting than that, he said. His eyes grew very soft when he smiled. What classes are you taking?

Sociology and Politics.

I studied something like that.

Doubt it. You probably did PPE at Oxford.

He groaned.

Ha! Oh my God, did you know Octavia Hammond?

She was a year behind me and a class ahead of me. Social class, that is. She ran around with a rather fast set, he said, delivering the last part in received pronunciation. How the hell do you know her?

She haunted a squat I lived in when I came to London.

What's your name?

Róisín.

You're Irish.

Please don't call the anti-terror squad.

Does that happen?

Every Monday my colleague asks if I've spent the weekend marching and rioting.

Christ. My name is Guy.

Guy Burgess. Guy Mottram in *Brideshead Revisited*.

I think you'll find it's Rex Mottram.

Shit. I knew that.

He laughed. Interestingly, you forgot the most infamous one.

Guy Fawkes? He's popular where I come from. A Catholic who wanted to blow up Westminster.

This Guy was descended from one of the Gunpowder Plotters, a Lancashire Jacobite, and his family was still Catholic. Sometimes he went to Mass with his father. Róisín liked that he didn't apologise for it.

They got into the lift together and he stepped off on her floor. Which is your office? he asked.

Down in the corner.

The one that's being guarded by a frightful woman with ghastly orange lipstick?

The very one.

I'm going to New York for six months. I hope you aren't still here putting microfiche in alphabetical order when I come back.

So do I. Good luck.

He stood looking at her for a few seconds, then walked to the staircase, disappearing through the door.

How's you, matey? said Eve in a child's voice.

Grand.

You've made a friend.

Not really.

Eve palpably smarted. She lowered herself into her chair and turned her computer terminal until she was no longer visible.

You were speaking to lovely Guy from M&A, said Françoise, pumping Muscadet fumes with every syllable. Róisín could not believe the amount of boozing that went on at lunchtime in the City, men returning to work at two smelling like her father.

At half three she excused herself and went towards the toilets, taking a detour down the back stairs to Capital Markets. Everyone was yelling and the air was opaque with smoke. She lit a cigarette and stood with her back to the wall so no one would feel her up, wondering what Catholic Guy was doing. It was the first normal conversation she'd had with anyone in the building. But the essay plan she was supposed to bring to class that evening existed only in her head and she hadn't read the prescribed chapter. Still, for an entire hour she'd forgotten to worry about the likelihood of running into Red. A band from home was playing in the Mean Fiddler later and Sinéad had made Róisín promise to go. Her reasoning – everyone would be there – filled Róisín with dread.

At five, the first lift to arrive was full. There was room in the next but she hesitated so long the doors closed and it travelled without her. She took the stairs, spiralling down the eleven floors to ground level, arriving at reception nauseous. Ahead, a girl who had started months after her called, Bye, boys! at the men behind the desk as she walked out. Mind how you go, Jen, one replied, the others waving. Róisín had worked here for ten months and doubted anyone would recognise her in a police line-up. Apart from Guy. Just her luck he was leaving.

Róisín landed into the front bar of the Mean Fiddler, chest heaving, and issued a croupy bark.

The fags are going to kill you, said Sinéad. She was waiting by the entrance.

I ran all the way from the Tube station with a bag of books!

Róisín made for the counter but Sinéad pulled her back. Fuck it, Róisín, we're missing the lads.

'The Lads', said Róisín in a deep voice. That's what they should have named their band. Jesus, though, it'll be like a GAA disco.

You're obsessed with school.

Upstairs, they slunk along the wall, Róisín searching the faces for Red's. It had been almost a year. For a while after she left the squat they kept in touch, him calling her at work and arranging to meet, Róisín knowing as she replaced the receiver he wouldn't turn up.

Finding a gap, Sinéad stopped. Róisín wedged her way in, bag bumping, wishing she'd had time to go home after class.

'The Impossibles', as the lads called themselves, were Shay Dempsey on acoustic guitar and lead vocals, Dessie Nolan on drums and backing vocals, and a pair of brothers from Carlow on lead guitar and bass. Dessie bashed the cymbals, and their first song was over. He was dressed for the job in a sleeveless T-shirt to show off his toned arms, combat trousers for comfort.

He looks like he's playing with a Fisher-Price activity centre, said Róisín.

Sinéad went on clapping, her curly hair an unruly halo against the stage lights. It reminded Róisín of the cover of a Dylan album Red had swapped with her for *Hunky Dory*. The exchange had been more symbolic than anything else; Red no longer went home by then, and both records were still in her mother's house in Ashgrove Lawns. Was he here? She found herself rising on her toes but it was hard to see.

Thank you very much, said Shay Dempsey in an Elvis Presley voice. This next song is for all of you. It's called 'Sealink Blues'.

It started slow, like a country ballad, Shay gently strumming his guitar.

An easterly gale, high water,
The ferryboat straining to get to sea.
'Let go, right time,' roars the master,
I find the shape of you on the pier,
I can't look, and I can't look away.

Please tell me he didn't write this song, said Róisín.

What's wrong with it? said Sinéad, a pinched look about her eyes. Was she irritated?

Nothing! It's surprisingly good.

A lock of Shay's hair had fallen over his right eye and one hand was cupped around the microphone. He was singing as if no one was watching, red plaid shirt open, the words *Safe Sex* printed on his T-shirt. The last time she'd seen him was the night Red drank the contents of his father's drinks cabinet. Or maybe she just thought it was the last time; in those days, she was so caught up in Red she took little else under her notice.

A few tracks later, Shay, shirt off, picked out the opening bars of 'Stairway to Heaven'. Maybe he wasn't so cool after all. As the crowd began to sing the first line, he abruptly stopped playing. Lads, have ye never heard of irony? he said.

When the rumpus had died down, Dessie Nolan tapped his drumsticks together three times. The place erupted.

This is the song that was nearly picked up by U2's label, said Sinéad.

Nearly.

You liked them a minute ago. Sinéad's tone was terse, what was wrong with her?

Down in the bar, Róisín went to the counter. It was the usual struggle to be served, men shouting orders over her head, until a man said, Hould on, boys, this girl was ahead of youse. He was handsome in the way of a Guard or soldier. Clean-cut, fit.

She bought two pints, thanking him as she edged away.

Ná habair é, he said, smiling.

She smiled back.

At first Róisín couldn't see Sinéad, but then she leaned out of a crowd in the centre of the room, beckoning with her finger like the dancer in the poster on the Underground advertising the Royal Ballet. As she handed Sinéad her drink, Dessie threw his arms around Róisín, the split ends of his ponytail bristling against her skin when she tentatively hugged him back.

God, it's been years, he said, do you never come home at all?

Sometimes I do. She smiled in spite of herself.

Shay was beside him. It's good to see you, Róisín, he said.

A blonde head ducked under his arm and a pair of delicate hands encircled his waist. Tina Doyle. Shay cupped Tina's chin like he had the microphone and slipped his tongue in her mouth, kissing her deeply. She was in a knee-length shift dress, peroxide locks in a long bob. When they had finished, Róisín mumbled that she'd really enjoyed the set.

Cheers, said Shay, and Tina widened her smoky eyes. Pattie Boyd hanging out of George Harrison, that's who she was like; in a few months she'd probably dump Shay for Dessie Nolan.

They stood in a circle, chatting about who was in London or Germany or America. Róisín, transfixed by Tina's metamorphosis, scarcely took it in. When Sinéad broke away to go to the ladies, Róisín followed.

Jesus Christ, the head on Tina. It's like she's taken a PhD in how to be a rock star's girlfriend. And she didn't say hello to me.

Did you say hello to her?

That's not the point.

Sinéad's face was warped with annoyance. Can you behave like a normal person for one night? Giving out about this one and that one. They were in front of the mirror, Sinéad trailing a wooden comb through her hair, frowning at Róisín between tugs.

It's really hard for me, meeting people from home.

Sinéad pulled her into a cubicle that had just become free, slapping her pint into Róisín's free hand. You're not the only one who had a shit time in school, she said, dropping her knickers and squatting over the broken toilet seat. Before the girls turned on you, I put in a good three years of being the butt of their jokes. *Your* jokes actually, because you were smarter than the others. If I can move on, so can you. She trailed a length of paper from the dispenser and wiped, flushing angrily.

Róisín stood blinking, too shocked to reply.

Look, I'm sorry, just please get over yourself, said Sinéad, kissing her cheek. She squashed past her and out the door.

So Sinéad had known all along about the name Róisín had given her. It wasn't smart or clever, it was mean: The Heif, because she lived on a dairy farm and because her little twelve-year-old body had briefly puffed out, filling her burgundy-coloured gym-slip, before stretching upwards. Sinéad knew and was the only one in the class to befriend Róisín when the girls turned on her too.

You'd better not be fucking crying, called Sinéad, knocking sharply.

Róisín dabbed at her eyes with a square of paper and left the cubicle. I'm a cunt, she said.

You're my cunt. Oh God, that sounded weird.

Back in the bar, in a group of men in leather jackets so scuffed her own looked plastic, she saw Red. Barry was there too, an unlit cigarette in the corner of his mouth. Catching her staring, he dropped his eyes and swigged from a naggin of vodka he slipped down his cuff.

Red looked in her direction and mouthed hello. Last time he was gimlet-eyed and skinny, the time before wretched, as if the soul was gone out of him. Tonight he was somewhere between.

She crossed the floor.

Look at you, all grown up, he said. There was no warmth in his voice, but she caught a spark of something as he looked in her eyes. He knew she'd been crying.

I was at work and then at college. I'm carrying this bag of books since half seven this morning.

You're doing well, he said, taking in her clothes. Under the leather jacket she wore a grey wool dress, double-breasted and pin-striped.

Not that well.

Still talking yourself down.

I'm a filing clerk. I spend forty hours a week putting microfiche in alphabetical order, bored to distraction.

Sounds like the chorus of 'Echo Beach'.

She offered him a cigarette. He refused, but each of his friends took one, smirking at each other as if she was a fool they had taken advantage of.

What are you up to, Red?

This and that, he said. Was it scorn that was curling his mouth?

People were drifting back upstairs for the main act. Sinéad put a pint in Róisín's hand, hugging Red briefly. See you up there, she said.

The guy beside them, a skinhead with a weak jaw, spoke in Red's ear. He listened, finger bent across his lips like a priest hearing confession. He can wait, he replied, the others simpering as if their beloved leader had issued an edict. All except Barry, who was rooting at his sleeve again. He looked terrible, cheeks pimpled by little blisters, shiny and pustular.

They were the only people left in the bar. Red glanced at her. Coming? he said.

A path appeared before them as they entered. Red was hard-looking, she realised. He stopped in the centre of the crowd. They were very close and it was an effort to avoid physical contact with him.

The opening song had been a hit at home and the whole room joined in for the chorus.

Red leaned over her shoulder. Not singing? he said.

Am I fuck. And neither are you.

Too cool, are you?

Not cool. I'm still a self-conscious mess.

Her use of 'still' had a whiff of desperation, a word selected to remind him of their bond. But then she felt his laugh on her neck and thought, We are OK, you and me.

The singer introduced a Bessie Smith cover, saying, 'Nobody Knows You When You're Down and Out' were the truest words ever written. Someone knocked into Róisín, pressing her against Red. She wished he would react to her body, welcome the weight of her, but there was nothing.

How's your lovely ma? he said.

She's all right. Lonely, I think, she said, looking back at him. He lifted his chin, about all he could do in the confined space to put distance between them. It made him seem angry.

What about Mary? he said.

She turned around fully. Mary will be four in a few days, she said in a rush, and she's funny and clever and gorgeous. I wouldn't even know her if it wasn't for you.

You would have got your head around it eventually. People do.

People do. Róisín wasn't that special.

Red spoke sometimes to his friends, clipped remarks that made them snigger. Out of habit, her paranoia flared, but they were making a plan to meet someone in Kentish Town. The singer had been drinking all through the set and was losing focus, coming in too late, forgetting words. This is a beautiful tune, will ye lot shut the fuck up? she slurred into the microphone. Róisín felt a shot of revulsion that nearly felled her. Was there no avoiding Irish people and their drunken melancholy?

The fury's like a force field, he said.

They were facing each other. She wanted to seize his hand and haul him through the crowd and outside, all the way back through the years to the weathered lock, the pair of them swinging their legs over the dreggy water. Red, she began, but he cut her off.

No one but me understands you? You'll be my friend forever and ever? he said, a spike in his voice. We both know that isn't true, Ró.

You never turn up.

It wouldn't have taken much to find me. And you don't understand me at all.

He was done with her. She reached up to embrace him, and after a respectable couple of seconds had passed, he squeezed her upper arms and released her grip.

Good luck, he said.

At the doorway she looked back. He was flanked by his unpleasant new friends, Barry Doyle by his side like a faithful servant. Red Camelin. Surrounded by people and entirely alone.

Sinéad was near the door with Dessie, a fresh pint in her hand, Tina and the others close by. Róisín made for the exit, too upset to face them, but her friend stopped her. Everyone was going to a house party in Gospel Oak, Róisín had to come, God only knew when they'd all be in one place again.

I couldn't if you paid me, said Róisín.

Fuck it, when you're out, you're out.

It was so unlike Sinéad, Róisín couldn't help laughing. You just want to ride Dessie, she said.

Outside, Róisín repositioned the bag of books on her shoulder for the walk to the Tube station. The man who'd made room for her at the bar was leaning against a lamp post, watching her. Don't go, you're great craic, he said.

Only for you I'd still be waiting to be served.

Ná habair é, I told you. Off home? His eyes travelled from hers down to her tits and back up again, so openly lascivious it was comical.

It's a work night.

Want company?

She almost walked away but was overcome with sadness. Red didn't want her but this chancer did.

Yeah, she said.

He slung an arm around her waist and drew her close. He was strong, something unguarded about the way he was holding her. Where do you live? he said.

Islington.

Glancing left and right, he led her across the street to a cab office. A young man was pacing in front of it, talking frantically to himself in a soliloquy that rose to a howl sometimes. He blocked their path. I'm eighteen years of age, he said, and I cannot live another day in this place. His speech had a Mayo inflection, like a lovely boy called John in her UCD class. A deliberate, almost archaic way of speaking English.

Róisín gave him a cigarette.

My name is Gabriel Stanford, he said, putting it behind his ear. What are ye called?

Róisín.

Paddy, said the chancer. Get off the street, lad. Go to the centre in Camden in the morning, they'll help you.

Are you really called Paddy? she asked as the boy staggered away.

He laughed and pushed the door open.

The office was little warmer than the street. In the strong light she could see that Paddy, if that was his name, was in his thirties. He had on a good wool coat, the sort a man who was doing well would buy.

Where to? said the controller from behind cloudy Plexiglass.

As she gave her address, she saw something pass between the two men.

Paddy spread his legs in the cab, asking where she was from, how long she'd been in London.

Where do you work? he said.

In a bank.

A sperm bank?

An uneasy feeling rippled through her. She never thought to ask anything about him.

Róisín put her hand to her face. It was stinging where he'd struck her, Paddy in the fine wool coat who was barely up the stairs before he said he wouldn't stick it in a filthy cunt like hers if his life depended on it. Her scalp was sore too, where he'd pulled her hair, ramming her face between his legs. At least it happened in the hall and not in her room with the twin beds, one with a My Little Pony duvet set she'd bought for Mary. She opened the freezer compartment, chipping at frost and ice to release a bag of peas. Placing it between her cheek and her shoulder, she unscrewed a bottle of bleach. For a second she considered gargling with it.

16

1 July 1989

A door slamming shut. The bark of a dog, a woman pleading, Leave him alone. The pause before the reply: Do him, Georgie. Do him. Róisín put her pillow – polyester and at three quid the cheapest one in Jones Brothers on Holloway Road – over her head but after a couple of minutes she was sopping with sweat. It was too hot to close the skylight and she tried to ignore the stomping, the moaning, the whelping and the wailing woman, praying they wouldn't wake her little sister. Fuck off, fuck off, no you fuck off, and Mary slid from her bed and got in beside Róisín.

Is that a fight, Rosh?

They're rehearsing a play.

Like my nativity play?

No. Christ.

She got up and pulled the Velux window shut. Throwing off the duvet, she coiled around her sister, feeling her small body soften with slumber. The street fell quiet and Róisín dozed off, waking to the rattle of her water glass on the bedside table. The first time she'd felt the tremble she thought it was an earthquake and was disappointed to learn it was a train moving through a tunnel far below. It was the only train of the day she was ever aware of, later ones melding with the sounds of the city.

They rose early, both groggy from interrupted sleep. She showered then put Mary standing under the nozzle. When

Sinéad came downstairs, they were having breakfast, towels around their bodies and heads.

Maisie McFluff, you might just be the cutest thing I've ever seen, she said, kissing Mary on the cheek. When she sat and poured herself a cup of tea, Róisín could see she was unhappy.

What's up? said Róisín.

I'm sick of it all. Sinéad was fingering a pluck in her jersey nightdress, working it into a hole.

That carry-on last night?

Being here. I miss Dessie.

It wasn't in her nature to be despondent. Róisín complained about living in London with little money, having nothing to go home for, Sinéad the one to jolly her along, saying it wasn't so bad, they would be back home one day and missing all the things they had been able to do here. You can't leave! said Róisín. Tell Dessie to move to London.

There's four of them in the band, it's not up to him. Anyway, don't mind me. Can I get you ready, Mary? You're like a little doll.

At ten thirty the buzzer sounded. The precise time-keeping made Róisín suddenly nervous.

The stench on the stairwell had risen in the heat, peaking as Róisín charged past their neighbour's flat on the first-floor landing. He only left to buy groceries or collect post from downstairs and had not, to Róisín's knowledge, had a single visitor since she moved in almost four years ago. Letters addressed to him arrived in British Legion envelopes, and he was old enough to have fought in the war. Maybe that had made him odd, or maybe it was just London.

She opened the door. Guy was looking at the ground, taking in the Jackson Pollock-style slakes on the paintwork, the red-brown splats on the pavement. Sudsy water was drying outside the pub two doors up. My neighbours were beating nine kinds of shite out of each other at two in the morning, she said. Fuckers cleaned their own doorstep and left ours like a nineteenth-century boxing ring.

What an analogy.

The Queensberry rules. Intermediate Certificate History, 1982.

Interesting. He was in a loose white linen shirt and chinos. She was always surprised by his appearance outside the office. The suit and tie he wore to work gave him ballast and without them there was a floppiness about him. She told him to hold his nose and run.

Ron must be dead down there, said Róisín, as she landed into the flat.

God forgive you, I saw him yesterday. I wonder should we have a word with him, Sinéad said.

We're here years and he hasn't done more than nod at either of us, we can't have a conversation about his personal hygiene.

Guy's hands were in his pockets, the beginnings of a smile on his mouth.

Oh my God, sorry. I'm Sinéad. And you're the Guy! It was gas, Róisín said, *I literally met a Guy*. Can't believe we're only meeting now.

Guy had walked into the new staff lounge – the bank had moved to a building in Broadgate – one day in May. Róisín was ashamed to still be there, although she was no longer a temp and had been trained to use a computer. Giving her a bundle of jazz cassettes he'd bought in the East Village, he asked her out. Since then he'd brought her to watch *À bout de souffle* in a cinema with Pullman seats that served wine, to a Ionesco play performed in the back of a pub, to Ronnie Scott's. On Sunday mornings they sometimes went 'dancing', which had sounded quaint until they were walking into Dingwalls and he was passing her an E.

And you must be Mary, he said, crouching. You look very pretty.

She was in a denim jacket over a floral dress. It's new, she said.

You look pretty too. He had straightened and was smiling at Róisín.

Her dress was a cotton kimono-style one that tied below her bust, olive green with a faint spriggy pattern in off-white. Thanks, she said, blushing like a fool.

You and Mary are insanely alike.

Mary's hair was cut in a chin-length bob like Róisín's. Lynne said it was the only way to manage her mad hairline, the widow's peak and cow's lick they'd inherited from their father. Róisín reckoned she'd have them in matching outfits if she could. Yeah, we could be sisters, said Róisín.

Mary smacked her own forehead, exclaiming, We are sisters, silly!

Everyone was smiling.

Sinéad pulled Róisín into the kitchen, saying she wanted cooking advice.

You're a better cook than I am, what are you at?

He's an angel of a man, please don't fuck it up. I can't do another winter with you like that.

Róisín was stunned. She hadn't told Sinéad about Paddy, pretending it hadn't happened, going to work the next day plastered in foundation to cover the bruising. Like what? she said.

You know well. Hardly leaving this flat for weeks on end, and when you did, getting paralytic drunk and picking up any ould toe-rag and bringing him back here. I don't know what got into you.

Mary joined them, looking at Róisín with concern on her little face. Had she heard them? Had Guy? Róisín picked her up and kissed her.

Sometimes you go too far, Sinéad, she said.

* * *

When she imagined Guy's home place, Róisín had seen a chunky detached house, built in the thirties, with bay windows and a garage painted battleship grey, like the ones in Bromley Lynne aspired to. But they were at a rambling cottage, roof visibly sagging in the middle, surrounded by a whimsically messy garden that was probably a couple of days a week work.

Dear God. Is your ma Anne Hathaway? said Róisín.

Far from it.

Mary had nestled herself in a climbing rose that was arching around a doorway. Take a picture of me! she said.

Come away, you'll get cut to ribbons. And I don't have a camera.

The three of them walked around the side of the house. She and Guy had been seeing each other for a couple of months and it felt soon to be meeting his parents. She combed Mary's hair with her fingers, glad to have her to fuss over.

A tiny corridor, tongue-and-groove panelling the colour of sand. Quarry tiles the colour of earth. Coats hanging from wooden pegs, a case of wine.

Guy's father was a fuller – if almost bald – version of his son. Nick, wonderful you could come, Róisín, he said, grabbing her hand.

You're like a hound with a hare, Dad. And this is Mary. Please don't shake her hand, her arm will come out of its socket.

Well hello, little Miss. Guy, I left your mother and sister there already. We ought to go.

A Saab and a sky-blue 2CV were parked on gravel to the rear of the cottage. She thought of her father's second-hand BMW; people like Guy's parents liked their status symbols solid or quirky.

Windsor Castle was on their right as they drove towards Henley. She tried to muster disgust, but it was gorgeous, the way it seemed to rise from the land amidst gentle humps of field.

As they passed a stand of old oak trees, Nick spoke. Is it like this where you come from? I've heard Ireland is beautiful.

We don't have oak trees any more.

Something like Dutch elm disease?

They were all cut down to build the British naval fleet.

Nick angled his mirror to see her face. God, the man was only being friendly, why was she going all 'up the Republic'?

She thought they would be picnicking on the banks of the Thames. Guy explained that the riverbank was mostly private property, under the ownership of stockbrokers or the Queen. A few miles on, Nick drove through the gates of a private college, saying Sarah had undertaken an MBA here.

'Undertaken' is a bit strong, said Guy.

It was a bloody nightmare.

Bloody nightmare, said Mary.

Way hay, cheered Nick, adjusting the mirror again.

We used to do that when Kate swore. She was like a fucking sailor, said Guy.

This time Mary cheered.

Róisín wasn't prepared for the scene that met them. A lawn, truly velvety, that dropped in gentle tiers down to the river. Men in panama hats and cricket caps popping open bottles, women in Laura Ashley frocks unpacking gingham-lined hampers on to squares of Black Watch and Stewart tartan, the water glittering behind them. Róisín had an impulse to rampage, kicking divots from the grass and pissing on their coronation chicken.

Here's Mum, said Guy.

She had never before encountered a woman so comfortable in her body, sashaying towards them with the bandy-legged gait of an ageing rock star. Up close it was clear she had been exposed to too much sun, her weathered face framed by blonde-streaked hair in a messy bun. Her eyes were the clearest and bluest Róisín had ever seen, and the most piercing, she thought, as the woman took her in. Sarah, she said, Guy's mother.

Róisín. Thanks for having us.

Sarah looked from Mary to Róisín. She could be your daughter, she said.

I wasn't that much fun in my teens.

There was a moment when Róisín thought she had said the wrong thing, but the blue eyes warmed with a smile.

Guy's sister, Kate, was holding the skirt of her dress out; it was made from the same fabric as Mary's. Twins! she cried. Mary held hers out too, delighted.

Róisín and Kate had met a couple of times, dancing like dervishes on pills Guy had given them. No drugs today, we'll have to get sozzled, she whispered as they embraced.

There was champagne and vacuum flasks of Pimm's. Róisín took too long to choose so Nick gave her a glass of each. Guy was on the grass, his arms around his knees. He patted the space between them and Róisín felt sick at the thought of moving. Everyone was watching so she sat between his legs. Mary clambered across, copying her position.

Kate began to sing the chorus of 'Rock the Boat'.

Behind Róisín, Guy's chest swelled with laughter. Was there an Irishman alive who would sit like that in front of his parents?

You live in Islington? said Sarah.

I do, with Sinéad, my friend from home. Above a betting shop and a reclusive pensioner.

It's an interesting area, though, said Guy.

There's something about your use of that word, said Róisín. As if it's interchangeable with shit.

They all laughed. Emboldened, she said the building backed on to a square of terraced houses. Most were in poor condition but the one behind had been renovated. Now there were svelte figures moving through ambient lighting to recline on couches the size of hovercrafts. She missed the old tenants, who had made a shebeen in the back garden and boomed dub from early morning, although she was in no position to dislike gentrification; in the launderette the other day, someone called her a fucking yuppie.

A fucking yuppie! repeated Mary.

Way hay, said Nick.

Love north London. We used to live in Primrose Hill, said Kate. She was balancing a straw hat with a folded-back brim on her fist, spinning it around.

Róisín waited for the others to comment but it was as though they'd silently agreed to change the subject. Sarah lit a cigarette. Róisín was craving one, but they would think she was a degenerate if she puffed with a child on her lap.

Sarah remembered she'd brought something for Mary. She rooted in one of the baskets and produced a book by Shirley Hughes.

DOGGER, spelled Mary. Róisín hugged her, hoping she'd never need to play word games in her head to get herself to sleep.

She's young to know her letters, said Sarah.

Róisín told her she'd worked in a bookshop at home. When people bought a gift for someone else's child they said, He's a bit slow. When they were buying for their own child they said, She's four, with a reading age of twelve. But my Mary actually is a genius, she finished.

Guy said you can tell a story. Sarah was frowning, as if smoking was a path to clear thought.

I don't know why he would tell you that.

He said you'd deny it. I work in PR. We have a vacancy for someone to write press releases, that sort of thing.

Boats were passing, people moving to the river's edge to wave and cheer. Guy hopped up and led Mary by the hand to the bank, bending to listen to her when she spoke. Róisín pondered all the things that happened that day, trying to make sense of it. How canny Sinéad was, unwittingly joining the dots between Guy and Red and the ugliness Paddy had brought into Róisín's life. Maybe Guy had been sent to deliver her. Maybe she could disappear into his gentle English manners and be someone else.

Róisín, Guy and Mary left as the sun was going down, the town washed in golden light. Even the station was beautiful, flowers spilling out of pots, the benches glossy with new paint.

They boarded the train. There were other Henley returnees around them, radiating drink and sunshine. Within minutes, Mary fell asleep on Róisín's lap, clutching *Dogger* as if it was a real dog.

This place is gorgeous, said Róisín.

I fucking hate it.

It was such a strong thing for him to say. His default demeanour was relaxed, open, but his face was tight. Wow, she said.

We left London because my mother was having an affair.

Jesus.

I was supposed to go to a local school with my friends.

Did they put you in school round here?

No! The local one is Eton. They sent me to a Catholic boys' boarding school in Hertfordshire. I was desperately unpopular. I had a stammer, it's still there when I'm sick or tired. They made me play rugby, which I hated – that's where the conk came from, he said, touching the bend in his nose.

Ah, Guy.

It's all right. How about you?

I hate where my mother lives too. We moved there because my father went mad as a result of making himself a legitimate target for Republican paramilitaries. Everyone in my new school hated me except Sinéad.

There's no need to be competitive.

She loved that he'd chosen to make her laugh. Beside her, he was himself again, or at least the self he presented to the world, a hamper on his knee that his mother had given him when they were leaving, smiling when he looked at Róisín. Living proof that there was a way to carry sadness and not destroy yourself.

She peeled back the cover on the basket. A wedge of Victoria sandwich, half a quiche and a copy of Fowler's *Modern English Usage*.

Did I not talk proper? said Róisín.

Don't be absurd. He opened the book and pulled out a couple of foolscap sheets stapled together, *Proofreader's marks* typed in bold across the top. She's serious about that job, he said.

They alighted from the train at Paddington. Mary was sleepy, so Guy put her over his shoulder, Róisín carrying the basket as they followed the sign for the Underground. A man in a black hat and colourful shawl was playing 'Feelings' on panpipes at the foot of the escalator, a crowd around him. Mary slid to her feet to listen. There were people coming at them from every direction and, afraid of losing her, Róisín took her sister's hand.

Can you spare a few coins, called a voice as they entered the tunnel to the Circle line, I'm homeless and hungry. He had the patter of a barrow boy, but his Irish accent made her look. A woman was hurrying away, head down. Miserable bitch, he called after her. Lots of people laughed, dropping coins at his feet.

Mary broke free and for a terrifying moment vanished. Róisín tried to cry out her name, but her voice wouldn't work. A gap opened in the crowd and she saw her, just a few feet away, petting a dog. Wilbur, you fucker, muttered Róisín, grabbing the child's wrist.

Red was angled like a set square, joints and bones jutting, all the flesh dropped away. His hair had lost its lustre, but it was still in spikes she knew he'd set with soap or cola. Wilbur knew

Mary, he said to Róisín, patting the dog's head. He knew her because he used to know you.

There was a moment when they could have embraced, but he scratched his arm distractedly and it was gone. Mary was holding out her book. You like dogs too? he said, kneeling and pointing at the cover.

She nodded. Dogger gets lost.

Ah no. I'm sure somebody will find him.

What's your name? said Mary.

I'm Red. And I know who you are, Mary McCaffrey. You got so big. He stood and glanced to Róisín's left, looking at her expectantly. She had forgotten Guy was there and began to panic, not knowing how to introduce them.

Red Camelin, he said.

Guy Walmesley, good to meet you.

He was behaving as though he was meeting Red for lunch at a brasserie on Fenchurch Street.

Lancashire Jacobite name. Are youse still Catholic?

We are. My God, I can't believe you know that.

Red was looking at the basket. Family outing to the Henley Regatta?

Guy smiled, but he was blushing deeply. He and Róisín might as well have had *Wanker* tattooed on their foreheads.

Do you live near here? said Róisín and promptly wanted to kill herself. He was standing on cardboard, begging.

He knew what she was thinking, for he said, I'm not homeless, just having cashflow issues. You know me, I'm everywhere.

A flâneur, said Guy.

It was the term Róisín had been trying to think of that first Christmas in London, when they'd walked miles. She said she'd come back to him with the right word but had been too far up her own arse, craving his full attention, to keep a promise. All the ways she'd let him down.

You still in Islington? Don't worry, I won't visit, he added, chuckling. That there was no accusation in it undid her.

I am, she said. She bent to pet the dog, unable to hold Red's gaze for another second. Wilbur looks great, Red. You've looked after him well.

He's seven now. An elderly gentleman.

Is that old for a greyhound? said Guy.

It is. Red scratched his arm, glancing behind them. They were bad for business.

She hugged him. His body felt like a carcass, as though it had been picked over.

Say bye-bye, Mary, she said, and bit her lip as the child put her arms around his knees.

Walking away, a lump like a chunk of baguette in her throat, she held tightly to Mary's hand, the basket bashing against her hip. Guy caught up with her, scooping Mary into his arms again. Did you give him money? whispered Róisín.

I'm sorry, I had to. All I had was a tenner. He shook my hand and sang a line, something about Daddy's arm.

There's a hole in Daddy's arm where all the money goes, she thought. A John Prine song he'd played on repeat, never thinking there'd be a hole in his own arm one day.

They got through the stench on the stairs and entered the flat. It smelled of the life she was trying to make. Dreft from the silk top she'd handwashed and slung over the shower rail above the bath, a lingering scent of fresh garlic from the kitchen. She lit a cigarette and pulled up the sash window. Guy was settling Mary on the couch. Admitting to Red that they'd been to Henley, using the word 'flâneur' to describe a man who was now clearly a tramp. Maybe she was angry because he had spoken to the person Red had been, perhaps still was under the hunger of addiction. Guy had given him money discreetly, so as not to humiliate him in front of Róisín. She had... Well, she wasn't going to think about that now.

The book Róisín had been trying to read was on the coffee table, John Healy's *The Grass Arena*. Every time she picked it up, she found herself stuck on the first line.

My father didn't look like he would harm anyone.

17

23 December 1989

A stairwell, its steps worn, smelling faintly of industrial detergent. Three flights to her father's door, greasy prints around the handle. Guy knocked, an official tone to the three brisk beats that might make her father stay in his seat with his yellow fingers round a cigarette, but the door opened.

His eyes were raw from lack of sleep. Come on on on on in, he said. Was it a catchphrase from a game show?

Guy Walmesley, good to meet you, Conor. He placed the shopping bag on the floor and took her father's hand in both of his.

Nice to meet you too, son. It was an endearment Róisín loved, he'd called Red *son* the last night he was in Sydenham. Addressed to the son of a Home Counties lawyer it sounded simple, parochial.

Guy was still holding her father's hand, sweet Guy who never said a bad word about anyone. What was wrong with her? People in the City would kill to live so close to work, he said.

Anyone with a modicum of pride would think he was being patronised, but her father was chuckling. I struck it lucky, he said. This housing is for respectable working people who are down on their luck. I had to go through a process, but by the end I had yer man well convinced.

He'd probably bored dozens of people in the pub with this spiel. What part did he think he'd fooled them with? Didn't he know he was down on his luck? And the state of the place. A pair of fawn armchairs and a fake-teak coffee table, a blocked-up fireplace. He glanced at the mantelpiece and deftly righted a pair of photographs that had been face down. Róisín in the hideous rust-coloured poncho she'd insisted on wearing for her confirmation. Mary in her first party dress, maroon velour with a tulle underskirt. Their mothers folded out of view.

Róisín carried the bag of shopping they'd bought to the kitchen, a tiny galley off the living room.

Ach, youse didn't need to bring anything, I've plenty in, her father told Guy.

A smell of stale cigarette ash from the bin, a hum of mould that made her panic until she realised it was coming from a once-white cloth in the sink, now the colour of lead. She looked inside a box of Quaker Oats. It was writhing with weevils.

The rubber seals in the small fridge were yellowed with age. *I've plenty in*, he'd said. A bottle of milk, Melton Mowbray pork pies, a tub of Flora. Eight cans of Tennent's Extra, a bottle of the cheap Soave she used to drink with Sinéad. She filled the shelves with fresh groceries. An egg, cheese and bacon flan, smoked salmon, prawn cocktail, two chicken Kievs. Mince pies and a rectangular slab of Christmas cake.

Her father came in, rubbing his hands in the way that made her heart sink. Taking two beers from the fridge, he said, Wee glass of wine? 'Tis the season.

It's a bit early.

I bought you those in case you're peckish, he said, pointing at a packet of Tudor pickled onion crisps. He'd remembered they were her favourite snack.

He insisted she take his seat. She hated the effect she was having on him, tremors in his upper body making his head wobble like a toy on a car dashboard. She sat on the arm of Guy's seat, the sharp wood almost cutting her arse.

Her father sat down, striking a match under a cigarette.

Where's the lighter Mummy gave you? said Róisín.

It's in getting serviced, he said, the lie glinting in his eyes.

Guy said Róisín was doing very well in her job, that she was a natural. He described their flat in the half-full way he saw the world. It was a great place, much like Conor's in layout but not quite so central. There were similarities – scratchy carpet tiles, large windows, cheap cupboards – but Bride Street had Aldo Jacober folding chairs, books and records and tapes, kitchen utensils from the Elizabeth David shop. And residents who were not actively obliterating themselves.

They talked the way men did, Guy and her father, about the weather and the fall of the Iron Curtain. Starter for ten, her father said.

Guy answered the rugby and cricket questions correctly and grinned apologetically that he didn't know anything about darts or snooker.

Where's the loo, Daddy? she said. Why was that word coming so easily today?

It's in the west wing, love.

In the hall, she peeked at his bedroom. It was not quite double, with a mock-teak nightstand and a wardrobe missing a door. The rack was full of clothes covered in polythene sheaths from the dry cleaner's, as if he had to be ready for a meeting at a second's notice; he hadn't worked for over a year. But his bed. It wasn't that it was old – she'd never seen a new mattress until the one Guy bought was delivered to the flat – there was no linen, just a tangle of blankets. The bathroom was worse. A seatless loo, a slash of blue Toilet Duck in the bowl like the mark of Zorro. A bar of Shield soap, deep grimy lines across its surface, the brand her mother used to buy because Róisín liked the ad. Did her dad suffer crushing nostalgia too, using groceries and old songs to find a way back?

In the living room, her father was pulling the ring from a beer can. It frothed on to the carpet. He pointed his toe as if he was about to grind it into the weft but, remembering he had company, went to the kitchen.

Guy already had another drink.

Please don't accept any more, she whispered.

He wouldn't take no for an answer. It's rocket fuel, I'm half-pissed.

Drink always made Guy a little giddy, but was he laughing at her father? God knows, he was laughable. So was Róisín, pitching up with a bag of provisions one might bring a pensioner in Surbiton for a man with the palate of a wino.

Lynne says you won't go to her for Christmas, said Róisín.

Aye, love, I'm working. Wish I could. Big day in the pub, he said, eyebrows rising, the way they always did when he wasn't telling the truth. Before, he lied so his family would keep him; now he lied to get away from them.

What happens in the pub? said Guy.

Was he slurring?

Christmas lunch with all the trimmings. There'll be thirty-odd people from all about the place.

Did Mary tell you what's on her list? asked Róisín.

Aye, she did indeed. She's up to high doh for Santa.

The previous week, Lynne and Mary had waited outside Block B for an hour in the rain. Giving up, they went to the pub on the corner to use the loo and found him at the counter.

I tried to persuade Róisín to stay here for Christmas, but she's determined to go to Ireland, said Guy, pronouncing it 'Island'. Cheap lager on his breath, his face open in a gormless smile.

The beer wasn't showing on her father; if anything it had shored him up. Róisín came to me one Christmas, you know, he said. She was with her pal, Red. Thick as thieves, they were.

* * *

I don't give a fuck about *Island*, she said outside, if I don't go home my mother will be alone.

Is this a back-handed way of saying you'll miss me? he said, putting his arm around her shoulder. When she didn't answer, he asked what she'd like to do.

Reach your current blood alcohol levels and keep going till I can unsee that flat.

By the pub her father pretended to work in – the one in which he was choosing to eat a turkey dinner with strays and fuck-ups like the *EastEnders* Christmas special instead of with his little daughter – Guy hailed a cab. He dozed off almost as soon as they sat. Róisín looked out the window. There was something decrepit about these edgelands that bordered the City, yet big money was pushing in, a Victorian warehouse converted into apartments breaking up a strip of dingy shops. Rents were rising, theirs manageable because Guy's income was thrice Róisín's plus bonuses. Her father was right, he had done well to convince the Peabody people he was decent.

And Red. Five years ago he had given her a home. Where was he now?

Let me out, she said, leaning forward to speak to the driver through the gap in the glass.

Where are you going? said Guy, rubbing his eyes.

Shopping. Go home and have a nap, I'll see you back at the flat.

She hopped out and walked to Angel. She would begin here and traipse every tunnel, every concourse, until she found Red.

Part Three

18

14 March 2007

The previous night, Róisín had said their father would be best represented by a pint of Tennent's and a letter from the Child Support Agency. The others laughed, then cried, but Róisín hadn't managed either since she'd heard he was dead. She and Mary had settled on a bowl of shamrock and a Tottenham Hotspur jersey. Laying them on his coffin, they joined their mothers in the front row. The organ sounded and they stood for the entrance hymn. 'How Great Thou Art', chosen because Conor had loved the Elvis version. No one was singing along. Róisín glanced back, afraid the church was empty, but there were twenty or thirty people. Irish people, presumably, who only sang drunk.

She took the altar steps. A reading from the Book of Ecclesiastes, she began. *For everything there is a season.* They were lines she knew from the song 'Turn! Turn! Turn!'. Her heart was beating so fast the words began to run away from her and she faltered at the end, confused that the last lyric seemed to be missing. Mary high-fived her as she passed to do the second reading. *When I was a child, I spoke as a child, I felt as a child, I thought as a child.*

The Mass responses came to Róisín unbidden. There was comfort in the mumblings, in the rhythms and pauses. Mary knew them too. Their father was out of her life by the time she was four but Lynne – who replied, C of E, I think, when asked her religion – took her to Mass because it was important to him, even though drink had become more important than anything. Róisín had last seen him in his flat, two streets away. Tics distorting his face like a plea, and still she could not forgive him. The priest gave him dignity she never thought he'd earned. His pride in his children, his Irishness, his Catholic faith. The struggle of his life and his lack of guile. Was 'guileless' not another way of saying 'pathetic'?

Men in black faded to bottle green read the bidding prayers, paper audibly shuddering as they thanked God for the love, friendship and happiness they shared with Conor, prayed for his sorrowing family and for those who'd gone before him, thanked those who had tried to help him, especially Father Timothy, the staff of the housing trust and Finbarr from the centre. At Communion time, the priest invited everyone to join the family at the altar. Those who had been away from the church could come for a blessing, he said, the sacrament wasn't a reward for good behaviour. Her mother looked at her with imploring eyes and Róisín followed her up the aisle, crossing her arms as Father Timothy whispered a benediction.

And then Thomas P. Clancy and Sons, Funeral Directors, hoisted Conor McCaffrey on to his daughters' shoulders. His brothers were behind them, a pair of his drinking mates at the rear, the hum of bachelorhood releasing when they raised their arms. The host was clinging to one of Róisín's wisdom teeth. When she was a child she had been warned it was a sin to chew, to munch on the body of Christ. She poked at the soggy wafer with her tongue as they followed the slow step of the chief undertaker towards the light, trying not to think about how little weight there was in her six-foot-two father's coffin.

Outside, cigarette smoke replaced BO and incense. Beautiful flowers, said Lynne, pointing at the mound of hellebores and rosemary and bluebells and ranunculi that Thomas Clancy was placing in the hearse between the shamrock and the Spurs jersey.

Across the road, Guy was parked behind a man who was a little familiar to Róisín. Cropped hair, slightly bulky from the gym, in a dark jacket like a hoodless parka. They began opening their cars like chauffeurs for the faded men, Guy removing a pair of booster seats and tossing them in the boot. The other man nodded at her.

That's Finbarr, said Mary, following her eyes. I think he's single.

Jesus. You would have me on the pull today?

They got into the funeral car – a Jaguar limousine their father would have loved – with their mothers. Lynne was in a Karen Millen tuxedo and spiky suede ankle boots. Earlier she had set about Róisín's mother with bronzer and draped her in a black coat with a fake-feather collar. Poor Una. She'd stood blinking at her reflection as though she was on a TV makeover show, afraid to say she didn't recognise herself.

How are you, Mum? asked Róisín.

Sad. The lovely big fella I met when I was seventeen was still in there somewhere. I hope he's at peace. What about you?

The usual.

Aye. Angry.

The small cortège went west of Angel, through Barnsbury. The traffic was slow and on Liverpool Road they came to a halt at the end of Bride Street. Amidst the rooftops Róisín could just about make out the attic conversion that was once her room. Their room.

Your old street, Rosh, said Lynne, squeezing her shoulder.

Yeah.

Trip down Memory Lane.

Mary remembered her My Little Pony bedclothes and walking to the Dome on Upper Street for hot chocolate. Una recalled how uncomfortable the settee was and that they had no television. Róisín glanced behind. Guy was craning left, arms around the steering wheel. They'd been happy in that flat, she hoped he remembered that.

The cemetery stretched from Finchley to Highgate. Parts of it were scraggy woodland, broken tombstones and weathered statues visible through bare trees. Her father's plot was in a well-tended part of the northern corner, an open grave swathed in folds of green baize like a collapsed snooker table. The priest led them in prayers. Lynne rooted in her big gold-strapped handbag and produced a bunch of red roses, its cellophane wrapping disturbing the peace as she doled them out. They tossed blooms and fistfuls of soil on the coffin. Mary was weeping. Róisín put her arm around her shoulder and rocked her to the *thwap* of earth on wood. She wanted to scream at their father, Look at what you had and you didn't care for it.

As they were walking away from the graveyard, Single Finbarr stepped from among his passengers. He was looking at her from under his eyebrows, his head turned slightly away. Róisín, he said.

She felt her mouth drop open. It was Barry Doyle.

Oh my God, she managed. But why is Mary calling you Finbarr?

Barry is an eejit's name. Or it was when I answered to it.

I don't know what's wrong with me, it's like I can't operate out of context. Mary says I have face blindness.

One of his eyebrows was arched. She was overdoing it. He said he was sorry for her loss, he'd been fond of Conor.

You're the Finbarr. This is nuts.

I suppose it is, he said, smiling. As a young man he'd been coarse-haired and now there wasn't a kink, some glossy product keeping it in place.

Come on, sis, called Mary.

Róisín told him she'd better go, that it would be a bad look if they arrived last, that she hoped he would come to the pub for lunch. He was still smiling, probably because she was chattering like a fool. He'd had work done on his teeth; everyone seemed to be wearing braces in their forties and getting veneers.

You met Finbarr, said Mary when they were in the car. Isn't he cute?

No.

Mary giggled. Róisín sent a text to Sinéad.

Barry Doyle is here. I'm not fucking able.

Her father's local was notable in Clerkenwell for not being a gastro pub. The manager had waived a fee for the room. He was helping the caterer set up at the far end and came to the entrance to welcome them, white shirt billowing out of his trousers. Conor was one of the best, he said, gone too soon.

Róisín thanked him, opening a bar tab and asking him to check in with her when it reached £500. Guy joined her at the counter. They had got the excruciating greeting – a hug that left her feeling nothing – out of the way before the service, but she sensed he was going to say something earnest. She lit a cigarette.

I hope you don't mind my being here, Róisín. Guy was not so much ageing as dissipating, eyes almost lucent, sparse hair beigeing rather than greying.

Don't be daft. You're good to come, she said, though she knew he was there for Mary. At first it bothered Róisín that they kept in touch, her ex-husband and her little sister, but Mary said she should not have to lose people who were important to her because they no longer had a place in Róisín's life.

Can I get you a drink? he asked.

A white wine. Put it on the slate.

He ordered eight pints of Guinness, eight Jameson, a sparkling water and a glass of Sauvignon Blanc. Towards the end, when every word that came out of his mouth irritated her, she used to tell him he sounded like the Duchess of Devonshire. As he removed notes from his wallet she noticed his new wedding ring. It was plain, unlike the ones they'd had made with a Celtic knot pattern that embarrassed her now. The outward show of Irishness, of heritage, when she was getting as far away from that as possible and didn't even invite her father. This one's on me, he said.

Thank you.

My mother sends her sympathy.

She pictured Sarah frowning as she asked him to relay the message, knowing the formality would hurt Róisín. Not that she deserved better.

For a moment neither of them spoke, stricken by the strangeness of being alone.

This area is pretty gentrified now, he said.

It was London talk, a sentence spoken to fill the silence, but he'd reminded her he'd been around here before, drinking extra-strength lager at midday, full of enthusiasm for the dump her father lived in. Fully gentrified now my da's gone? she said.

I'm not going to rise to that, Róisín.

She watched him carry a tray of pints across the floor and felt unexpected tenderness for him. He had held her all that night as she cried for her father, not knowing she was crying for Red too. She'd traipsed the Underground until the last train but hadn't found him.

Barry joined her at the counter, sniffing a tumbler of ice and lemon before pouring Perrier over it.

You're driving, she said.

I'm sixteen years, ten months and eleven days sober.

He looked well, skin clear beneath a close shave, cording in his neck and hands from exercise. How profoundly the drink had shown on him at twenty.

Is 'congratulations' the right response?

Yeah. Thank you. And it's all good, like I'd be dead otherwise. Over his shoulder, Guy was collecting the rest of the drinks.

So you helped my father. What was it, addiction counselling or something?

I work for a mental health charity, he said, a soft 't' at the end of 'health'. Over two decades in England and he still hadn't mastered the *th* sound. His accent had not so much mellowed as mutated, the intonation slightly cockney. Our business is loneliness, I suppose, he added.

Jesus. Do youse offer a family rate?

Now the tears wanted to come? She wiped her eyes.

Ah, I'm sorry, Róisín. Conor was doing great. He was part of our meitheal programme, working in our garden, decorating flats for other service users. Not everyone who starts where he did makes so much progress.

Where did he start?

His shoulders lifted in a sigh. He told her Conor wasn't able to mind himself. Years ago he would have been admitted but these days treatment was a prescription and six sessions of CBT and away you go. It wasn't enough. The housing trust contacted us because we have a cara network, he said.

She didn't know why it made her feel better to hear words in the Irish language. Meitheal, work gang. Cara, friend. And the way Barry had spoken them. Silky and glottal at once.

You were his cara?

Usually it's a volunteer but I took the call. He was great company.

Did he do the starter-for-ten thing with you?

Barry smiled. I never met anyone who knew so much about sport.

He learned all that in the pub, she said. Unfairly, because her father had done the pools, watched *Grandstand*, *Match of the*

Day, *World of Sport*. He even watched swimming and tennis. Jesus, she said, I can't say a good word about him, it's like a form of Tourette's.

He loved you. He was Róisín this and Róisín that.

More tears, it was gruelling talking to Barry.

Are you trained to drag emotion out of people? she asked.

I am actually, he said, giving her a tissue.

Her mascara left semicircles on it like false lashes. I must look a state, she said.

No. Just a tiny bit there. He took back the tissue and blotted beneath her right eye. Her body remembered him, afflicting her with a hot twinge between her legs. I'd better sort myself out in the jacks, she said, and left him at the bar.

Mary was at the mirror with two friends. From the back they were like a Ronettes tribute band. Róisín snatched a wand of eyeliner from her hand. What has you all hot and bothered? said Mary.

Barry Doyle. Finbarr or whatever he calls himself now. He lived in the squat in Pimlico.

Oh my days, you shagged him.

Her friends giggled and made *twit-twoo* noises.

I swear you're a witch, said Róisín. Fix my face.

Mary cleaned her up with the tissue she'd used in the cemetery and ordered her to shut her eyes. Grief makes people horny, you'll probably shag him again, she said, drawing on Róisín's lids.

Feck off and mingle, you.

Mary raised a middle finger, her lips smacking in a kiss, and traipsed out. She'd made Róisín's eyes vampish. Ridiculous. *I'd better sort myself out in the jacks*, as if she was running off to masturbate.

Mary had joined Guy at the counter, her head resting on his shoulder. He was the nearest thing to a father she'd had. Conor hadn't been up to it and Lynne's men were always divorced and too busy avoiding their own children to bother with her. After Róisín left, it was Guy who'd persuaded Lynne to send her to a better school for her A levels. No mean feat, considering Merv the Perv, Lynne's second husband, thought the university of life was all a person needed to get on. Mary insisted that without Guy she wouldn't have got on a PhD programme at all, let alone a funded one.

Róisín's glass was empty. She ordered another, drinking a third of it in one go. The faded men were at the edges of the room. One of them was approaching her, his hand on Barry's forearm. He was thin as a stick, his upper body swinging from side to side like a pendulum because his left hip sat a good three inches higher than the right, jutting at an unnatural angle. He must have been in agony.

Muiris wants to meet you, said Barry. He'd taken off his jacket and was in a grey lambswool jumper over a soft-collared white shirt. His torso was almost triangular.

Muiris lifted his chin as if it was a terrible burden. I'm sorry for your troubles, he said. Your father was a fine man.

It had taken so much out of him she felt tears gather again. Thank you, Muiris. How did you know him?

I met him at the centre.

Her father had sought the company of men like Muiris? She'd imagined him swapping Spurs lore with broken London spivs, too young and aspirational for his countrymen, never feeling Irish enough to pass himself amongst them. Muiris is a meitheal man, Barry said.

With gentle prompting from Barry, Muiris told her he and Conor had set the potatoes a few days before he died. That he was a gas man, God rest him, always in good form, and he'd miss him sorely. After a few minutes, he shook her hand and turned, a manoeuvre so full of pain it was difficult to look.

Barry stayed beside her. Imagine moving through the world like that, she said.

He thinks he's blessed because he's alive and not in a wheelchair.

Didn't you turn out well?

He glanced up at her and laughed a little. Fucking brilliant, yeah.

She took a sip of her wine and lit a cigarette. Barry had always needed props: a joint and a can, a pint and a Benson. New Barry – Finbarr – had his arms loosely at his sides. Did my father tell you I ruined my marriage?

He never said a bad word about you.

Her mother was coming, eyes fixed on Barry. Oh Jesus, Róisín told him. Prepare to be interrogated.

I heard that, said Una, looking from one to the other.

Mum, this is Barry Doyle. Sorry, Finbarr.

Ach, are you the man was being lauded from the altar? Isn't that lovely. She embraced him, patting his back.

Good to meet you, Mrs McCaffrey. Myself and Róisín lived in the squat in Pimlico at the same time. My sister Tina was in her class in school.

Call me Una. So you stayed in London?

I'm here twenty-two years.

Róisín bought one of the wee lock-keepers' cottages down by the canal. She has it beautiful, you should call in next time you're home.

Barry's smile was converting to a smirk. In fairness her mother's attempt at matchmaking would not have been more obvious had she dug Róisín in the ribs and winked. If only she'd go away. Mary spared Róisín further mortification by raising a glass above her head and pinging it with her rings. Grub's up! she said. Fill your boots!

I'd better round up Conor's brothers, said Una.

Róisín swallowed the rest of her wine and watched her mother make her way to the back of the room. That wasn't embarrassing at all, she said.

Barry placed his hand on her lower back. Come on, Róisín. We'll get the dinner.

There was an electric soup tureen filled with beef in Guinness. Jersey royals dripping in butter, a whole ham in slices. A salad of butterhead lettuce, tomatoes, beetroot and hardboiled egg.

I see your name in the paper sometimes, he said.

Yeah, I'm world-famous. Eight hundred words a time on lighting and paint and what not to do when designing a kitchen.

Shallow, easy things she knew because she had shrugged off the difficult things.

Why are they not coming? said Mary, pointing a serving spoon at the men.

They're shy, said Barry. Lash food on to plates and I'll drop them over.

What the hell's going on? hissed Mary when he'd left with the first two. A strand of her beehive had come loose and Róisín tucked it behind her ear.

It's a frigging nightmare. My mother asked him to call to my house next time he's home.

She needs to ask him to bonk you. The sexual tension is off the fucking charts.

Please stop.

Mary let the tongs she was holding drop. Fuck, he's coming back. You're on your own, I can't bear it.

Róisín served huge portions, following Barry's instructions to *Lorry it on, especially the spuds*. When everyone else had a plate, Róisín began to fill one for him. He refused potatoes, saying he was training for an endurance event.

Jesus.

I substituted one addiction for another. Look, I told Muiris I'd eat with him.

I'd better eat with the mother. Please don't come near us.

The banquette seating went around the walls in an L-shape. Barry was perpendicular to her, amidst the men, each of them forking food into his mouth with a rhythm that was almost mechanical, as if there was a stopwatch running and the plate would be whipped away if they didn't finish on time. In case he thought she was ogling him, she moved to the chair opposite.

I don't recall any mention of a Finbarr, said Róisín's mother, laying down her knife and fork; she had only taken wheaten bread and a quartered egg, much of which was still on her plate.

We called him Barry then, I told you.

Is he still in touch with Red?

I don't know.

Robert Camelin's funeral was awful. You should have come with me.

I was arranging my own father's burial!

Una attended every funeral in the town, a down payment on a decent attendance at her own in a place that wasn't hers, but surely she could have drawn a line at paying her respects to a man she suspected was a monster?

Poor Dolly was all by herself. Three sons and not a sign of them.

Hell slap it into her. Awful woman.

You can tell her what you think of her in person. She wants you to go and see her.

Mary and Guy joined them. He sat at Róisín's right, giving her a conciliatory smile.

Una asked him about his children. How old were they now? Were twins a handful?

It never feels like work, he replied. He used to say that about Mary, when Róisín apologised for having her so often.

What a good man he was. And what a relief to have got away from him.

No one asked to see photographs of his children, as though there was an unspoken consensus that poor childless Róisín would not survive the sight of his progeny.

Time for a toast, said Lynne, placing a cluster of flutes and a wine cooler on the table. She popped a bottle open and splashed Prosecco into the glasses, a tennis bracelet glittering below her satin cuff. God, Róisín loved her, she'd been saving her life for over twenty years.

When everyone had a drink, Lynne raised her glass and clinked it against Una's. To our girls. You did your dad proud.

Hear, hear! said Guy.

You sound like you're on Prime Minister's Questions, said Mary. It was the sort of thing Róisín used to say to him, only without the hatred.

I screwed up the reading, said Róisín. I thought there was a line missing.

Pete Seeger added an extra one when he made the verse into a song, said Guy.

The bollocks, said Róisín.

She stacked the dirty plates and carried them to the buffet table. Lighting a cigarette, she checked her phone. There was a reply from Sinéad.

BD is there??? Dessie says he's buff as fuck.

Róisín laughed out loud.

A little later, Barry came to say he was taking Muiris home. Mary threw her arms around him, crying a little. Lynne did the same, saying she was ever so grateful. Then Una was on him, whispering God knows what into his ear.

Róisín stood facing Barry, willing her body to embrace his, for her mouth to gush gratitude and grace. It felt like minutes were passing, the four of them watching her.

Come to the door with me, he said.

He introduced her to some of the other men. They were friendly now, audacious from drink. As Muiris was getting to his feet, Barry leaned in and kissed her cheek. It's good to see you, Róisín.

That cursed stirring again, could he see it in her? Smell it? You too, she said.

A pause and then they both spoke at once, neither hearing the other. You go first, said Barry, eyeing her sidelong, a glimmer of the shy boy he'd been.

I asked if you know where Red is.

The smile in his eyes disappeared so slowly Róisín wondered if it had been there at all. I haven't seen him since 1990, he said.

That long. God.

Róisín was one to talk. She had last seen Red in 1989. Swanning through Paddington station with champagne on her breath and him on a cardboard box, begging.

Muiris reached them, the poor hip cocked, shaking Róisín's hand. Barry opened the door ahead of him and didn't look back.

An hour later, the crowd had shrunk to about a dozen people. Róisín, Mary and their mothers amongst the men.

The night's not done till there's a song, said one. He seemed elderly, a jumper over a shirt and tie, a jacket over that, but he was probably in his sixties with just a year or two on her father. The photograph on the funeral leaflet was from the Lynne era. How had her father aged?

There were Irish drinking songs, country songs about drinking. Country songs about love and loss and loneliness. Lynne and Una swayed as they sang, the pints flowing.

A man who hadn't taken his woolly hat off all day cleared his throat and began to sing.

I wish I was in Carrickfergus.

She saw Micksy as clearly as if he was slumped at her feet. Red standing sentry in his Dennis the Menace jumper, disgracing bystanders into paying to listen. Why did his mother want to speak to her?

19

6 April 2007

Dolly Camelin still lived in the house overlooking the fake lake, on the other side of which was the hospital people drove to Dublin to avoid. Róisín's image of it was from the night Enda Gilhooly pulled up after the disco, a recollection clouded by Red's revolting cocktail and the dark evening. Now it had mock-Georgian double-glazing and a circular sunroom. Róisín walked up the driveway and pressed the bell. A swan beat its wings on the water behind her, and she turned to see a mother with a pram hurry away, a plastic bread bag flapping from the handle.

Red's mother opened the door. Where her bouffant do had been there was a leopard-print cap and the wisps of hair that escaped it were white. She was in full make-up, gold on every item: her shoes, blouse and the slim belt that cinched her waist. Good enough for her, she said, watching the commotion. Rotting the poor creature's guts with cheap sliced pan.

I'm Róisín McCaffrey. My mother said you wanted to see me.

I know who you are. Come in.

Like Dolly, the sitting room was heavily decorated. Róisín did not like its look, but had been writing about interiors for long enough to know it was rare for someone to have such conviction in their personal style. Red had taken after her, with his particular tastes, and it made Róisín warm to the woman who was now sitting on a sofa as puffy as a meringue and eyeing her sharply.

A large painting of a naked woman coiled around a human-sized salmon, eggs spilling out of one or both of them, was hanging on the wall above a dining table at the far end of the room.

Wow, Róisín said.

He bought that, Dolly spat. Disgusting thing to be hanging over you when you're eating. I'm going to sell it, not that I'll have much time to enjoy the proceeds.

There were other pictures with the same garish, slightly sexual vibe, but no photographs. A family with three sons and no trace of them.

I should be offering you tea or something, said Dolly. Her face was so thin the mechanics of her jaw were visible as she spoke.

I had lunch at my mother's.

Your mother is a good person, she said. Registering Róisín's surprise she added, I asked about her in the town when my Redmond was going to your house all the time. I didn't worry about him so much then.

You knew about us?

What you must think of me to say that, said Dolly. A bump the size of a twenty-cent coin on her chest, a cable running beneath her skin to a vein in her neck. She caught Róisín staring, touched it. It's a portacath for cancer drugs. I've a year. He got cancer too. He died in agony.

Oh no, said Róisín.

You think I'm sad about that! she shrieked in a girlish giggle that sounded unhinged. They offered him the hospice but I kept him at home. I used to hold his morphine pump away from him, and him squirming. Big strong man that he was crying in pain. Ha!

I'm sorry.

Dolly brushed a piece of lint from her skirt with the side of her hand, looking at it bitterly as if she was sweeping talk of her husband away with it. I'm not sorry, she said. You lost your own father.

A month ago. It felt like he was gone a while.

I wish my boys had lost their father a long time ago. I wish my little treasure was buried, I used to say to people. They thought I was joking. I suppose you're wondering why I asked for you.

I presume it's about Red. Redmond.

Top of the class. That bad bastard drove him away. The others are gone too, one in Australia and the other won't say where he is.

I lost touch with Red a long time ago.

Dolly had been worrying at a scar on her wrist, a small glossy crater. Oh, this old thing, she said – the woman missed nothing – as if she was being coy about a piece of clothing Róisín had admired. He gave it to me one Christmas night. That same Christmas actually, the one when my own son looked at me and I turned away from him. I did my best when I got home but I was sad. My husband didn't like me to be sad, she said, delivering the last sentence in a childish whine, as if he wanted her to be happy.

I always bought him a big cigar for Christmas, she went on, in that lovely shop at the end of Grafton Street. He lit one after the port and cheese and stubbed it out on me. In front of my other sons.

She crumpled forward, looking suddenly desolate. I'm tired, she said, her fingertip in the cigar burn. Find my boy for me. Tell him it's safe to come home.

Beautiful on the outside, Red had said about Christmas with his family. That St Stephen's Day, twenty-four hours after their father had mutilated their mother with a luxury stocking filler, Red and Andrew Camelin brawled on the main street. Róisín got into her car and lit a cigarette. She thought of the mood that fell on Red as they walked to Nathy's hovel of a house on the back lane. Andrew must have told him what happened and blamed him for not being there. And who knew what Robert Camelin had said in Red's ear after Mass on Christmas morning. She started the engine, glancing back as she reversed. Dolly was at the window, watching her.

The baker's doughy children were still lobbing out Black Forest gateau and coffee slices and two of the drapery shops had survived but the town was now a satellite of Dublin, according to the property supplements, new housing developments and industrial estates bleeding into the countryside. A motorway had taken heavy traffic off the main street and it had an air of prosperous bustle, expensive boutiques selling flouncy clothes to the horsey set, a couple of good restaurants. Her mother's favourite addition was an M&S Foodhall. Earlier she'd given Róisín a list, unnecessarily, as the order was always the same.

Parking behind the shopping centre, she ran in and began to fill a basket. Part of the bakery section had vanished, a display of Easter eggs in its place. She'd read somewhere that modern humans, having lost the ability to hunt and gather their own food, navigated supermarket aisles with an unconscious desperation, and a change in layout could send them into panic. She imagined herself turning over shelving and screaming for crumpets. The staff probably wouldn't be surprised; Sinéad joked that Róisín was so odd and solitary she was at risk of getting a nickname. She found the rest of the bread section beside the wine and after some dithering bought a bottle of Rioja, reasoning that its full body and plummy finish would stop her from demolishing it in a single night.

At her mother's house, she unpacked the groceries on to the kitchen table. It was the one she'd always had, now covered by a couple of yards of oilcloth with a sweet-pea pattern. The kitchen units had been replaced by Shaker-style cabinets, an extractor fan eliminating the steam that used to blacken the walls. Her mother was not quite leaning against the worktop, as if it was hot or dangerous. You forgot the crumpets, she said.

They didn't have any, lied Róisín.

You're later than you said you'd be.

I went to see Dolly Camelin.

Her mother's chin seemed to retreat. You never said! How was she?

Completely mental and scarily sane. You should have heard her about the husband, she said, putting the chilled food in the fridge. I always kind of knew he hurt them but I didn't think he was a total sadist.

Oh, he was a bad article. He called here one day to tell me Red was a compulsive liar and a thief, that he was a bad influence on you. I chased him.

Róisín stopped, a quiche in her hand. Why am I only hearing this now?

The child felt safe here. I didn't want him to know that man had been next or near us.

All the times Róisín had stormed in and out of this kitchen accusing her mother and Enda Gilhooly of nosiness. They'd only ever wanted to help Red.

She walked Una into the sitting room, lowering her into the ugly armchair one of her quacks had sold her: wipeable, with arm and footrests that went up and down. It enraged her that after working on her feet for nearly forty years her mother was doomed to eternal agony. Róisín lit the fire, bashing a peat briquette to shards against the lip of the hearth to make kindling. It was a trick of Red's; kneeling where she was now, fifteen and acting like the man of a house that wasn't his. Red in need of a home, Róisín desperate for a friend. Was that all it had been?

Are you hungry, Mum?

Her mother twisted her mouth. My appetite came and went. Dolly was here one day too.

Jesus Christ.

It was that Christmas Eve. God, you had me up the walls, storming about London in one of your strops with nowhere to go. Red was gone nearly a year and she didn't know where he was. She thought I might because he'd spent the previous Christmas here. When youse phoned she was standing beside me. She heard his voice, God help her.

God help her my hole. Did she not want to speak to him?

I passed her the receiver but youse were gone. She started panicking that she'd been missing too long, she'd told the husband she was nipping out to buy wrapping paper. I gave her a couple of sheets of mine, cheap tat that tore if you so much as touched it, oh she wasn't a bit impressed, by the way.

And then what?

She said she was happy youse were together, although there wasn't a sign of happy on her. Head to toe in winter white and her dinky new hatchback outside when no one had a decent car, but she was like something going to the gallows walking down the drive.

She withheld morphine from him.

That must have felt great.

There had always been lovely houses along the canal but a showiness had crept in, cobblelock driveways and bay trees in huge glazed pots. Her cottage had been recently renovated when she bought it and she'd spent the last seven years undoing the supposed improvements, hiring a Kango hammer to smash up the fully tarmacked frontage, planting a cottage garden like Guy's mother's. In winter it was a dank, straggly mess, the wages of its wild summer colour. Now there were clusters of green blades, narcissus about to open.

Inside, she threw a couple of logs in the range. She stood at the sink and lit a cigarette. Her kitchen window overlooked the lock. All the hours she and Red had passed there, swinging their legs over the dark water. *He's not what people think*, he had said of his father. Was it fear or stupidity or innocence that had stopped her asking what he meant?

20

1 May 2007

In Micksy's place a different man, slurring in an Eastern European language. Róisín walked past him and hailed a black cab.

Jane Austen House, she said, opening her diary to find the full address.

Churchill Gardens, love, replied the driver, ignoring the satellite navigation system on his dashboard. Hop in.

You have the Knowledge.

Took me four years, he said, smiling at her in the rearview mirror. Fifty thousand miles I clocked up on my old Yamaha.

The exterior of the Bull and Crown was lead grey, its white logo in Arial. Bistro chairs on the pavement outside, a waiter taking an order from a pair of blonde women in sunglasses. They had almost driven past the squat when she picked it out, unremarkable now that it was being properly maintained.

The driver left her in front of Mary's building. It didn't seem possible that a complex of council flats built in the sixties could be appealing, but the balconies were bright with flowers, freshness in the breeze that was coming off the Thames.

Mary's squeals were audible before she opened the door. Hurling herself at Róisín she burst into tears.

Ah, what is it?

We're going to live together, Rosh.

It was like having a puppy. Or maybe a child, not that Róisín would know.

We are, said Róisín, wiping Mary's face with her sleeve. I still can't believe this place. There was a brown leather couch, books in stacks on a G Plan coffee table, a cowhide rug.

God bless Merv the Perv, said Mary fondly, the rent's really low for Zone Two. Lynne's second (ex-)husband was Mary's landlord. She'd assured Róisín that as far as she knew he wasn't a pervert, just a philanderer, and she'd invented the nickname to make Lynne happy when he broke her heart. Right, let's settle you into my bijou maisonette.

They went upstairs, Mary insisting on carrying the suitcase. She had offered Róisín her room with the double bed. Róisín opted for the other, as she was unlikely to have company. Mary left her to unpack. The spare room was small but had everything Róisín would need: a tall chest of drawers and a narrow clothes rail, a chair upholstered in wavy fabric she recognised as knock-off Missoni. There wasn't a desk, but she could write at the kitchen table. She put her clothes away and brought her toiletries to the bathroom. Half a shelf had been cleared for her, a pine one ringed from oil and acetone. It would be nice to live with someone again, especially when it wasn't a husband.

A sweet scorched smell was coming from the kitchen. She followed it down.

You didn't bring much, said Mary. She was blistering red peppers at the hob, her arms bare to the shoulder. There was a new tattoo.

It's summer and you have a washing machine. I might even go shopping. What's that on your arm?

Mary angled her elbow. It's a shamrock.

I should get the Spurs emblem tattooed on mine.

Danny Blanchflower's face, said Mary, tittering.

Pat Jennings's big hands. Have you any wine?

Mary pointed at the clock on the oven. It was twenty to five. You just got here and my six o'clock rule is out the window, she said. There's a bottle chilling, open it.

The fridge was covered with Instamatic photographs of Mary and her mates practically snogging each other.

Are they all bisexual as well? said Róisín, which Mary found hilarious.

Róisín watched her sister pound the pepper flesh into a sauce with nuts and garlic. Sipping wine and chatting as she put hake under the grill and wilted spinach with a spritz of lemon. At her age, Róisín was living off cheap mince, at least until Guy turned up. And did nobody in London eat white carbohydrates any more?

They sat down to eat.

How have you been? said Mary, refilling their glasses. And if you say 'grand' I'm going to choke you.

I'm OK.

You're not, though. I think you should talk to someone.

I'm talking to you, aren't I? It was meant to be funny, but Mary looked like she was going to cry again.

They went outside to the balcony with a second bottle. Solar-powered fairy lights were beginning to glow and the table had Frida Kahlo stickers on it. You could put me out of a job, said Róisín.

Can you believe these were council flats? said Mary, no more able than Róisín to accept a compliment. That once there were people running the country who believed everyone deserves a good life?

She had brought a tin pencil case, a present from Róisín when she was six or seven. Mary had loved fancy stationery, collecting pieces of decorative paper that she traded in school and put in order in the night when she stopped sleeping for fear of bad things happening to her father. She opened the box and took out a tuft of grass and cigarette papers.

This is fucked up, said Róisín, watching her roll. There's a Hello Kitty logo on the lid.

Mary giggled and sparked a lighter under the joint. Inhaling and holding it in her lungs, she passed it to Róisín. Was Red his real name? she said.

Redmond Camelin. It's a French Huguenot surname. He loved that it was different.

Róisín told her about the day she carried the letter, finding him swinging his legs against the wall, tall, dark and handsome. About Tina, the year she'd spent with no one talking to her.

Fucking bints. I'd have been your friend.

Róisín laughed, but it hurt to think about it. I'd made friends as a child, she said, but we moved and I couldn't find my place. Or maybe I didn't know my place. Aside from Sinéad, I'm not in touch with a single girl from school.

But Red Camelin wanted to be your friend, said Mary. In the dusky light she looked like a little girl. Even with a spliff.

She told Mary that Red rarely went home, and then moved out altogether. That he was run out of town at sixteen.

You told me that before, said Mary.

There was something Róisín hadn't shared. She took a swallow of wine. In '84 I came to spend Christmas with Dad and Lynne. My mother nearly had to beat me on to the boat. When I got to the flat in Sydenham, Lynne opened the door. She was holding you. They hadn't told me there was a baby and I left.

Don't blame you. Idiots.

I had an address for Red. He was in the squat in Pimlico by himself. I never wanted to see any of you again, but he made me go back. For you.

Your best pal.

If I'd been a friend to him I'd know if he was alive or dead.

Stop feeling sorry for yourself. Here, for fuck's sake, she said, lobbing wine into their glasses.

Where do I even start looking?

Contact Finbarr. He works in that field, and he was Red's mate too, right?

Barry's reaction when she asked about Red: the cold way he spoke, walking away without saying goodbye.

Jesus. The thought of asking the piss artist formerly known as Barry Doyle for help. Forgive me, the former piss artist formerly known as Barry Doyle.

Harsh, sis. Finbarr was so good to Dad. I wish he hadn't found him, it must have been awful.

He what?

Finbarr went to visit Dad. When there was no answer he got the duty manager to let him in.

Róisín knew the caretaker had opened the door but had no idea anyone else was present. Why did no one tell me this?

Mary had folded her arms. It didn't take a body language expert to see she was annoyed. You didn't ask for details, Rosh, you never did. I thought you couldn't handle it.

It was to her credit that she didn't say, You weren't interested. All the calls Róisín had taken from Mary and Lynne and her own mother, treating them as if they were prattling about something trivial. As if her father wasn't important.

I let you down, said Róisín.

Fuck off, said Mary sweetly. It's cold. Let's go inside.

Róisín washed up, beginning with the glasses. Mary dried them and put them away, then stood looking at Róisín for a moment.

What? said Róisín.

You're here because of Dad and you don't even know it.

In the morning, Róisín waited until Mary had left before going downstairs. It was only seven thirty. She'd put herself to sleep spelling YOU LET THEM ALL DOWN, dozing off before she'd paired the letters. She opened the fridge. There was sparkling water she knew Mary had bought for her. The thoughtfulness made her feel monstrous.

Drinking from the bottle, she brought her laptop to the couch and opened her inbox. The interiors editor to whom she had submitted a *what's hot in chairs* list wanted her to remove her favourite – Franz West's 'Onkel-Stuhl' – because it was 'a bit mad'. Too hungover to argue, Róisín replied that she would send a new draft soon. An advertising feature on a garden centre was overdue but she couldn't face doing that either. She made herself tea and toast, texting an apology to Mary for being atrocious. The reply came immediately: *Fuck off. Contact Finbarr. Xxx*

Barry Doyle shared his name with a personal trainer in Firhouse, a teenage rugby player in Limerick and a realtor in Portland, Oregon who swore Tipp would always be home. He didn't seem to do any social networking. A search for Finbarr Doyle found him on his organisation's website. His image was an 'ugly' as they called them in PR: smiling uncomfortably in harsh lighting. Educated at Mile End University and City University he'd become director of the service in 2002, having begun as a support worker in 1996. On the home page there was a collage of photographs including one of him shaking the hand of a minor royal, which must have nearly killed him. Róisín began to compose an email but writing to Barry was hard. Typing and deleting over and over, after a couple of hours she went back to her original message. She didn't know until last night that he'd found her father's body. She was sorry and grateful and embarrassed. She had come to London to search for Red and hoped Barry might agree to meet her. The tone still wasn't right, but he probably wouldn't reply anyway. Adding her mobile number, she pressed send.

21

4 May 2007

Over the next couple of days she redrafted the chairs article, including one upholstered in a luxe fabric her editor would like, resenting putting her name to something that resembled a hotel furniture brochure. For the garden centre she wrote a feature on crocosmia and Japanese anemones because it was too late to promote summer colour. She'd told herself she'd start looking for Red once her work was done but she had no idea where to begin. There was no reply from Barry. Mary kept apologising for saying he'd know what to do, promising to ask the manager of her soup run to put feelers out. Guy must have recruited her, he'd been doing voluntary work for years. Waking in the morning determined to do better, be better, full of a 'this is the first day of the rest of your life' enthusiasm that made Róisín homicidal.

Out of excuses, she went on the internet. Several organisations in Britain searched for missing persons. For hours she clicked on mission statements and pleas for donations. And profiles. Joseph from Hackney with the broad smile who looked younger than his forty-six years. An out-of-focus Duncan from Oldham who carried his pain in his bent neck. She read trends and statistics. The most common reasons for adults to disappear were mental health problems, homelessness and relationship breakdown. Most of those who disappeared were children. Looked-after children were more likely to go missing (one in five compared with one in a hundred) than children who were not looked-after. The term confused her and more searching revealed it referred to children in the care of a local authority, fostered or institutionalised presumably. There was an argument for concluding some of them were not being looked after very well. Most people turned up; still there were thousands of missing people in the UK.

A man from north Antrim answered the Salvation Army line. He told her that because of the high volume of enquiries it was only possible to trace blood relatives. She thanked him and, as she prepared to hang up, he said, Sorry, are you still there?

She was indeed, she told him.

I'm sure you've done this already, but you should contact the General Register Office.

It was a moment before she understood what he meant.

A woman called Debbie with a lilting Scouse accent explained how to go about applying for a death certificate. Although the records were not yet available digitally, an application could be made online or by post or telephone and the more information she could provide the better. All Róisín had was his name and date of birth. Debbie put her through to Bev who put her on hold. A few minutes later Bev came back to say there was no death certificate for a Redmond Camelin. It's strange, she said, there isn't a single Redmond Camelin on record. Often uncommon names are handed down through generations, but his is unique.

He'd love that, said Róisín. A polite silence at the other end. Maybe she should have said: would have loved.

She changed into her trainers, desperate to walk Joseph and Duncan and the not-looked-after children out of her head. Taking her phone from her bag, she saw there were new messages. One from Sinéad: *Your mother really likes crumpets.* One from Mary, she wouldn't be back until after nine. One from a London number.

* * *

Barry watched her come in. He'd probably seen her dallying outside, hoisting her stretch skinny jeans up, a cigarette in her mouth.

Howaya, he said, standing. He had on a long-sleeved sporty top, the collar standing up like Eric Cantona.

She was nervous. As she pulled out her chair her bag swung against a wine glass on the table. He caught it and stayed on his feet until she was settled.

Whole burnished hams hanging above the counter, Moorish tiles behind it. Sturdy wooden chairs her editor would have hated. This is great, she said.

A woman he worked with recommended it, he wasn't in the West End often, he told her. A waitress carried over a blackboard and propped it against the next table. They served little plates and she recommended they order three per person. Barry asked for a large bottle of sparkling water. They were both looking at Róisín.

Water's fine.

Have a drink if you want one. I won't fall off the wagon and do a Henry Sellers on it.

There was too much relief in her laugh. She asked for a fino sherry.

Did you have far to come? he said, reading the board.

Pimlico.

Pimlico? he repeated, looking at her now.

Mary lives in Churchill Gardens.

Right. Which of these would you not like?

I don't love kidneys and the prawns will be drowning in oil.

When the waitress brought their drinks, he ordered one of every dish but those Róisín didn't want. It was refreshingly uncomplicated.

How long are you here for? he said, drawing his shoulders slowly back and wincing. Róisín wondered what kind of 'training' left him sore in restaurants and ordering nine tapas.

Three months, she told him. She could work anywhere, all she needed was a laptop, and Mary had a spare room until August.

What about your lock-keeper's cottage?

She looked for a sign that he was making fun of her, but he just seemed interested.

I rented it out for three months to a writer from here.

Don't check your messages. She's probably been put through the window of Yankee Chicken.

He hadn't been funny when they were young. Or confident, she thought, as he filled her water glass with a flourish that would have required four or five pints in the old days.

The food was coming, a couple of plates at a time. For a few minutes they ate without speaking. We're like the men at my father's funeral, she said.

Yup. Getting the feed, he said, tipping a lamb brochette on to her plate.

She should have taken off her blazer, it was making her feel constricted. Swigging the dregs of her sherry, she asked the waitress for a glass of wine.

I'm so sorry you found my dad, Barry. Finbarr. But I'm glad too, she said. Christ, I'm shit at this.

I get it. Thank God he wasn't there long, that a friend found him.

A friend. Her father's unmade bed, weevils writhing in Quaker Oats. All the years she'd shunned him.

Barry put down his fork and leaned across the table. Ah, Róisín.

Jesus. I don't cry.

Not strictly true, he said, passing her a napkin. It's grief, it does its own thing.

It's a pain in the fucking arse.

Still at the anger stage?

Fucking raging since 1967.

He laughed, heartily this time, wrinkles appearing that she hadn't noticed before.

My father's funeral brought back a lot of stuff. Being in London too.

He speared the last of the patatas bravas and popped them in his mouth, chewing slowly. Stuff like Red, he said after what felt like an hour.

She told him there was no death certificate and that the agencies she contacted only dealt with blood relatives. His head was moving, almost imperceptibly, but she didn't know if he was saying yes or no. If it's hard to talk about forget I asked, she said.

I was in AA for years, three meetings a day sometimes. It's all fucking talking.

Did it help?

For a while, until I realised I was addicted to the meetings. Now I'm addicted to exercise. There's always going be something.

Not even with Sinéad, who knew everything – almost everything – about her, would Róisín be so candid. She was racked by a dreadful sense of responsibility; it would be easy to destroy him.

The waitress cleared their dishes. Barry asked for a crema catalana and a decaf cortado. Herself could do with another glass of wine, he said.

Am I presenting as a lush?

Only a small bit.

She laughed.

So you want to know about the last time I saw Red, he said. He was stretching backwards, pulling his shoulders down. She made a mental note to text Sinéad confirming that he was indeed buff as fuck.

Red and Barry had stayed in Pimlico for a couple of years after Róisín moved out. Greg went back to Arkansas, leaving

Wilbur, and a couple of others moved in, scum punks Red knew from dealing. One evening four men smashed in and beat them out of the place, zapping them down the stairs and on to the street with a cattle prod. They weren't hoods, more like soldiers. Octavia had been hanging about for days at a time and it was likely her father was behind it. They moved into a squat in Oval, a party house. Barry didn't turn up on the building site once too often and he was sacked.

In fairness, I'd had plenty of chances, he said, passing Róisín a spoon and putting the dessert between them. But without a job I couldn't keep it together.

Taking in a breath, she physically braced herself for the details, but he didn't elaborate. Besides, she'd seen him in the Mean Fiddler in November 1988, drinking from a naggin he kept up his sleeve, his face ravaged by whatever else he was doing to himself.

It was just drink with you, though.

Yeah. Until I became a heroin addict. He ate a mouthful of custard, licking the spoon. I was doing the odd drop for Red but I was so fucked I didn't know one day from the next and he was no better. The lads he worked for came looking for their money. They gave me this, he said, lifting aside the collar of his shirt. There was a scar running from below his ear to his throat, the sort she'd read football hooligans gave each other with two Stanley knives, purplish and gouged-looking twenty years later.

Jesus Christ. What did they do to Red?

He got out the back. I never saw him again.

He saw her disgust, confusion. He was a junkie, Róisín. They're not known for valour and honour.

At that time, Róisín was in Bride Street with Guy. Doing her little PR campaigns, cooking out of unillustrated paperbacks borrowed from his mother.

Barry insisted on paying, saying it was the least he could do after dumping all that on her.

Outside, she lit a cigarette. Barry was leaning against the exterior wall, left knee bent and his foot flat on the brickwork. He asked her for a drag, closing his eyes as he sucked.

It's weird the things you miss. I used to love hanging about like this, acting the corner boy, but I could have done without the rest of it. He dragged again, and passed it back to her. I'll help you look for Red, Róisín. But if you find him, you're on your own.

22

9 May 2007

He'd told her to wait by a bronze figure of a milkmaid. Somewhere in *Mrs Dalloway* Peter Walsh recalled *an absurd statue* in Regent's Park, surely this one. 'Matilda' was atop a grotto, right hand shielding her eyes, a bucket in her left. Róisín put the bag from Pret A Manger under her arm, aware she was scowling.

Barry was crossing the street, looking like he was trying to keep a straight face. Poor Matilda, I'd say you've the shite scared out of her, he said, taking the bag.

I was starting to feel her ridiculousness is a reflection on me. You should have given me an address.

I like getting out of the office at lunchtime. Most days I run here.

Do you want a fucking medal?

He burst out laughing.

His building was just a couple of streets away, a two-storey structure from the eighties with vertical blinds. He introduced her to a woman at reception. Her name was Eileen. She told Róisín her parents had come over in the fifties and she'd grown up in Cricklewood.

Eileen was a champion Irish dancer, said Barry. Róisín didn't know whether he meant she'd been very good or won actual prizes.

They went upstairs to his office. It had been painted in cheap brilliant white with too much blue pigment. A metal bookcase was full of policy documents and folders, leaflets printed with the National Lottery thumb in an open box on the floor. The only decoration was a Swiss cheese plant on a muddy dinner plate. She touched a leaf and it drifted to the carpet.

He laid out the food she'd brought on his desk. Thanks for this, it's great, he said, clearing away the few personal items, a pair of glasses and eye drops. A homemade postcard was propped against the monitor. It read:

sometimes you climb out of bed in the morning and you think,
I'm not going to make it, but you laugh inside
remembering all the times you've felt that way.

Is that an AA thing? she asked.

Charles Bukowski.

Between mouthfuls of salad he asked what she was writing, how did she pass the time? After each question he looked up at the last possible moment. She used to think him sleekit, the way he struggled to make eye contact. Now she could see the courage in it; he was shy. She wished she had more to tell him. During the day she walked and pitched articles to editors. In the evenings she cooked for Mary. All she'd done about looking for Red was read heart-scalding accounts of homelessness on the internet.

He went off to get them tea, leaving a leaflet with her that gave a history of the centre. She tried to take the information in but was distracted by the card. She turned it around. In French cursive, it was addressed to Finbarr Doyle at a flat in Camden. No message, just *Cx*, like a pretty algebra problem. Replacing it, she speed-read the brochure, hoping he wouldn't quiz her on it, looking up guiltily when he came back.

You still make me feel like I'm missing something, he said, sitting in front of his PC. He'd remembered she liked her tea strong with little milk.

She pulled her chair next to his. After a single sip, he put his mug down abruptly and stretched like he had in the tapas bar. Róisín could see where the discomfort was; knew she could loosen it by massaging his shoulders.

He began typing a description of Red that he would circulate to affiliate organisations. *Redmond Camelin. Irish. 6 ft 1 in. 40. Black-haired, possibly greying. Last seen in Vauxhall area of south London in 1990. Known to his friends as Red.*

Want to add anything? he said.

There were lots of things. Tidy, until he wasn't. Generous. Funny. Clever. Private. Elusive. Loyal, until he ran out on Barry. Precise in his tastes. Obsessed with the Huguenots and then the Georgians.

Wears a handknit black and red mohair jumper, she said.

Yeah, Barry said, smiling. Hair standing on end, hands in his back pockets.

Neither of them had a photograph. The most recent one in Dolly's possession had been taken when he was fourteen. After Róisín went to visit her a fantasy had begun to form. Sitting on the bonnet of her car alongside the Camelins' house. Red, grey at the temples, a little shook, glancing at her from the step of his family home, pleading for reassurance, Róisín nodding in encouragement as he pressed the bell. Dolly flinging the door wide and embracing him, her hair grown back, miraculously cured. Is it totally naïve to believe I'll find him, Barry?

He pressed save and swivelled to face her. Do you think you're going to find him?

Well, yeah, there's no death certificate.

He was staring at her as if she was a crazy person who'd come in off the street.

What? You said you'd help me.

I said I'd help you look, Róisín, there's a difference. He was an intravenous heroin user. It's a brutal life, it's unlikely he survived it.

You did.

He shook his head.

What?

I didn't share needles. It was the eighties, Hep C and HIV were rampant.

I'm so stupid.

You're better off not knowing anything about that world, it's hell. Every day I thank God I had a saviour.

Who?

Tina.

Róisín almost spat out her tea.

Jesus, your face, he said. She turned up a couple of days after Red left and read me the riot act, saying she'd tell Daddy. Hilarious looking back on it, but she got me in for a spin-dry.

He let her smoke out his window. Behind her, he was listing wet houses and dry houses and needle exchanges and shelters, all the places someone like Red – if he was alive – might be. It was too much, what she was asking of him.

Thanks, Barry. Shit, I can't remember to call you Finbarr.

He kept typing for a few seconds then swivelled his chair to face her again. You can call me whatever you like, he said.

They sent the email to over twenty accounts. Barry said it was a good start, there were places in Greater London they could try later, dozens more in the rest of the country. It hadn't entered Róisín's head that Red might not be in London, but she kept that to herself.

He brought her around the building. There were two meeting rooms, three consulting rooms, a function room with a stage and a piano, a little kitchen. Throughout, posters bearing the name of each county were hanging on the walls.

Kildare's getting reframed, he said, pausing.

I'm from Down.

You're a fucking handful, he said with the sideways look. She swallowed and her lips made a smacking sound. He pushed the door open and they stepped into a courtyard. For a moment they hesitated, desire still on them, before Barry snapped himself out of it. A couple of elderly men were sitting on a bench, smoking. At the far end, Muiris, his poor hip cocked, was leaning on a spade. Beside him was the man who'd sung 'Carrickfergus' after her father's funeral, still in his woolly hat. His name was Timmy. There were six hazel potagers. One was full of wildflowers, the sort you bought in a pouch of mixed seeds: poppies and camomile and borage. Another was a jumble of artichokes, nasturtiums and bright annuals, a diminutive version of her garden at home. Two contained rows of vegetables such as scallions, beetroot and courgettes. Muiris was tending the furthest pair, which were twice the height of the others with neat rows of potato plants. He told her the beds were Conor's idea, he'd seen something like them in the paper.

She plucked out a tiny spurge plant. My garden's full of these, she said.

When the plants are happy, the weeds are too, said Muiris.

She put her fingers in the soil to follow a bindweed stalk. It was tangled around the base of a cosmos plant. Can I? she said.

G'wan ahead, said Muiris.

She lifted the plant from the soil and shook it, combing the roots with her fingers to remove the weed. Placing it back in the hole, she brushed the muck from her hands.

Maith an cailín, said Muiris.

Maith an cailín. Good girl.

It's the battle of my life, she said.

Barry was against the wall in his corner-boy stance, watching. He winked at her like an old farmer, with a slight flick of his head.

She found another strand and did the same, and another. Barry had to send some emails and left her there. The men teased each other gently sometimes. They said there were different weeds at home. Muiris remembered one that the women used to dye wool red in Connemara – Barry had said he'd been in Letterfrack, the worst of the industrial schools. Mostly they worked without speaking, Muiris scooping compost from a sack and patting it around the base of the potato plants, Timmy watering. It took her so far away from herself she didn't notice when Barry rejoined them.

You look like you've been in the fields, he said, examining her hands.

She has the touch, said Muiris, like Conor.

God, you're using your degree better than I am, she said when they were indoors.

They give me more than I give them. You should come back.

I will, I love Muiris. And those potagers. Who knew my father could see something through.

He opened his mouth to speak, then seemed to think better of it.

What?

Your father got the idea from an article you wrote. He showed me your name on the page.

Lynne came striding off the 18:05 from Bromley South in a white trouser suit with boot-cut legs and wedge heels. A couple of railway workers were watching, one of whom let out a whistle. Mary confronted wolfish men on construction sites but her mother was clearly enjoying the attention. Jesus Christ, said Róisín. You're like Sharon Stone in that slow-motion scene in *Casino*.

Gotta take it where you can get it, said Lynne, leaving a sticky kiss on Róisín's cheek that she rubbed away with her thumb. Are you all right, darling?

Just tired.

Exhausted from bawling all the way home from Camden, she thought.

Outside, they got in a black cab. The driver kept adjusting his mirror, checking Lynne out too.

At home, Lynne lived on calorie-counted ready meals and pillow packs of washed rocket. For nights out she went big, in this case a fancy Italian place in the style of a grand café on Sloane Square that was known for its theatrical service.

My treat, she said as they were seated, asking the waiter for two Bellinis. She took off her jacket. A Tiffany necklace, silver with a heart, around her neck. She'd been to her timeshare in the Canaries twice since the funeral and her tan was so deep that white spots had appeared on her chest and arms. Still, she looked better than she had at thirty. The worry that was on her then, skint in the flat in Sydenham, waiting for Conor to come back from the pub.

The drinks arrived and they ordered a tricolore salad and Parma ham with melon and a main course of seafood pasta they planned to share.

Lynne clinked her glass against Róisín's. Mary said Finbarr's helping you look for Red, she said. I'm sure he has some leads, he's been living in London all this time.

He hasn't seen Red since 1990.

Lynne was looking at her expectantly. It wasn't that she was shockable but it was Barry's story. Barry who worked from morning to night to stay clean.

A rumpus from the next table, a waiter wringing his hands, pretending to cry. Róisín began to panic he would do it to her, she wouldn't know where to look, and when the starters came she was afraid to lift her head.

Róisín told Lynne about the email they'd composed and sent around.

Poor lost boy. You were so mad about him and he about you, but I never saw anything sexual in him.

What do you mean?

Men check women out but he was oblivious. You were so lovely and there for the taking, but I thought he wasn't made that way.

I know I'm irresistible, but just because he didn't want me doesn't mean he was asexual.

Was he with other girls?

Róisín shook her head, the image of Octavia in his arms forming. I don't know, Lynne.

So why, darling? Why are you so hell-bent on finding him? You can't save people, we both learned that much from dealing with your father.

You didn't abandon Dad altogether.

I had Mary, I couldn't. Many's a time I wished I could, mind. Look, things were hard for you.

Róisín sometimes wondered if she'd hurt herself more by staying away. It had suited her to believe her father didn't care about her and the thought of him reading an article she'd written was tormenting her. How was he, Lynne? At the end?

Oh my God, you're crying. He was doing well. It had been awful for a while. Mouldy food, bluebottles hatching like there was no tomorrow and his clothes so worn and grimy they were fit for the bin. Merv didn't like me going round there, he was ever so jealous, so Mary bore the brunt of it. She asked for a meeting with the housing trust and they contacted the centre.

They had finished their Bellinis. As Lynne ordered a bottle of white wine, her phone throbbed. She read a message, a smile playing on her lips; Mary said she'd been seeing Merv the Perv again.

He'll fuck you about, said Róisín.

I'm a slave to love, Rosh.

When they stopped laughing, Lynne told her that Finbarr had visited Conor and brought him to the centre to meet people. He'd loved the nights of music and talking, the gardening.

There were hints that he wanted to get sober, but by that stage his liver was failing, he was yellow. Besides, said Lynne, Finbarr reckoned it was more than alcohol addiction. He thought your dad carried a deep sadness.

When your daddy wasn't well, her mother used to say. She hadn't been able to accept Róisín's depression, suggesting she'd caused it herself. All those black clothes, all the sad books, she'd rail. Róisín didn't know what it was, but got her GP to prescribe her Prozac as it was coming off the conveyor belt. He'd asked if there was depression in the family and Róisín had said no, just alcoholism. Nature or nurture? She didn't know.

Have you thought of talking to someone? You never mention the baby, Rosh.

When she moved home to Ireland Róisín visited a therapist, a humourless German woman with French plaits. She said Róisín had low self-esteem, hated herself so much she couldn't see the good in anyone else, and asked her why she wasn't married. I was once, which is probably once more than you, Fräulein, replied Róisín. She never went back.

I don't talk about that, Lynne.

All right, darling. I'm sorry. We love you, that's all.

The mains arrived and Róisín began to divide the shellfish.

You're such an older sister, said Lynne. Sharing fairly.

You're just being nice.

I'm not. I wish you could see that.

Róisín ate without relish, necking the Pinot Grigio she normally loathed.

That time you came to me in a state, said Lynne. Was it Finbarr?

Good Jesus, no one gets away with anything round you.

Did you like him?

No.

Do you like him now?

No.

Lynne clapped her hands. You little liar!

She ordered a pudding she called "tisamiru", winking at Róisín, the mispronunciation a way to flirt with the waiter. How could her father not have fallen for her?

23

19 May 2007

She knew the shape of him from a couple of hundred yards, glad, as he got closer, he wasn't in cycling shorts. He straightened up and let his breathing settle. Are you waiting long? he said, I left in plenty of time.

I'm pathologically punctual.

Yeah, you were an early riser too, he said as he removed his helmet, reminding them both he'd been briefly familiar with her morning habits. He swung his leg over the crossbar and stood holding the handlebar, head slightly tilted. She thought he was going to kiss her, but he bent to rip off his bicycle clips.

Did you run this morning too?

Five miles. I'm addicted, I told you.

Across the river, the sun was striking Battersea Power Station. A pair of Irish developers had bought it the previous year for £400 million.

Fucking notions. Not so long ago they'd have been doing the digging, said Barry.

When they reached Mary's place he paused at the plaque on the wall. *Ah lads, there's no one like Jane!* he said, as if he was repeating it.

Who said that?

Thomas MacDonagh. In his final class in UCD before he gave up his life for old Ireland.

She'd tossed interiors magazines around the coffee table so he wouldn't think she'd tidied for his visit. Mary came running downstairs and threw herself on him. Róisín's chaste greeting at the riverbank seemed loaded in comparison. It was surprising to watch them. She had presumed they'd exchanged a couple of phone calls, but they were easy with each other.

Róisín put the kettle on and took a bottle of sparkling water from the fridge, pouring Barry a glass.

Do you have some at room temperature? he asked.

Are you taking the piss?

Seriously, you wouldn't pour freezing water on a plant, would you?

I've seen your plant, it's fucking parched! Pulling a bottle from the cupboard, she slapped it into his hand. Mary, do you have a thermometer?

They stood eyeing each other, then Mary giggled and they all fell about the place laughing.

Róisín made tea and they sat at the table to drink it. Barry had received an email from a needle exchange, he'd sent it on to Róisín. She opened her laptop. A member of staff who'd been there since the eighties remembered someone who fitted Red's description. He was with a girl.

Octavia, said Róisín.

Who the fuck is she? said Mary.

Octavia Hammond. She was our neighbour in Pimlico.

A squatter?

Barry was picking at a nail. Explaining Octavia would entail disclosing his heroin use. Róisín wanted to spare him her sister's questions but Mary had taken the laptop and was typing.

Jesus Christ, she said. Look at this.

Listings in *Debrett's* and *Burke's Peerage*, tracing Octavia's aristocratic lineage back centuries. She didn't seem to have married or borne children. There was a mention of an antique shop in Bath called Industry and Idleness that specialised in Georgian prints, furniture and ephemera.

You have to go there, said Mary.

Barry looked up at the ceiling as if he was begging for strength.

I'll check it out later, said Róisín.

Bloody dozens of mentions of her father. Mary's eyes were moving down the screen. She stopped abruptly. This is weird.

What? said Róisín.

There was a link to a WordPress article about a House of Commons paedophile ring, but when I clicked it had been removed.

Róisín thought for a moment she might vomit. Barry shook his head: *Say nothing*, he was telling her.

Mary pushed the laptop at Róisín and stood up. Better get ready, she said, and went upstairs.

Barry tugged Róisín's sleeve. Are you OK?

I don't know. You?

I don't know either. You couldn't make this shit up.

Sorry if Mary made you uncomfortable. She gets very engrossed in things.

She's full of life.

Mary thundered back down with an overnight bag and hugged them both, briefly bringing their heads together. Don't do anything I wouldn't do, she said as she left.

Jesus, muttered Róisín.

That was some exit, where's she off to?

Babysitting my ex-husband's children.

How does that feel?

Really weird, thank you for asking. She loves him, though.

They went on to the balcony so Róisín could smoke. Barry had brought sunscreen and was applying it to his face. She was about to tease him for being vain when he told her he'd had a melanoma removed from his cheek. Occupational hazard of being a paddy on the buildings, he said.

Barry at eighteen, ashen from dust, coming in the door with a bag of cans. You worked so hard, she said, and the rest of us scratching our arses.

You made a life here.

Yeah, and then I trashed it.

When did you go home?

Two thousand. New millennium, new me. Shame I had to bring myself along.

I need to teach you some affirmations. He looked over the railing. It's great here. Can you believe the way we lived, and us only kids?

He sat down again, moving his chair to avoid the sun but it was beating down on them. They went back inside, sitting on the couch.

There was something off about Octavia, he said. Hosting dinner parties for her father as if she was the wife, no mention of a mother. Red's da was a fucking weirdo as well.

If she'd been with anyone else, Róisín would have opened a bottle of wine. Instead she sat sipping tepid mineral water, wanting to cover her ears. For Red's eleventh birthday, Robert Camelin took him to the beach with some of his friends. None of the boys wanted to get in the water but Robert wheedled them in, rolling up his trousers and encouraging them to splash about with each other. Red was standing apart from them, telling his father they wanted to get out. He ignored him, snapping with his camera. Like it wasn't unheard of for photographs to be taken at a birthday party, said Barry, but in wet togs?

She had known there was something dreadful in Red's family but her imagination had never taken her beyond picturing violence, which in itself was so disturbing she tamped the thought down every time it tried to surface. I couldn't get my head around anything more sinister than the da giving out slaps, she said.

All das gave out slaps, said Barry, but I know what you mean. That story was out there, we used to giggle about his da being a 'kiddie fiddler' but when Red stopped going home it was like we couldn't make the connection.

Octavia is like me, said Róisín. He told me that. The expression on Red's face in the drawing room that night came to her again. She'd been harried for years by the thought that he'd chosen Octavia. He had, for reasons Róisín was incapable of understanding.

Barry had a theory. He'd gone to a Hogarth exhibition in the Tate a few months ago. It made him think of Red and Octavia lounging about the place like the last of the Georgians, or maybe they'd been on his mind before he went there. Red's Tom Rakewell obsession was like how adults talked about the 27 Club after Kurt Cobain's suicide, worrying that teenagers were mythologising rock stars who died young. *A Rake's Progress* was Red's version of that. He couldn't bear to be ordinary; if he was going to destroy himself he was going to do it like a dandy.

She'd made a Spanish tortilla in case he was still there at lunchtime. They ate it on the couch. Neither of them mentioned Red or Octavia, she sensed he was as wrung out by it as she was. They talked about London, its changing skyline. In Southwark, she told him, a pair of office blocks were draped in white, ready for demolition. She'd read that Renzo Piano had designed a slinky glass-and-steel iceberg to stand in their place.

They'll have to blow them up first, he said. Do you love all that stuff?

Yeah, but I'm at the low end: interiors. Actually just writing about interiors, which is the dregs.

How do you get work?

I send pitches and hope someone bites. Last week it was a feature on the Derek Hill house in Glenveagh. Nine alternatives to black granite worktops which I sent to an English magazine because Irish people love cooking in glittery darkness. And something on the death of brown and cream because I'm hoping to kill it off.

What's wrong with brown and cream?

He got up to leave at five, saying he had to go to a dinner. Taking a book from the pannier on his bike, he handed it to her.

Thank you.

You're welcome.

They were both grinning idiotically. Mary's a tough act to follow with the meeting and greeting, she said.

That's all right.

When he was gone, she opened a bottle, filling a wine glass almost to the brim. Stretching out on the couch, she called her mother. In spite of her back problems, Una answered almost immediately. It made Róisín feel like a source of worry.

Are you ringing from one of those bloody mobiles? said her mother. It'll cost one or both of us a fortune.

Me, you're on a landline.

Aye. Well.

Sinéad had been in a few times, bringing her messages. Her youngest is always with her, Síofra, she said. Gorgeous wee thing, big mop of curls like her mummy's and full of personality. How are you getting on there?

Róisín told her about the reply Barry had received from the man who remembered Red, without adding it was a needle exchange.

That nice fella was at the funeral?

Yes.

Oooh.

Stop. Have you heard from Dolly?

She's not able for the chemo, her legs are burning. God love her, not a minute's luck since that bastard died.

Róisín hesitated, careful to phrase the next question without upsetting her mother, who had been kind to Red. Do you ever wonder if there was more than violence going on in the Camelins' house, Mum?

Every single day.

Róisín had a sudden memory of overhearing her father speaking to Red on the fire escape in Sydenham.

Daddy told Red he knew his da from the pub, but then he got weird and wouldn't say any more.

Her mother paused. Jesus. The wee lounge boy.

A young lad had been employed on Saturday nights to collect glasses and take orders at the tables. His mother was Pauline, the pub cleaner. Róisín remembered her, she was friendly and pretty, even though the town had given her a vile nickname – Slap the Rasher – and made jokes about how many men had fathered her children. One day she came in shouting that Robert Camelin had been at Kyle and she was going to the Guards, but then it wasn't mentioned again.

That's atrocious!

Her mother told Róisín to wise up, saying the likes of Pauline would be demolished by a half-decent solicitor and she probably didn't want to put the child through a load of police interviews. Conor suspected Robert Camelin had paid her off.

How old was Kyle?

Thirteen or so. My God, when I think of it. The town swarming with priests and teachers and police, the whole bloody lot of them turning a blind eye. I didn't do enough and neither did Enda. We didn't ask the right questions. Nobody did.

The book Barry left was called *I Could Read the Sky*. An elderly Irish emigrant was recalling his life from his bed in a London boarding house. There were stark, beautiful photographs. Some had been taken in England, but most were from Ireland, images of what emigrants had left behind. She loved the opening line.

This room is dark, as dark as it ever gets – the hour before dawn in winter.

Róisín forgot about her glass of wine and kept reading. Early on, the man made a list of the skills he'd brought to London.

What I could do.

I could mend nets. Thatch a roof. Build stairs, it began.

When she reached his other list she texted Barry.

This book. I'm fkn destroyed.

I know... he replied. *It's all of them... All of us...*

What I couldn't do.

Eat a meal lacking potatoes. Trust banks. Wear a watch. Ask a woman to go for a walk. Work with drains or with objects smaller than a nail. Drive a motor car. Eat tomatoes. Remember the routes of buses. Wear a collar in comfort. Win at cards. Acknowledge the Queen. Abide loud voices. Perform the manners of greeting and leaving. Save money. Take pleasure in work carried out in a factory. Drink coffee. Look into a wound. Follow cricket. Understand the speech of a man from west Kerry. Wear boots or shoes made from rubber. Best P.J. in an argument. Speak with men wearing collars. Stay afloat in water. Understand their jokes. Face the dentist. Kill a Sunday. Stop remembering.

24

24 May 2007

She had lined up enough work to keep her going for a couple of months. Scraps of wallpaper and fabric, leaflets and flyers, photographs that already looked great on her laptop. As she walked around ideas came to her scattergun and sometimes she felt better about her work than she had for years. She had made pitches not just to pretty glossy magazines, but to serious specialist ones in which she'd have scope to examine social history and provenance. She felt her heart flutter at the sight of a cane chair in the window of an antique shop in Notting Hill, or a piece of sculpture in the East End, carried away with the possibilities it opened, but the feeling would soon be replaced by a sense of almost existential pointlessness. The only salve was the garden.

She worked hard in the mornings so she could go to the centre in the afternoons. Her weeding had been so ruthless there was little for her to do but she hung around all the same. Occasionally she'd bring the men something she'd baked, a tea brack or currant soda they spread with Kerrygold and washed down with tea. Barry joined them sometimes, joking that it was like lunchtime on the buildings, but usually he was too busy.

On her eighth or ninth visit, she brought curly kale seeds that she'd ordered on the internet. Muiris was delighted, it was something they could grow in the winter when it was too cold and damp for anything else. Like Róisín's mother he rarely sat, saying it was easier to stay on his feet. Róisín had presumed his terrible gait was the result of an accident on a site but Timmy told her he'd left Letterfrack that way after years of beatings, it was just worse now because arthritis had set into the old fractures. At one point she looked up and saw that Barry was against the wall in his corner-boy pose, watching. She waved but he didn't come near her, just replied with a slow flick of his head. The others were by the potato potagers, speaking in low voices. Maybe she was getting in the way.

When she was leaving, Muiris came swinging towards her, a paper bag in his hand. The others stood around him, smiling shyly.

A few Golden Wonders for you. The ones your father set.

His body stiffened as she hugged him, but when she released him his eyes were shining.

Barry was at his desk, the end of a biro in his mouth. He glanced at her over the rim of his glasses and, realising she was crying, came to where she was standing in the middle of the room. She held open the bag.

My father planted these.

Muiris was scheming for days. All the intrigue.

I want to cook them this evening. Will you eat with me?

They bought lamb chops and French beans, butter and a carton of full-fat milk. Barry told her to choose wine, but she was sick of drinking, opening a bottle while she waited for Mary and guzzling most of it herself because her sister just wanted to go to bed. As they passed Camden Town Tube station, she stopped. I pulled a whitey against that pillar, she said, pointing. Fucking state of me.

I remember you that night. You were in one of those granny dresses with a full skirt you used to wear. Your hair in a clip.

She walked on, suddenly shy of him.

He lived on a Victorian terrace of sand-coloured brick, plasterwork and window ledges in cream. Brass plates that read *CBA* were screwed to the door in descending order. His was flat C, on the upper floor. His bike was in the hallway, helmet hanging from the handlebars. A door at the top of the stairs opened into a bright kitchen-living room with a bay window. It was decorated in the browns and creams she wanted to send out of fashion, the only vivid colour from a spongeware bowl piled high with fruit. An expensive blender sat on the counter beside it.

He took off his zip-up top. Underneath he had on a T-shirt that appeared padded, like the jerseys rugby players wore now, but it wasn't. It was from his triathlon club. I can do them because you taught me to swim, he said.

You didn't need much help. Just some technique.

There were four chairs around a white table. Róisín had four too, and a couple of spares in the bedrooms, but rarely needed them all.

He went to a fake-oak shelving unit full of books and CDs and put on music.

A Tribe Called Quest, she said. I haven't heard this for so long.

I missed nearly a decade.

They talked as they prepared the food. She told him she'd rushed in several proposals and now deadlines were looming. She thought she could work anywhere but she missed the routine she had at home.

What's that?

I wake at six, throw a log in the range. Make tea, go back to bed and read for a couple of hours. In the summer I walk by the canal before anyone is up, then I write till two and have lunch with my mother.

He told her about his work. A man in a flat so full of newspapers and rubbish all you could see was a pair of blue eyes. Can you help me? he said when they found him. It was mostly men;

the women coped better, perhaps because nursing and caring was a sisterhood.

The potatoes were floury and she wasn't sure how to cook them. Barry knew, pouring all but an inch of water off after the pot came to the boil, leaving them to steam, covered, on the lowest setting.

When they sat down to eat she felt overwhelmed.

They were grown to be eaten, said Barry. Enjoy them.

Wrapping his hand in a tea towel he picked up a potato, peeling away the skin with his dinner knife. He dropped it on her plate, repeating until they had three each. Muiris says Golden Wonders are as close to the old lumper potatoes we ate before the famine as you'll get these days, he said.

She wondered if Muiris had told her father that as they set the sprouting tubers. Her father with his uneasy sense of identity.

Did my daddy tell you much about himself?

Not really. He had two daughters. He supported Spurs and Glasgow Celtic. Down and Belfast Celtic when he was a young fella.

When I was a child he joined the RUC.

She waited for the recoil, the questions, but he didn't say anything. It encouraged her to go on, to tell him about her father's breakdown after being stationed in south Armagh. The three of them leaving the north. Conor leaving Róisín and her mother in the south.

The lives people have, he said.

Your own's been fairly eventful.

Yeah. Quiet now, thank God.

She didn't know anyone who still said 'thank God'. They sent good vibes into the universe, or thanked fuck. It was lovely, she thought.

A fine meal, he said, when they were finished, bualadh bos to us.

Bualadh bos. The Irish for round of applause. It literally meant banging of the hands. Róisín loved it, she could almost see people in cloaks and brooches applauding a bard.

She took out her cigarettes and he brought her on to the fire escape. There was one of these off the flat in Sydenham, she said. I went outside to call my da in for breakfast one morning and he hid a can of Tennent's from me. Mary was only a baby.

Ah, Róisín, he said softly.

I'd brought Red along. In the middle of the night I got up to heat a bottle for Mary and he sobbed all over the three of us for hours. I knew then they were both fucked, my father and Red, so they are mixed up for me.

Barry took the cigarette from her, dragged. I know that, he said, handing it back.

I need to go to Bath. To Octavia's shop.

He was looking through the mesh to the ground, his arms folded. He reminded her of a PE teacher or a coach, raised veins and sinews. You should go, but I'd better sit it out, he said. Too close to my chaotic past.

After they washed up, he made a pot of tea and brought it to the couch. He fiddled around with an iPod, playing more tracks she'd forgotten she liked. At nine he switched on the news. The three-year-old who'd been taken from her bed in a holiday resort in the Algarve was still missing. Her mother was skin and bone and holding the child's favourite toy. The screen kept switching to an image of the little girl, zooming in on her eyes, which the reporter stressed were slightly different colours. Róisín thought of Mary at that age and started to cry again. She blew her nose and looked at Barry, ready to apologise for all the weeping. The sun had almost set and he was reclined against the back of the sofa. Hitting the off button on the remote, he patted his knee. Get over here, will you, he said.

She'd never really seen the point of French kissing, considering it something you had to endure before fucking, or something you had to settle for when sex was not available, a teenage thing, prodding around each other's wet places. It wasn't like that. Their tongues licking gently, rhythmically, legs entwined like when they were young. How hatefully she'd spoken to him then, how she'd looked at him.

I was a cunt to you. I'm so so sorry.

Broke my heart, he said, with a little laugh.

Stop messing, Barry, I'm serious.

So am I. It's all right, you just didn't like me back. One of his hands was on her hip, the other in her hair.

I kind of did like you, though.

Do you want this? You and me, I mean.

Yes.

Want me?

Yeah.

OK, he said. Stay.

She brought her bag to the fire escape, lighting a cigarette and texting Mary that she wasn't coming home.

Whore x, Mary replied.

Barry came out and took a drag, kissing her before going back in. She liked the way he did it, without saying anything, disappearing through the door.

Inside, the kettle was boiling. I'm sorry to say I have a routine, he said.

I'm leaving now.

Smiling, he held up three boxes of herbal tea. She asked for rooibos with a drop of milk. Carrying the mug made it easier to enter his bedroom. He chucked her a T-shirt and told her to use the bathroom first. Among the scrubs for blackheads and tubes of factor 50 there were products for women. Maybe they belonged to the algebra problem who'd sent the postcard, or maybe he still picked women up.

She got into his bed. Another bookcase, a Mexican pine mirror over a black cast-iron fireplace. A spider plant, its offspring trailing on the floor. She nestled into the brushed cotton of his bedding with her tea and tried not to panic.

Barry returned damp-haired, in baggyish checked boxers. He got in beside her. How are you doing there? he said, slurping from his mug, a hand on her thigh.

Full of spuds and milk and rather sober.

Rather sober, is it?

Yes, rather. Jesus, I spoke like that all the time when I was trying to be an English person.

He moved his fingers, stroked her. For a couple of minutes they nursed their tea in silence, then he took her mug and put it on the bedside table with his.

Choose some music, he said, handing her the iPod.

No.

Suit yourself. He fiddled with the dial and the opening bars of 'Dearg Doom' thumped from a speaker on the floor.

Jesus!

He played air guitar to 'Wonderful Tonight' and she tried to snatch the device from his hand. You're no craic, he said.

There was something around his neck on a fine gold chain, a tiny bronze medal.

She touched it. What's this?

That'd be St Monica. The patron saint of alcoholics. Are you going to be able for being with a recovering headcase?

Yes.

I was fucking crazy about you, Róisín, he said after a while.

She began to reply, making a joke of it, but he shushed her and kissed her hair. Let's get some sleep. God bless, Róisín McCaffrey.

She woke a few times in the night. Barry slept heavily, stirring when she did, nuzzling into her. At six, her body clock snapped her awake. There was a mug of tea on the bedside table. Barry was in running gear, lit from behind by the light from the hall. Kissing her on the mouth, he left. All the things he had to do every day to keep himself right.

He returned slick with sweat, walking stiffly. I'm going to jump in the shower, he said.

Don't.

She got out of his bed, standing in front of him. He pulled the T-shirt over her head and yanked her knickers down. She ran her finger around the waistband of his shorts but he caught her hand. I get tested all the time but I should put something on, he said.

She lay back on the bed and waited.

Are you freaked out? he said, over his shoulder, latex snapping.

No.

Turning back, he enfolded her in his body. I can't get you close enough, he said. A taste of salt on his skin.

There were other scars. He didn't know how he'd got them, waking bruised and bleeding with no idea whether he'd had a fall or a fight. She felt the little holy medal on her skin sometimes and made a promise to the God he was so fond of never to do anything to hurt him.

Afterwards, he hugged her tight, rubbing her arse. You OK? he said.

Yeah. You're good at this. Even when we were young. It's very un-Irish of you.

The mother gave me a copy of *Everywoman* when I was sixteen.

Insanely cool move for an Irish mammy.

It was and it wasn't, he said, lying on his back and pulling her across his chest. There was some kind of message in there about my father. He came back from Lebanon in '82, wandering the house at all hours, freaking out over everything. One night he moved into the spare room and stayed there. My mother was very pretty and he'd been proud of that. She had to give up her job in the civil service when she got married and all she had was the way he looked at her. And then he didn't see her any more.

Barry Doyle and his hard-won wisdom. She kissed his breastbone. Strange, the way things turn out, he said.

It's completely fucking mental.

25

14 July 2007

A soft, white mizzle, as if the sky had descended into the streets of Bath, her ballet flats slithering on the wet cobbles. She'd arrived early, but a queue was already forming outside the Roman Baths, a pungent whiff coming from inside. Octavia's shop wouldn't open for another hour so she walked around the city, giving in to the craving and buying a pack of cigarettes. With Barry, she smoked little. He'd be back from his run, reading the previous day's *Irish Times* on the brown couch, twirling the dial on his iPod from time to time.

She stayed with him most nights, watching films from the late eighties and early nineties, his missing years. During *Betty Blue* he said, I always thought you looked like her.

I did in my hole.

You do.

OK, I'll grant you the hair.

And the tits.

Tits sounds vile.

Breasts then. And I never knew what you were thinking.

I think I had dissociation.

The little girl was still missing, no longer the first item on the news. Róisín resisted teasing him about the sex education his mother had given him until Chaka Khan came on a playlist and she turned 'I'm Every Woman' to full volume. There was lots of sober sex, lots of tea and reading in bed. Talking late into the night, lying on their backs, looking at the ceiling.

She went into a small hotel to get out of the rain, ordering Earl Grey tea because it felt like the appropriate thing to do. It was highly perfumed, like licking the inside of Lynne's make-up bag. Her phone trilled, a message from Barry.

Sorry...again...

They were meeting Tina and the jockey husband for dinner later, a celebration of Barry's fortieth birthday. *The things I do for you*, she replied.

Her phone rang, making her jump. What's up?

Talk dirty to me.

I'm drinking tea in a genteel dining room.

Christ, your voice.

What about it?

Nordie and kind of scratchy.

It's the fags. Have a wank.

The couple at the next table turned to her in horror, Barry's laughter reverberating down the line. Róisín hung up. Her phone trilled again.

That's not what I meant by talk dirty...

Oops

Lol come round early...

She left the hotel, stomach queasy with nerves. She'd set out that morning worrying that Octavia would not be in her shop; now she was worried that she would.

A young man was putting out a black sandwich board. *Industry and Idleness* printed in Caslon, an eighteenth-century font, thick and thin lines in each letter, the 's' resembling the cursive 'f'. The sign over the door was in the same script. Róisín entered, a bell chiming in her wake.

It was instantly disorienting, like stepping back a couple of centuries. Handel's *Water Music* was playing. The walls and ceiling were a deep, brackish green, almost black, framed prints on every available inch. Persian carpets on the floor, repurposed oil lamps glimmering in recessed alcoves. Huge pedestal vases of eucalyptus and laurel gave the impression the outside was coming in. There were cabinets of Georgian ephemera: theatre tickets, programmes, pamphlets of rhymes; glass-fronted armoires full of crystal and silver. A twelve-seater table in the middle of the room displayed a dozen or more candelabras.

The young man was replacing candles, lighting as he went along. He was skinny with a baby-white complexion, an eejit-genius air about him, like a contestant on *University Challenge*. He smiled as she approached him, a lit taper in his hand that he appeared to have forgotten about until it burned his fingers.

How can I help you? he said, blowing it out.

I'd like to speak to Octavia Hammond.

May I ask your name?

Róisín McCaffrey. What's yours?

William, he said. She looked for a trace of Octavia in him, but there was nothing. Anyway, her entries in *Debrett's* and *Burke's Peerage* didn't list any children.

William, Octavia and I used to know each other. Is she here?

He asked her to wait, not saying whether Octavia was there or not, and went through a doorway at the rear of the shop. She looked at the prints. There were architectural drawings like the ones in the Soane Museum. Portraits of men in tail-coats, cartoons depicting the dandies of the day they nicknamed Macaronis. Most were pornographic. A portly man, rosy testicles the size of grapefruit spilling out of his britches, his cock buried in a girl swathed in layers of petticoat. Another girl performing fellatio on an austere elderly gentleman behind a yew tree in the corner of a graveyard, a funeral procession passing a few feet away. Each of them wearing an expression of slight surprise.

Behind the counter – a mahogany desk – there was a window, beyond that a yard full of fireplaces and doors in various stages of restoration. William was on the threshold of an outbuilding at the rear, throwing his hands wide, looking back towards the shop. Octavia came out. Róisín stepped away from the desk, returning to where she'd been standing by the table. Watching the door, her heart hammering, as it opened.

If it isn't the Little Match Girl, Octavia said, walking towards her. Twenty years later and she still had the power to make Róisín feel shit. In some ways she'd not changed. Hair still a rope over her shoulder, albeit with a few wiry white threads sticking up. But the comely cheeks were gone, leaving sharp blades above sunken pockets, her skin thin and open-pored.

I sent you an email.

You did.

I'm looking for Red.

I gathered that.

The effort of not beating her to death with one of her Georgian candelabras was gargantuan.

His mother asked me to find him. She wants him to know his father is dead and it's safe to go home. She has cancer. The treatment isn't going well.

Octavia sighed. That's unfortunate, she said. She might as well have laughed.

A fury was rising in Róisín she hadn't felt for years. She tried to quash it but could hear it in her voice when she stepped forward, saying, Listen, love. You're the last person to have seen him.

Octavia stood pulling the cuffs of her cotton jumper over her knuckles. Nonsense, she said eventually.

You were seen in a needle exchange in Elephant and Castle. You're alive and well, what the fuck happened to Red?

The rear door opened. Is everything all right? said William, head lowered as if he was afraid to witness anything.

Leave us please, William, said Octavia calmly. She went to the front door and locked it.

I haven't seen Red since 1991. We were in a flat in New Cross. My father took me away and I never saw him again.

Did you look for him?

Octavia's face was changing, the fear leaving it. Did you look for him, Little Match Girl?

I'm looking for him now.

When did you last see him, out of interest? She was enjoying herself, watching shame bloom on Róisín's face.

'Eighty-nine.

Paddington station. He told me you saw him and kept on walking.

I spoke to him!

You walked past him and only went back because your little sister had stopped to pet Wilbur. Reaching for the snib, she clicked it open.

Róisín walked on to the street, resisting with all her strength the urge to scurry away like the rodent she was. It was no longer raining but the temperature had risen, a sickly mugginess in the air. At the end of the road, she turned the corner and lit a cigarette, hands as unsteady as Micksy's.

She boarded the train that was waiting on the platform, an earlier one than she'd planned to take. A message came over the tannoy that refreshments were being served from a trolley. She walked through five carriages to find it, buying four miniature bottles of vodka, ignoring the server's surprise when she refused his offer of a mixer. Taking the nearest free seat, she drank until there was nothing left.

The ticket inspector shook her awake. Paddington, he said, last stop.

There were several messages from Barry. He hoped she'd found Octavia. His sister had been texting him since early morning, warning him they weren't to be late. Never in her life, even when she was being mentally tortured by her in school, had Róisín felt less like seeing Tina Doyle and she couldn't face her brother either. Texting Barry that she needed to nap and change, she took the Tube back to Jane Austen House.

As the effects of the vodka faded a heaviness had descended and she'd drunk the remains of a bottle of wine she found in Mary's fridge. Barry didn't seem to see it on her, backing her into his bedroom.

You look so good, he purred, one hand cupping her cunt, the other stroking her neck. She was in a floral tea dress she'd bought in Top Shop when she was fresh from being fucked and cuddled and served mugs of Barry's Gold Blend in his bed, feeling almost pretty. Now it felt like a disguise, something she'd worn to conceal her wickedness. She pulled it over her head and off.

They got on the bed, Barry's shoulders against the headboard, Róisín crouched over him, his fingers in her hair. As she undid his zip his hand flattened. He'd encouraged her to go down on him before and, sensing her unease, let it go. Because it was his birthday and because she hated herself so much she deserved to be debased, she took him in her mouth. She was trembling. Barry let out a moan, mistaking her fear for excitement, and caressed her scalp as he thrust upwards. She worked for as long as she could but he was pressing, burrowing, her throat filling. Afraid she would vomit, she drew away. Her heart was beating very fast and she'd broken into a sweat.

Barry, realising something was wrong, sat up. It's OK, it's OK, he said, thank you, I'm sorry, I know you don't like it.

* * *

Tina offered Róisín her cheek but averted her face before she connected with it. She was in a long-sleeved sequinned mini-dress, golden hair almost reaching her waist, lime, basil and mandarin perfume overlaying the rancid pork notes of fake tan. John Joe, the jockey husband, flung his arms around Róisín, saying it was great to meet her. He was tiny, with the face of a matinee idol and an incongruously deep voice. You could nearly smell the money off the pair and the staff were circling. Barry was attentive to Róisín, hooking his little finger around hers, settling her at the table. He'd been terribly gentle after her freak-out, thinking he'd put her under pressure, not knowing she wanted him to annihilate her. It made her feel tender towards him, the lovely fool of a man who saw vulnerability where there was only filth.

They toasted Barry with vintage champagne and he raised a flute of Sanpellegrino, glancing at Róisín as if he was in need of help. Forty, said John Joe. You don't look a day over thirty-nine. Your sister's looking well on it too.

Irish twins, Barry said, smiling fondly at Tina. How many months are we apart?

Ten and a half. Disgusting.

Twenty-eighth of August, said Róisín.

Tina's mouth was curling. What?

Your birthday.

It's not weird at all that you remember that.

Róisín couldn't raise her head as Tina described her month of celebrations, a catered party in a marquee at home, a shopping trip to Dubai, a weekend in the George V in Paris and various lunches, almost complaining about the complications of having so many friends. Róisín's fortieth had been a midweek break in a spa hotel with her mother, a fortnight after she buried her father. Three nights of butter-rich table d'hôte dinners in an almost empty dining room, menus that embarrassed Una.

Leading her into the swimming pool felt like they'd gone to Lourdes.

The maître d' arrived, slabbering over Tina, saying it had only been a fortnight since he'd seen her. It hurt to watch Barry's face register that his sister had been in London and not contacted him.

You're always working, said Tina. She said she only attended the big race meetings for prizes and photographs but sometimes travelled with John Joe when he was riding in places no one had ever heard of, like Lingfield. She'd leave him and go 'up to town'. John Joe was champion jockey that year.

I couldn't give a shite, I just want to keep riding, said John Joe. Realising the comic potential of what he'd just said, he banged the table and raised his glass. Sure, we all want to keep riding!

The service became almost invisible. Róisín, relieved that Tina and John Joe were heavy drinkers, sipped steadily. Barry asked about his nephews, remembering their ages, the stages they'd been at the last time he saw them. John Joe said they were all mad for the horses, the eldest up at the crack of dawn to muck out the stables, going on practice rides with his father at weekends and during the holidays.

Tina didn't acknowledge his questions and moved on to talking about the town. Who had left, who had come back for the Celtic Tiger. Who was married from school. Who was not married, for which she lowered her voice. Who had children, who did not have children, or, as she put it, 'had no family', because a family could only be a nuclear one. A cruel expression, Róisín thought.

So you two, she said. How did you get together? God, were you at it in that squat?

Barry smiled, shaking his head.

We were actually, said Róisín, at it like rabbits. Under the table, she moved her hand along his thigh and touched the bump that was growing in his trousers, pressing his balls the way he liked.

The fuck are you doing, he whispered, but he was looking at her like he wanted to eat her.

Gas woman, said John Joe, winking at Barry in approval.

Róisín was enjoying herself so much she didn't notice that something was happening. John Joe was reading the label on the wine bottle. Barry, elbow on the table, was supporting his chin with splayed fingers.

You didn't have a family, did you? Tina was speaking carefully, as if she was repeating herself.

I have my mother. My father died in March.

I meant you and your husband, did you have a family?

We didn't have children, if that's what you're asking.

I couldn't imagine you, I suppose. This one had brains to burn, she told John Joe.

Barry touched Róisín's knee. OK? he mouthed.

She nodded and lifted her glass. It was full again. She didn't know how much she'd had to drink. John Joe ordered a bottle of Vosne-Romanée that he pronounced Vosnay-Romano. At two hundred quid a go, the sommelier didn't appear to care what he called it. The main courses arrived. She couldn't concentrate on what they were saying, could hardly eat. When the plates were cleared she stood; the recent ban on smoking indoors was an excuse to go outside.

She was lighting up when the door banged. It was Tina.

Finbarr said you're here to find Red Camelin, she said, taking a cigarette from a silver case and sparking a matching lighter under it. Do you have him helping you?

Róisín began to reply but Tina inhaled deeply and blew the smoke out. I swear to God, if you're using him.

I'm not.

You'd better fucking not be. You have no idea the state he was in when Red rang me. Tina looked alarmed then.

Red phoned you? When?

Jesus, if Finbarr knew that. Nineteen ninety. Red rang the house and I picked up. He said Barry was in big trouble and someone needed to go and get him. I couldn't tell the father, he was mental enough, and the mother wasn't able for more grief.

I don't understand why you haven't told that to Barry.

Red said he needed to think someone cared about him. Tina tapped her cigarette slowly, eyes narrowed in contempt. You'd better not tell him either. Just find Red and leave my brother the fuck alone. Why he's saddled himself with you I'll never know.

Róisín found herself laughing. For a year I walked into school wanting to be dead. Because of you.

Tina made a noise like one of her husband's horses and went back inside.

It was easier after that. Tina was visibly relaxed, as though she'd expunged her rancour for Róisín. John Joe told them stories. The crazy things he had to do to make his weight, blocking the bathroom door and running the shower until he'd sweated pounds. Riding horses feeling so light-headed it was like flying, fainting after his first pint. Meeting the Queen Mother and getting knocked into next week by the bang of gin off her.

When dessert came, there was a miniature cake, a glossy gâteau opéra. *Finbarr 40* written on the plate in chocolate. Barry was smiling. It was good to see him happy.

She wanted to go to Jane Austen House but he was still fussing. In his flat she went to his room, stripping and lying in his bed. Barry brought her a glass of water and took his clothes off too, the beginnings of an erection pointing vaguely at her. She normally loved that he wanted her, reaching for him before he got in, but now it seemed absurdly trusting.

Skin on skin, he said, the words he always used as they turned to each other. She was supposed to say: it's good for us; he'd joked that it was part of his routine now. When she didn't, there was a twitch of concern in his eyes. She could put his head off so easily.

He kissed her mouth. She felt drunk and hungover at once. I didn't clean my teeth, I'm foul, she said.

I don't care, he said, kissing her again.

She lay on her back.

Barry went up on his elbow. The shit Tina was at earlier, he said. I'd never ask you something like that.

Is that your way of asking me now?

Maybe, I don't know.

There was a pregnancy.

She didn't elaborate but he nodded as though she had. You don't know a fucking thing, she wanted to scream. She hated the way he was bent over her with that counsellor face, Barry Doyle who understood all the sadness in the world. Barry Doyle the metrosexual who kept a basket of women's skincare in his bathroom. She rolled away and out of his bed, picking up her clothes from the floor. She caught a glimpse of her reflection, her stupid made-up face, puffy beneath the foundation and blusher. Her own badness looking back at her.

He sat on the edge of the mattress. You're leaving? he said.

I can't take any more, today was too much.

I should have said something to Tina, told her to shut the fuck up.

Yeah, you should have.

What happened in Bath, Róisín? You landed in so late I couldn't ask you and then it got weird and we had to leave.

Weird because I couldn't give you a fucking blow job?

No!

I should go home.

Stop. Did you find Octavia?

She hasn't seen him since '91.

Hey, come on, why won't you look at me?

Róisín forced her eyes to meet his, but after a couple of seconds could not endure the scrutiny. I'm tired, Barry.

You'd been drinking when you arrived.

Most people drink.

She looked at him now, keen to see him wilt, and St Monica glinted at her, a warning. For just a moment he flinched. He probably had a strategy for being goaded about his sobriety.

What is it, Róisín?

I'm never going to find him.

It's a hazardous life, you know? You'll find a way to explain it to his mother.

He thought she was doing it for Dolly, when it was to assuage her own rotten conscience.

He talked her into bed. You can tell me anything, he said, anything.

A midwife asking if someone was coming but she was alone, she said, her husband was out of the country. A hospital toilet, a bloody mass like raw chicken livers cramping out of her all through the night. A screen, almost black, as if Neil Armstrong might bounce slowly across it and put a flag in her uterus. A terrible quiet.

26

24 July 2007

A warning on the home page read: *Please be aware that some images might be distressing*. Róisín took in a breath and clicked. There were hundreds of unidentified bodies, going back to the sixties. Most could not possibly be Red – 'Male 60–70' or 'Female 30–40' – but she felt compelled to look anyway. The images hit her like slaps. The artist's sketch of a young man who had hanged himself under a railway bridge in Surrey that captured the relief in his face. A bra taken from the body of a woman washed up on a Welsh beach, warped underwiring hinting at violence. Scars, tattoos and the heart-scalding contents of pockets. She glanced at her phone, wanting desperately to speak to Barry, but he already had one foot in this realm of the lost and forgotten. And he knew if it had been left to Róisín, her father could have been part of it.

Mary came downstairs in an outsize *Looney Tunes* T-shirt, tendrils of backcombed hair protruding half-heartedly from her head. A stoner Medusa.

Where are you off to today, Dora the Explorer? she said, toeing Róisín's backpack.

A flower shop in Hampstead. Wanna come?

I can't, sis. Meeting my supervisor.

Róisín poured her a cup of tea. God help anyone trying to supervise you.

I'm reverential around male authority, it's fucking weird. Mary's face had crumpled into a guilty-looking scowl, an expression she'd worn as a small child when afraid she was in trouble. Róisín didn't know why she sometimes spoke to her like that. It was the way Una still spoke to Róisín, making unfunny jokes that left her feeling like she didn't understand herself.

Ach, pet, I'm a stupid bitch.

You're making it worse, cried Mary. Putting yourself down too.

Róisín felt tears forming. She couldn't let Mary see them, she would think she'd made her cry. You're the best girl, Mary McCaffrey, she said, leaving the table. I'm going out for a fag.

On the balcony, she lit a cigarette. The lavender and heuchera she'd potted when she arrived were humming with small bees, a perfume like roses wafting from the scented pelargoniums. It gave her a lurch of homesickness. The writer who was renting her place had promised to mind the garden, but Róisín doubted she would take as much care of it as she did.

Mary came outside, letting the door bang behind her. I've just seen what you were viewing on your laptop, she said. Are you mental?

I don't know where else to look.

You clicked on a woman who is clearly Chinese! Jesus, Rosh, what are you like? Get out like a normal person and enjoy London, have a whirl on the London Eye, take in a fucking show, I don't care! Just stop bloody torturing yourself.

OK.

OK? You're shutting me down. Mary was holding her T-shirt across her body as if it was a cardigan, her colour still rising. Where's Finbarr, Rosh?

He's busy.

That's a lie.

It probably is, said Róisín, squashing the tip of her cigarette between her fingers, but that's what he says.

Something had shifted the night of his birthday dinner. When she was being easy on herself she concluded she had embarrassed him in the restaurant with her groping and fawning, or that he was annoyed that she'd been drinking, or that he wanted a girlfriend who gave head without boking. In darker moments, she suspected he'd seen into her black, treacherous heart. For a few days, she texted him. Did he want to walk, eat? When would be a good time to help Muiris in the garden? He replied promptly, the ellipses that had promised more replaced by full stops. There was an audit at work. He was short-staffed. So many reasons not to see her.

Fix it, said Mary.

He doesn't want that. Anyway, I'm leaving soon, thank fuck, so it doesn't matter.

Mary stood staring at her for a moment. As Róisín went towards her she turned and went back inside.

Róisín had visited five flower shops and this was her favourite. Terracotta pots of hardy herbs displayed like a primrose theatre outside. Blooms clumped by type and colour in hand-blown vases on a large table in the centre of the shop. She introduced herself, explaining she was writing a feature. The florist was called Rosie.

We have the same name. Róisín means 'little rose', she said.

Rosie laughed and thanked her for not asking if she'd changed her name by deed poll. Róisín chose flowers – orchids, roses, carnations, peonies, baby's breath, all in white – and asked her to make an arrangement.

Are they for a birthday?

They're for my sister, said Róisín, writing *Please forgive me, I'm a stupid cunt* on a card.

Rosie glanced at the message and went into a fridge behind the counter. These are on me, she said, coming back with sprigs of lily of the valley.

As Rosie snipped and layered, twisting the stems into a posy, Róisín took photographs. Her phone rang. It was Una, Róisín had been ignoring her calls for days. Sorry, she mouthed at Rosie and stepped away.

Mum, she said.

Mum, indeed. I thought I'd have to introduce myself.

I'm in a shop.

So you can't talk to me, very convenient.

I'll ring you later.

Don't bother your head. I went to see Dolly. She hasn't a lot of time.

Jesus.

Go on about your business.

Her mother hung up.

Rosie was wrapping the posy in cellophane. Maybe Róisín should send flowers to everyone she'd hurt or failed: Barry, Dolly, her mother. Her father, but it was too late. For the first time, it wasn't repulsion that swelled in her at the thought of him. She arranged for delivery to Jane Austen House after four and paid for a pot of rosemary.

Rosemary, that's for remembrance, said Rosie. You're having quite the day.

Outside, it was so warm the road was shimmering. She hailed a cab and clambered in. The driver watched impatiently as she placed the plant between her feet and secured the seat belt, but his eyes softened when she told him where she wanted to go, a respectful silence falling on him as he passed through the cemetery gates. How different it was in summer, trees lush with leaves, broken tombstones swallowed by their foliage. She directed him to the far corner and asked him to wait.

Walking towards the stand of trees on the west side, she couldn't help take in the inscriptions. Ellen (Nellie) Watts, 1910–2003, was buried with three of her children and the husband who'd left her a widow at thirty. Joshua John Regan, 2005, had lived for a single summer. She and Mary hadn't yet chosen a headstone, but as she got close she saw that it had been marked by a St Brigid's cross woven from hazel. The meitheal men had been here and she hadn't. Her regret was so overpowering she felt weak. Kneeling on the warm earth, she placed the rosemary at her father's feet. She told him she loved him, she missed him, she was sorry. Kissing her fingers and touching the cross, she told him she'd be back in March with a bowl of shamrock.

Eileen, who Barry had claimed was on annual leave, was behind the reception desk. Hello! Finbarr said you'd gone, she said.

How cleanly he'd removed Róisín from his life.

I'm around for another few days. Are the lads here?

They're in the garden. Go on through, they'll be delighted to see you.

Muiris was by the potatoes, his poor hip cocked, beaming as she walked towards him. Arra, Róisín, he said.

You made a St Brigid's cross for my daddy's grave.

We did indeed. Conor left a bag of sticks.

Shticks. And the big bashful smile. How she'd miss this man.

It was a lovely thing to do, Muiris.

'Twasn't only myself. Finbarr brought us over there last week.

Timmy came through the door with a tea-tray, spoons tinkling in mugs. Barry was a couple of paces behind him, a packet of Mikado biscuits in his hand. On seeing her, his face registered no surprise; Eileen must have told him she was here.

How are you, Róisín? he said.

I went to my father's grave this morning.

That's great, I'm happy for you. Genuinely.

Genuinely. Acknowledging there was a possibility he might not be happy for her.

I came to say thank you.

Conor was one of our own.

Barry had visited her father, cared for him, he had even found his body. Still, a bitter, empty part of her was disappointed he hadn't gone to the grave for her.

They each took a mug of tea. Are you going ateing those bishcuits yourself, Finbarr? said Timmy.

Barry ripped open the packet and held it out so they could each take one, his solemn expression an absurd foil to the gaudy packaging. Róisín shook her head, seized by an impulse to laugh.

Timmy said she'd picked a good time to go home, with the fuchsias red in the hedgerows.

Deora Chríost, we called them, said Muiris, the tears of Christ. We weren't allowed pick them.

Barry listened, the terrible politeness still on him. You're away home, so, he said suddenly, as if he was thinking aloud.

I am.

Will you come back, do you think? said Muiris.

I'd like to.

How could she come back when Barry didn't want her here? She told Muiris she'd send bulbs: giant alliums and a variety of anemones called 'St Brigid'. He nodded without looking up, perhaps sensing something was wrong. Shaking her hand, he swung out and away from them, and she said goodbye to Timmy. Behind her as she crossed the yard, Barry was hovering like a bouncer at closing time. God, you really can't wait to get rid of me, she said, stopping dead.

Not here.

Where then? Please, will you give me five minutes?

Whatever, his shoulders said as they rose.

They sat on a bench. Róisín lit a cigarette.

He was still holding the packet of Mikados. Did you choose those? she asked.

Yeah.

Gee biscuits.

What?

They look like vaginas.

He took in the folds of pink marshmallow, hairy with coconut, the slash of red jam up the middle. He burst out laughing. You're the most vulgar woman I've ever met.

Thank you, she said, desperate to prolong the levity, but he was placing the packet on the bench between them, as if he was shutting down the connection it had offered.

He told her he'd taken the liberty of going wider in the search for Red, forwarding the message to organisations beyond Greater London. The city's poor had been pushed out to surrounding counties, Essex and Bedfordshire and Kent; it was possible he had ended up somewhere like that. If the new round yielded any leads he would contact Róisín, he had her email address.

Thank you, she said again, and again he shrugged.

Red was my friend too, Róisín.

Barry, I need you to know that I see what you are and all your goodness.

It sounded extravagant, gushy, and he replied with a derisory *tssk*. I told you, I get more out of it than I give, he said.

Why don't you want to see me any more?

I want to see you all the time. The scar on his neck was bright, it happened when he was angry or flustered.

I don't understand.

You don't trust me. All the things I told you, shit I've never told anyone. I thought you were doing the same, but in two months you never told me you lost a baby.

A little quiver of horror went through her. She never used the B-word. It had been a malformed clump of cells, an aberration. Not a baby.

You are the only person apart from Guy I've spoken to about that and he doesn't even know those details.

She tried to take out another cigarette, forgetting there was one in her hand. Barry pulled one from the pack, lighting it for himself. I'm so sorry, he said. I swore I'd never speak to you again rather than bring this up.

She remembered a Frank Spencer misquote that had made her father laugh. *A trouble shared is a trouble doubled*, she said.

What does that make me, a whingeing trauma junkie?

No! Some things are too fucking hard to talk about. It's just a sad thing that happened, Barry. It has nothing to do with you and me, she said, laying her hand on his.

He glanced in the direction of the potagers. If the boys hadn't been across the yard she supposed he would have swatted her away. Nothing to do with you and me, he repeated. Like you and Red.

So this is what it's really about, thought Róisín.

I came to London to find Red. You knew that.

Yeah, he said, withdrawing his hand. Looking for the love of your life.

I haven't seen him for nearly twenty years.

But you love him.

It was almost insufferable. The demand for truth, even when he might hear something that would hurt him.

Of course, what kind of question is that?

More than me?

She hadn't told him she loved him. How had they got into this? Ah, come on, she cried.

That's your answer. Jesus. Fuck this shit, it's too hard.

Maybe it was. And since she'd probably never see him again, because as usual she had fucked everything up, she would give him another reason to despise her.

He listened without looking at her, the absurd biscuits between them on the bench.

You're a beautiful soul, Barry Doyle, she said when she had finished. Rising, she left him to process the scene she'd described. Red begging in Paddington station. Holding Róisín's gaze for a split-second. Watching her walk away.

27

28 July 2007

Mary had been thrilled with the bouquet – it was the first time anyone had sent her flowers – until she read the card, saying, *I'm a stupid cunt* isn't funny. Róisín's insistence that it was just Irish humour had gone some way to making it better but a stilted atmosphere still permeated Jane Austen House, Mary policing Róisín's every word and gesture, Róisín wishing she was back home with no one to annoy but herself. She took to the streets of London to avoid it.

At first, a self-consciousness came over her that she hadn't felt since her teens. She didn't understand it until she was queuing for the cloakrooms in Tate Modern behind a man and a woman so absorbed in each other they didn't notice when the line moved, fingers reaching to touch as if they were making sure the other was really there. It was how she and Barry had carried on, pawing each other like chimps, oblivious to all around them. She had let herself get used to it, fool that she was. As she went upstairs to the galleries, she had a sudden memory of walking into the Turbine Hall and seeing Eliasson's *Weather Project*. She had been alone that day too but had felt Red so keenly that for a mad moment she saw him tilt his face to the vast earthly yet unearthly sun setting in a mist. He was always with her.

In the Soane Museum she joined a tour. As they moved through the rooms, she realised her memory of the place was impressionistic, a blur of Pompeii red and Portland stone. But other aspects of that visit came back to her so sharply it was like a visitation. The rapt expression on Red's face as he listened to Octavia, his disappointment that Róisín did not see what he did in *A Rake's Progress*. She waited around until two and went to the Picture Room, squashing in. The guide was slipping on white gloves, visitors edging forward. It was just a story, she thought, as he folded back the panels, a life told in eight pictures. Fortune and misfortune and love and loss and crime and punishment, not some coded beckoning into darkness. Barry had so much more insight.

She did the National Gallery 'Grand Tour', tramping Soho for replicas of its famous paintings. Caravaggio's *Salome Receives the Head of John the Baptist* was by the entrance to the sex shop she'd passed with Red, Bronzino's *Venus and Cupid* on Greek Street. On Lexington Street, she found a Gainsborough and crossed the road to a small restaurant that could have been decorated by Octavia. She ordered quail and a bottle of burgundy and thought of Red's swagger in the Chinese. What he might have become, if he'd had a chance. Too cool for her, probably.

Today was her last in London, a scorcher, the light milky with heat. The estate was quiet, blinds and curtains drawn against the sun. She walked away from the river, turning on to Lupus Street. At the junction with the road they used to live on she waited to cross, but it felt wrong to approach the house from that direction. Walking on, she boarded a train at Pimlico, taking the two-minute trip to Victoria.

Outside the station, the drunk she had seen when she arrived three months earlier was in Micksy's spot again and she silently cheered him for claiming a place for himself in this vast, disinterested city. She gave him a cigarette and set off on the route she had taken at seventeen with a rain-slaked sausage bag on her back.

The stucco on the surrounding buildings was dazzling and she was thirsty, sweating through her dress. All the tables outside the Bull and Crown were taken and she went inside. Little had been done to the interior – carpets and wallpaper stripped away, floorboards and plaster washed white – yet it was unrecognisable. The original bar still stood. Its intricate beauty had been hiding in plain sight, unable to compete with tartan carpet and flock wallpaper and Terry's belligerent bulk. She sat where the jukebox once was and ordered a beer and a bag of crisps. The waiter said they didn't stock bar snacks and brought Marcona almonds. 'Is She Really Going Out with Him?' came from the speakers, the song Sinéad had sung to tease her about Red. It felt fateful.

Octavia's house was now a place of indeterminate business, *APEX* spelled in simple graphics on a chrome plaque that suggested dark-money shenanigans. A van was parked outside number 48. She stepped under the portico. The front door was ajar. The house was at the end of a refurbishment project, paint cans where they used to stack empty gas canisters. Entering the hall, she rapped the door to the drawing room. A radio was on and a man was singing along to Rihanna's 'Umbrella' with the gusto of one who thought he was alone. She rapped again and turned the knob Barry had fixed rather than kick the door in. In the centre of the room, a painter was up a tall ladder, daubing at the ceiling rose with a narrow brush.

Excuse me, she said.

Oh my Gordon Bennett, he said, momentarily buckling before he descended.

I'm sorry, I tried to knock.

He was her own age. There was an edge to him, flat-top hair zapped with silver, green ink on his forearm, the bottom leg of a Celtic cross. You're Irish, he said.

So are you.

My dad's Dublin, my mum Kerry.

All-Ireland final day must have been some craic in your house.

Carnage, love, he said, with a smile. What can I do you for?

I lived here a long time ago. It was a squat then. The last one in Pimlico.

I did my time in squats, but they weren't like this. More ink on his fingers, the sort people got in prison. Aware she was staring, he put his hands in his pockets.

It got hairy here, in the end... She let her voice trail off. Who was she telling?

They went to the kitchen. Her feet knew what to do, tripping lightly down the five steps. The Aga had been reconditioned and attached to shiny new pipework.

She opened the back door. This was like a jungle, she said, surveying the cleared garden. Shrubs and trees all the way up to the window. We did a winter without electricity.

Must have been fucking Baltic.

It was. And really fucking beautiful.

They had used so little of the house then. Now every door was open, but she didn't care about those other rooms. She showed him where Dawn's huge photographs had stood, the moth-eaten rug. She told him about Barry's Guinness sign and the orderly arrangement of empty bottles. At the entrance to Greg's room she braced for the reek of Wilbur which would surely lurk in the floorboards for as long as the house stood, but it smelled only of paint and varnish. And Red's room. She felt the snap of cold linen. Saw him on his back, hand on his heart.

Her last stop was Millbank. At first she couldn't find the ditch, circling back and back through leafy streets. She was about to give up when she recognised the block of flats to her left. Looking down into the trench, phrases from *David Copperfield* came to her in fragments but she couldn't assemble them into the passage Red had recited. His own words came to her, though. 'Can you not feel it? All those wretched lives layered up underneath us.' *Can you not*, because he knew she wouldn't understand. She thought of the 'looked-after' children who'd vanished; human lives reduced to unclaimed carrion on a missing persons website. She could feel it now.

There was a note from Mary. She had gone shopping with Lynne. They'd be back by five, after which they would eat, drink and be merry for tomorrow big sis was fucking off home to the old country. Róisín filled a glass with water from the fridge and drank it, then another glass. The flowers were thirsty too, the peonies blowsy like pom-poms, the rest in various stages of wilt. She changed the water, trimming an inch off the stems and stripping them of slimy foliage.

She sat on the couch with her laptop. There were nine replies to pitches, all but one acceptances, enough work to keep her going until Halloween. Logging out of her email, she entered the missing persons site. The banner on the home page horrified her every time: *Can you help us identify someone?* Clicking on 'Male 20–40, 1994, Greater London', she hoped she would be of no help whatsoever.

Upstairs, she packed the case she'd come with and the new one she'd bought to accommodate the swatches and brochures and books she'd gathered. Her phone buzzed. She hated the sound now, the hope and then dismay that it wasn't Barry. It was her mother. She was sorry no one could pick Róisín up but she would see her tomorrow. She missed her and was happy she was coming home. Replying with a single *x*, Róisín lay on the bed and cried.

When Mary and Lynne came back she was downstairs, showered and blow-dried with a full face of make-up.

I told you that was your colour, Rosh! cried Lynne, stroking the sleeve of the dusky pink silk top she had given Róisín. Mary was smirking; it was the last thing Róisín would have chosen.

They drank champagne, Mary at the hob, the shamrock tattoo flashing as she chopped and seasoned. She told Róisín to put on some music, there was an eighties mix on her shuffle. They tapped their feet and sang along. Then a Luther Vandross track came on. Tune! said Mary. Turn it up.

Lynne's face collapsed. I love that song, it reminds me of your dad.

Jesus. I'm sorry, said Róisín.

It's all right, I only remember the happy times. He wasn't a bad man, Rosh. Maybe you'll forgive him one day.

She already has, said Mary. I went to the grave yesterday. All the other ones have plastic flowers. Miss Ideal Home left a pot of rosemary in weathered terracotta and a rustic cross.

Róisín told them the meitheal men had put the cross there, woven it from hazel, that Barry had driven them to the cemetery.

Sweet man, Finbarr, said Lynne, running her fingers under her eyes.

When Róisín didn't reply, Mary turned from the cooker. You OK, sis?

Róisín laughed a little. I'm heartbroken.

Mary embraced her from behind, oily hands crossed at the wrists.

Lynne drained her glass. Right, she said. Let's get pissed.

They drank a second bottle of champagne and two of wine with dinner. Afterwards they brought their glasses on to the balcony. The sun was falling away to the west, hardly a breath in the air. The old lady next door came out. Lynne went to greet her, hugging her over the dividing wall. Mary produced her pencil case and began to skin up.

Peg was Merv's mum's best friend, said Lynne, taking a seat. Every time I see her she tells me he was a randy little git. I told her he still is.

Christ, I'm sick in my mouth, said Mary.

I only give him my body sometimes. Lynne took the joint from her.

I have questions about your parenting of my sister, said Róisín.

She told them about her walk, leaving from Victoria, the workman showing her around number 48. There was no trace of him, she said, of any of us. But I felt like he was on the streets with me.

You'll always have him, said Lynne.

Róisín reached for the spliff, picturing Red a touch away, invoking Plato to avoid being her boyfriend. He'd thought he was doing her a favour, but she was too besotted to see it.

28

29 July 2007

Róisín gripped the edge of the kitchen sink and dry retched. I'm fucking poisoned. How much did we drink?

I'm not telling, you'll vom for real. Oh, sis, I'll miss you.

I'll miss you. And you, Lynne.

Outside, the taxi driver tooted his horn. Róisín said goodbye, hugging them both, and wheeled her cases down the path. She lost control of the larger one and the driver leapt from his cab to catch it before it crashed into his door. Served him right for not helping her, she thought, sitting in the back. On the doorstep, Lynne and Mary were guffawing so hard they could barely stand.

He left her at Victoria coach station. In the past she'd used the dingy entrance to the bus hangar and had forgotten it had a grand art deco façade. Inside, it was like an airport departure lounge, people crowded under the information boards. She noted the number of her bay and wheeled her cases through the throng. The new one with the lively castors spun away from her again and a man caught it. She raised her head to thank him. It was Barry. Did you never hear tell of cheap flights? he said. She had wanted so badly to see him but now he was here, making a lame joke, she was annoyed.

I'm on a sentimental journey. What do you want?

There was someone hovering behind him, eyes roving from the board to Róisín. Barry turned, putting his hand on the stranger's elbow. Andrew, this is Róisín.

Andrew Camelin. The flagon bouncing along the pavement, the frenzied look in his eyes. *Home? You left us there.* There was still rage on him, a tensile set to his upper body, the stubborn chin. He looked as hungover as Róisín, beer stains on his sweatshirt, dried sleep on his lashes.

Oh my God, was all Róisín could say.

They shook hands. He found it hard to maintain eye contact and she recalled him at Mass, skittering around the pew in Red's combat jacket. Your mother will be so happy to see you, Andrew, she said.

Either that or she'll die of shock. He spoke like Barry, the flat tone of home lilted by years in London. He said he needed water and they followed him to the shop, waiting outside with the luggage.

Fucking hell, Barry, could you not have prepared me? she said.

I heard he was in one of the Medway towns but I didn't know if he'd agree to meet me let alone go home. An hour ago he was in two minds.

How's he doing?

Not great. There's a wife and two kids he's barred from going near and he lost a job over drink. If he wants to sort himself out I'll try to help him.

Andrew came out and handed Róisín a bottle of water. You look like you need it, he said and she saw a trace of Red in his wry smile.

Late one? said Barry. He was looking at her top, the pink one she'd worn the previous night, more spattered than Andrew's.

I was doing the 'Walk of Life' with Lynne and Mary at four o'clock this morning.

They love you, he said.

You don't, she thought.

They walked to the barrier, showing their tickets. Barry talked his way through, saying he had to help Róisín with her luggage. In the hangar, there were hordes waiting for buses to Southampton and Brighton and Bournemouth, a smaller group queuing for Dublin. Barry stowed her cases. He embraced Andrew, slapping his back in a brotherly way, saying he could ring him any time. Andrew joined the line. All he had with him was a little backpack.

I made you feel shit, said Barry.

I kind of am shit.

Because you walked by Red? I could write a book about shame. Let it go.

The driver was slamming the hold shut. Are ye getting on or what? he said.

So this is it? said Barry. He was looking up at her from under his eyebrows like he had when they were kids, as if he was afraid to hear the answer.

We already said goodbye. Thanks for finding him.

She boarded the coach.

Andrew was in the centre of the back seat. Choose a side, he said.

She sat on the right, with a view of the street. As they left the building, she saw Barry standing where her father had jangled his BMW keys, where the man from Scramogue had shredded his ticket. Red Camelin arriving here at sixteen, banished from home, a grand in his pocket. Muiris, Timmy and the hundreds of thousands who'd gone before them.

Barry held up his hand. Pressing hers to the window, she wished things had turned out differently.

She and Andrew opened their water bottles, sucking until the plastic had collapsed inwards.

We need tea, she said.

And food.

When were you last home?

'Eighty-five. So the evil emperor is gone?

Since March.

I hope he died screaming.

Róisín would let his mother tell that story, she'd enjoy it. Andrew rounded on her, perhaps taking her silence as disapproval. Do you know what he did to us?

I do now.

You've been looking for Redmond, he said, tearing at a rag nail on his thumb.

Yeah.

Barry said he was a smackhead. Do you think he's dead?

I hope not.

She thought about the missing persons website. If she could provide DNA or dental records there was a better chance of finding out if Red was one of the cases. But how could she ask?

He said he was tired and shunted away from her, nestling himself where the window met the seat. In repose, he had a pious appearance, the hangdog face he'd inherited from his father arranged in an expression of supplication. Imagine looking in the mirror every day and having a monster look back at you, she thought.

He woke a while later, blinking in surprise. Where are we?

Somewhere in the Midlands. We'll be stopping soon.

Thank fuck. I'd do time for a cigarette.

Me too. Are you OK?

I swore I'd never go back. Everything was so fucked up. I hated Redmond for walking away, but after he left the abuse stopped. I think it rattled the father that he was out there and might tell people what he'd been doing. Like the sick cunt never touched Jonathan, not that way. The shit he did to my mother, though. I hated her too. What a family.

He twisted his knuckles in his eye sockets. They came away wet.

The driver stopped in Birmingham for a twenty-minute break. Long enough for a shite and two fags, he said as they got off.

They smoked with the urgency of addicts. I've been on the batter, he said suddenly. I don't want her to see me like this.

You can clean up at my place.

OK, he said, but his face seemed to fall.

They filled a basket with sandwiches and bananas, salt and vinegar crisps and Lucozade. World's best hangover cure, she said.

Yeah. That and a pint.

She worried all the way to Holyhead that he would go straight to the bar on the ferry, but he found them a table in the lounge. His eyes were brighter, an air of poverty in the baggy-kneed tracksuit bottoms and knock-off trainers. He'd picked up a newspaper that had a supplement on the new Premiership season. He was a Man United fan and asked if she had a team.

Spurs, maybe.

Sorry for your troubles.

Her father would have enjoyed the banter. *Starter for ten.*

They went on to the deck to smoke. It was dark, a stippling of cold rain on the breeze. The boat had left the port and was in the open sea, water churning behind them like molten metal.

How bad is she? he said.

Pretty bad.

I'm no good with sick people.

There'll be nurses going in and out, you'll have plenty of support. I'll call up every day, I live five minutes away.

Barry said you were sound.

So did Red and look how that turned out, she thought.

An announcement said motorists and those who had travelled by bus or coach should return to their vehicles and foot passengers should join the queue for the gantry. For the first time in all her years of coming and going she felt a tiny thrill; she was nearly home. Her phone rang in her pocket.

It was Barry. He'd arranged a pick-up.

You didn't need to do that.

She offered.

She?

My sister. Tell Andrew to get your bags from the coach.

What the fuck?

Stop acting up, it'll save you two bus journeys. Can I come and see you?

Yeah.

She hung up.

They disembarked, Andrew insisting on wheeling her cases. She suspected he was nervous and glad to have something to do. She was nervous too, as they walked along the line of cars parked by Dun Laoghaire ferry port. Barry hadn't told her the make of Tina's car and it was unsettling to pause and gawp in each windscreen. A slim, tanned hand emerged from the open window of a white Range Rover, knuckles heavy with diamonds.

The boot's open, said Tina.

Andrew dragged the bags away.

It's kind of you to do this, said Róisín, steeling herself for the retort, *I did it for my brother*.

I was horrible to you in London. Finbarr gave out shite to me. Tina was blushing beneath her tan. It gave Róisín no pleasure.

We still bring out the worst in each other.

Andrew volunteered to sit in the front. He was carrying himself differently, practically preening. Tina had always had that effect on boys. They talked about horse-racing and their children. Andrew's were nine and eight. Irish twins, he said. They stopped in a shopping mall off the M50 to pick up a change of clothes for him. He was impatient as they queued at the till then began to walk back towards the clothing section. Róisín followed him. Andrew, please, let me buy them, she said.

I can't pay you back, he snapped. Earlier, she would have put it down to anger but it was pride and trepidation and all the hurt.

You can. Do you like gardening?

I hate it.

That echo of his brother again.

As they turned off the motorway, Andrew peered out the window. How different the main street must have looked to him, with its M&S Foodhall and the hanging baskets the Tidy Towns people put up in summer. In other ways the place hadn't changed at all. When she offered Tina directions to the cottage, she knew which house Róisín had bought and when, how much she'd paid for it; seven years of seeing almost no one and everybody still knew her business. Or maybe they just knew what they wanted to know. Andrew could testify to that.

Two mins! she texted her mother.

Right at the lights, past the school and the church, left by the perimeter wall of the estate. The canal had been dredged a couple of years earlier, the harbour in the town cleaned up and reopened. A Waterways Ireland van was parked by the lock, a man in a high-vis jacket looking left.

They got out of the car, both of them thanking Tina.

Róisín started to walk away but Tina called her back. Come round for coffee in the morning, she said. You can meet the lads.

This was a step too far. Is this Barry's idea? she asked.

No. Look, he wants us to get on.

OK. Fuck's sake, though.

Tina's face widened into a smile. Fuck's sake is right. See you tomorrow.

Una was standing in the open doorway, straighter, somehow, since Sinéad had taken her to an osteopath. Róisín walked towards her, Andrew trundling the cases along the path.

My God, whispered her mother. Is that Andrew?

It is. But Dolly...

Her mother pinched her cheek. But nothing. You brought her son back.

Una opened her arms for him and he let out a sob. He didn't think anyone would remember him.

There were voices coming from the bank. The lock was opening. The odd flashy cruiser came this way, inept sailors Helly Hansened from head to foot. This craft was a barge, a houseboat painted in bright colours with a grass roof. It passed into the channel and the lock-keeper closed the gate behind it, crossing to shut the one on the other side. A gush of water and the vessel rose. She watched until it had floated out of sight, praying to God that Red had got away.

ACKNOWLEDGEMENTS

I am grateful to my oncologist, Professor Paul Donnellan, and the staff of University Hospital Galway who continue to look after me. And to those who work in medical research – in particular the legend who figured out how to use Chinese hamster ovary cells against melanoma – I owe you my life.

NOTES

The text of *Stations* features the following words from other writers and lyricists:

The epigraph from Plato's *Symposium* is from the translation by Benjamin Jowett.

The epigraph from Jimmy MacCarthy's 'Missing You' is from the album *The Song of the Singing Horseman*.

On page 19, *Commemorate me where there is water* is from the poem 'Lines Written on a Seat on the Grand Canal, Dublin' by Patrick Kavanagh.

On page 21, *Go placidly … all persons* are lines from the poem 'Desiderata' by Max Ehrmann.

On page 35, the line of dialogue *If I said you have a beautiful body would you hold it against me?* is a reference to the title of a song by the Bellamy Brothers. The passage from *The Symposium*, by Plato, was translated by Benjamin Jowett.

On page 75, *Every idiot who goes about … dumping a hamper on the table* is a passage from the novel *A Christmas Carol* by Charles Dickens.

On page 78, *A sluggish ditch deposited its mud at the prison walls. Coarse grass and rank weeds straggled over all the marshy land in the vicinity* is a sentence in *David Copperfield* by Charles Dickens.

On page 89, *I wish I was in Carrickfergus … Come all ye men and I'll lay me down* are lyrics from the traditional Irish ballad 'Carrickfergus'. This particular version was popularised by the Clancy Brothers and Tommy Makem.

On page 93, *They sweated blood … McAlpine's Fusiliers* are lyrics from the song 'McAlpine's Fusiliers' by Martin Henry.

On page 111, *The only true wisdom is knowing you know nothing* is a common formulation of a statement widely attributed to Socrates.

On page 128, the lines *Nor sought he friend to counsel or condole, / Whate'er this grief mote be, which he could not control*

and

… though he loved but one, / And that loved one, alas, could ne'er be his are from the poem 'Childe Harold's Pilgrimage' by Lord Byron.

On page 179, *There's a hole in Daddy's arm where all the money goes* is a line from the song 'Sam Stone' by John Prine.

On page 180, *My father didn't look like he would harm anyone* is from *The Grass Arena* by John Healy.

On page 224, the phrase 'an absurd statue' is borrowed from the novel *Mrs Dalloway* by Virginia Woolf.

On page 225, the lines *sometimes you climb out of bed ... all the times you've felt that way* are from the poem 'Gamblers All' by Charles Bukowski.

On page 234, the line *Ah lads, there's no one like Jane!* is a reference to a statement attributed to poet and playwright Thomas MacDonagh, a leader of the Easter Rising who would go on to be executed.

The passages on page 241 are from Tim O'Grady and Steve Pyke's book *I Could Read the Sky*.

And the line *Rosemary, that's for remembrance*, on page 266, is from Act 4, Scene 5 of William Shakespeare's *Hamlet*.

A NOTE ON THE AUTHOR

LOUISE KENNEDY grew up a few miles from Belfast. She is the author of the acclaimed short story collection, *The End of the World Is a Cul de Sac*, which won the John McGahern Prize. Her debut novel *Trespasses* has been translated into over twenty languages. A *Sunday Times* bestseller, it won Eason Novel of the Year at the An Post Irish Book Awards, Book of the Year for Debut Fiction at the British Book Awards and the McKitterick Prize. It was also shortlisted for several awards including the Women's Prize for Fiction, the Waterstones Debut Fiction Prize and the Barnes & Noble Discover Prize. In 2025, *Trespasses* was made into a limited TV series by Channel 4. Before starting her writing career, Kennedy spent nearly thirty years working as a chef. She lives in Sligo.

A NOTE ON THE TYPE

The text of this book is set in Fournier. Fournier is derived from the *romain du roi*, which was created towards the end of the seventeenth century from designs made by a committee of the Académie of Sciences for the exclusive use of the Imprimerie Royale. The original Fournier types were cut by the famous Paris founder Pierre Simon Fournier in about 1742. These types were some of the most influential designs of the eight and are counted among the earliest examples of the 'transitional' style of typeface. This Monotype version dates from 1924. Fournier is a light, clear face whose distinctive features are capital letters that are quite tall and bold in relation to the lower-case letters, and *decorative italics, which show the influence of the calligraphy of Fournier's time.*